A High Whisk Situation

Oxford Tearoom Mysteries

Book Twelve

H.Y. HANNA

11 24

CONTENTS

CHAPTER ONE

When life gives you lemons... keep calm and head to Scotland.

Well, I'm sure the original author of that quote never expected *that* variation, but it was certainly apt in my case. It wasn't an abundance of sour citrus fruits, though, but rather a flood of sewage water that threatened the mundane peacefulness of my life...

"It's totally gone, luv. Rusted right through. You're goin' to need a whole new system," said the plumber as he sat back on his heels, wiped his hands on a dirty rag, and eyed the twisted network of old pipes with relish (no doubt thinking of what the "whole new system" was going to put in his pocket). "Reckon I could squeeze you in before my next job, but you're goin' to have to close for a week."

1

"A week?" I stared at him in horror. "You want me to shut the tearoom for a week?"

The plumber shrugged. "No other way. Not unless you want your customers smellin' everything I bring up."

I shuddered. It had been bad enough the last few days when I'd had to explain to irate customers that there was no working toilet available—not something you want to announce to big tour groups and families with young children after you've been plying them with multiple cups of tea!

And people might rave about how much they loved the period features and quaint atmosphere of the converted Tudor inn that housed my tearoom, but somehow they drew the line at experiencing authentic fifteenth-century plumbing. I knew the Little Stables Tearoom had already copped some negative reviews online because of this; its reputation would sink completely if things got worse.

"All right," I sighed. "Just... can you please do it as fast as you can?"

"Sure, luv. I'll have it done for you in a jiffy," he said cheerfully.

Which—as anyone who has had experience of British tradesmen knows—probably meant that he would only drink seventeen cups of tea a day, have twelve cigarette breaks, and knock off at three thirty instead of three.

Still, I didn't have much choice, and after I showed the plumber out the front door and readjusted the

CLOSED sign, I went into the kitchen to break the news. Two women looked up expectantly as I stepped inside the door: Dora my tearoom chef, a stocky, grey-haired matron with a wonderful knack for creating gorgeous baked treats and a brisk manner that belied her kindly heart... and Cassie my best friend and partner-in-waitressing, whose sensual resemblance to an artist's muse belied her own brilliant talent with the paintbrush. While they could not have been more different, at that moment they were both wearing identical expectant expressions on their faces.

"Well?" said Cassie. "What did the plumber say?"

I relayed the bad news, bracing myself for their dismay. After all, both Dora and Cassie had worked as hard as I had over the past year to make the tearoom a success, and I knew they'd both be appalled at the prospect of being forced to close for business. To my surprise, though, Cassie beamed and exclaimed:

"Actually, that's brilliant! You can come with me!"

I looked at her blankly. "Come where?"

"To Scotland, of course," said Cassie. "I'm heading off this weekend, remember? I'm teaching that painting workshop at Aberglinn Castle in the Highlands."

"Oh... yeah, that's right," I said, wondering how I could have forgotten when I'd had to make changes to the menu and seating arrangements to ensure that we could manage while Cassie was away.

"My contract comes with room and board," Cassie continued excitedly. "And apparently there are twin beds in my room, so you can stay with me. I'm sure they won't mind. It'll be perfect: you can just lounge around and relax, or go and explore the castle grounds while I'm teaching the workshop. The castle's been converted into a posh hotel, you know, and it's up in the Scottish Highlands. The countryside is spectacular. You could try fly fishing or go hiking—"

"Cassie, I can't go gallivanting off to Scotland while work is being done on my tearoom!"

"Why not? It's not like you're going to be holding the spanner for the plumber, are you?" Cassie said. "You can't do anything while this place is closed, so you might as well take advantage of the situation. And you're well overdue for a holiday."

"Cassie's right, dear," Dora chimed in. "You've been working so hard; it's high time you took a break."

"It's not a break that I need, it's a new plumbing system," I muttered. "Besides, you've both been putting in long hours too—"

"Not like you," said Cassie. "You've been working like a madwoman, especially in the past few weeks. It's not healthy, Gemma! Do you realise you haven't taken *any* time off since the tearoom opened nearly eighteen months ago? And don't mention that trip to Vienna," she added, giving me a mock glower. "Spending most of your time investigating a murder doesn't count as a proper holiday."

"It's not like I haven't tried to take a holiday," I said irritably. "But every time I've organised something, it's ended up being cancelled because Devlin—" I broke off.

There was an awkward silence. Then Cassie took a breath and said, in a determinedly cheerful voice, "Well, let me tell you, that's one of the perks of being a single girl. No more worrying about the stupid workaholic boyfriend. No more contorting your life to match another person's schedule. You just suit yourself." She grabbed my arm. "Come on, Gemma— it'll be our own 'girls' trip'! We'll have a brilliant time."

I shook my head, but inside I could feel myself beginning to waver. It was true that I had been working like a maniac in recent months. But I had desperately needed to keep busy—to distract myself and take my mind off a certain Detective Inspector Devlin O'Connor who had turned my world upside down when he suggested that we "take a break" from our relationship.

Okay, so Devlin had nearly lost his job and his chance at an all-important promotion because of my meddling—er—I mean, attempts to help in an investigation, so perhaps it had been understandable. And he *had* been right that we needed to sort out the various thorny issues between us, including my tendency to get personally involved in other people's troubles, and his tendency to dedicate every waking hour to his job. It was ironic, really, because the reason we clashed so often was because we *both* tended to put strangers' needs before our own, albeit in different ways.

Still, I had always thought that we'd work through those "thorny issues" *together*, and I was shocked and hurt when Devlin had suggested some time and space apart to help us find some answers. Not that I showed him how shocked and hurt I was, of course. Oh no—growing up in a repressed upper-middle class household had provided me with the perfect training for the classic British "stiff upper lip", and I had made sure to maintain a cool, nonchalant façade ever since. It was exhausting, though, and I knew that Cassie could see the strain. One thing about having a best friend who had known you since primary school was that they could see right through you.

"Well, okay, maybe I *could* do with a break," I conceded. "But I could just stay in Oxford so that I'm nearby, in case there's a problem with the renovations and—"

"No, no, you *must* come to Scotland with me," insisted Cassie. "There's a reason the plumbing packed up right now. It's like it's meant to be!"

I stopped and looked at her, surprised by her vehemence. "Why are you so keen for me to go to Scotland?"

Cassie blinked. "I... well, like I said, I've already got this place sorted so it's the perfect arrangement—"

"Yes, but... you sounded like there's a specific reason you need me to go."

"Well, of course there's a reason—the reason is because you need a holiday!"

I narrowed my eyes at her. The thing about childhood best friends is that it works both ways. "No, there's something else—something you're not telling me, Cassandra Jenkins."

She gave an exaggerated shrug. "What do you mean? I don't know what you're talking about. I just think it's a fantastic opportunity and you should seize it. Not just to have a break but also to... to do some research!"

"Research?" I said, momentarily distracted.

"Yes, you could see it as a sort of... er... business development trip. You know, a chance to check out the baking in the Scottish Highlands, maybe pick up a few tips and ideas from local tearooms and bakeries." She snapped her fingers. "In fact, now that I think about it, I seem to remember that Aberglinn Castle offers a special afternoon tea to its guests. Wouldn't you love to try that, see how they do things?"

"Well..." It was true that I loved sampling and comparing offerings from other establishments. Part of it was professional curiosity and part of it was that I just loved the ritual of English afternoon tea: the beautiful fine bone china, the fragrant tea leaves steeped just long enough to produce the perfect cup, the delicious, freshly baked buns and tarts, and the warm, buttery scones... I would have loved to see the Scottish interpretation of this classic tradition, and Cassie was painting a very tempting picture; a "work" reason for the trip certainly made it seem more acceptable to abandon my tearoom and go.

"Well, I for one would *love* to sample some traditional Scottish baking," declared Dora, smacking her lips. "They do all these scrumptious cakes and desserts. I love clootie dumplings, with all the flavours from the dried fruits and treacle and cinnamon... mmm... and that lovely, moist, rich Dundee cake... oh, and cranachan, of course. You'd think it's just like a trifle but it's *so* much nicer! Maybe it's the Scottish raspberries or maybe it's the whisky," she chuckled. "And of course, nothing beats their famous shortbread It's one of those things that seems so simple—only three ingredients!—but it's so tricky to get perfectly right."

"I think your shortbread is delicious, Dora," said Cassie loyally.

Dora waved a hand. "Oh, it's not bad, I suppose. I've got a good recipe. But I'm sure it can't compare to proper shortbread made in Scotland. Plus, there's nothing like learning from a local baker." She turned to me and nodded emphatically. "I'll be sending you with some homework, Gemma. You can use some of your time to take notes for me."

"I haven't said I'm going yet," I protested.

"Aww, come on!" said Cassie impatiently. "Look, if you don't get away—I mean, *completely* away—you'll never have a real break from things. You know how it is: if you stay in Oxford, you'll just end up getting sucked back into stuff. You'll be doing emails, admin, accounting, and you won't be able to help yourself coming out to Meadowford-on-Smythe to check on the progress in the tearoom..." She paused, then added with a sly look: "*And* you'll be roped into your mother's latest crazy schemes."

Oh God. She was right. The thought of being at a loose end for a week, with no way of escaping my mother's bossing and interference, was more than enough to sway me.

"What about Muesli?" I asked, glancing across at my little tabby cat who had—once again—sneaked into the tearoom kitchen despite our best efforts and was now happily curled up on one of the chairs by the table.

"She can stay with your parents, can't she?" said Cassie.

"I think they were planning to go away this weekend. Mother said something about being invited to stay with friends in the Cotswolds."

"*I* would offer to look after Muesli, except that I think I'll use this chance to visit my sister in Bournemouth," said Dora apologetically. "I was planning to go next month, but since I won't be needed here, I might as well go now."

"Don't worry, I'm sure the Old Biddies will be happy to have Muesli. It's only for a few days. We can close the tearoom this Thursday, walk across the village to drop Muesli off at Mabel's house, and then you can fly up to Inverness with me on Friday morning," said Cassie. She looked at me eagerly. "So that's all sorted and all you need to do is think about what you're going to pack!"

Her excitement was infectious, and in spite of myself I felt a flutter of anticipation. Suddenly, the thought of getting away from the tearoom, Oxford, the stresses of everyday life—of having a complete change of scene—was incredibly appealing.

"All right," I said, smiling at my best friend. "Scotland, here we come!"

CHAPTER TWO

I turned the key in the lock and stepped back, looking up at the building in front of me. In the late-afternoon light, the half-timber framing, whitewashed walls, and thatched roofing of my tearoom looked more picturesque than ever, and when I turned to look down the village high street, the quaint stone cottages and distant view of the Cotswolds hills reminded me yet again why hundreds of thousands of tourists flocked here to visit every year.

I felt a twinge at the thought of leaving all this cosy familiarity. Was I doing the right thing? Other than a few instances when I had been forced to temporarily suspend business (including the time an American tourist was murdered with one of my own scones!), I had never closed the tearoom completely and gone away like this. The Little Stables had filled my whole life, ever since opening it over a year earlier, and now I felt a sudden panic that, when I returned, everything I had achieved might not be here anymore.

"Don't be silly," I muttered to myself. "It's not as if you're leaving forever. You're only going away for a few days."

"Gemma? What are you doing, standing there talking to yourself?"

I turned guiltily and hurried over to join Cassie, who was waiting next to our bicycles.

"Nothing... just doing a last check," I said. I threw a final glance over my shoulder at the tearoom, then turned determinedly away.

"*Meorrw!*" came a little voice, and I glanced down to see Muesli peeking at me through the bars of her cat carrier, which had been placed beside my bike. Her green eyes were wide and excited, and she sniffed the air with anticipation. Obviously, her feline senses had picked up that something was different—this wasn't the usual trip home after work.

"It's all right, Muesli, you're not missing out. You're going on your own adventure with the Old Biddies," I said as I picked up the carrier and placed it in the front basket of my bicycle.

"Yeah, and let's hope it doesn't involve any mystery, mayhem, or murder," said Cassie, rolling her eyes.

I grinned. The "Old Biddies" was our affectionate nickname for the geriatric foursome who were probably Oxfordshire's most notorious senior citizens. Mabel Cooke, Glenda Bailey, Florence Doyle, and Ethel Webb had a talent for meddling matched only by their passion for playing detective, and they topped it all with an uncanny ability to insert themselves into any murder investigation that caught their fancy.

"They seem to be going through a relatively quiet spell recently, though," I reminded Cassie.

In fact, there had barely been a single suspicious figure, mysterious footprint, or "sinister overheard conversation" reported to the local police in the last few weeks.

I gave a hopeful smile. "Maybe they'll keep out of trouble while we're gone. I mean, they should be busy enough with their usual bingo games and gossip sessions at the village post office."

"Don't you believe it," said Cassie darkly. "I'll bet when we get to Mabel's place, we'll find them gathered in the sitting room, poring over some clue from an imaginary dead body."

As it turned out, Cassie was wrong. When we arrived at Mabel's cottage on the other side of the village, we did find the four little old ladies assembled in the sitting room. But rather than dissecting a gory murder, they were engaged in that most innocent of English pastimes: having afternoon tea. And with them, to my surprise, were my parents: Professor

Philip Rose and Mrs Evelyn Rose.

"Mother!" I cried as Cassie and I were led in. "I didn't realise you and Dad were coming over?"

"Volume, darling!" said my mother, giving me a scandalised look. "Remember, a lady never raises her voice above a well-modulated murmur."

I resisted the urge to roll my eyes. My mother was the living, walking embodiment of a Victorian etiquette manual. Still, I couldn't help a twinge of envy and admiration for the way she managed to look so composed and elegant, perched on the sofa sipping tea, her hair perfectly coiffed and her starched-linen dress without a single crease or wrinkle. The weather had been unseasonably warm this summer, and Cassie and I were a hot and sweaty sight just from wheeling our bicycles across the village.

My father gave me a gentle smile over his spectacles. "Mrs Cooke kindly invited us to tea, and your mother and I thought it would be a lovely opportunity to see you before you left for Scotland. You're departing early tomorrow morning, I believe?"

"Yes, we're flying up to Inverness and then taking a connecting train to Fort William," Cassie answered him. "I suppose we'll then try to find a bus that will drop us near the castle. Otherwise, it'll have to be a taxi, which will probably cost an arm and a leg," she added ruefully.

"Never fear," said Mabel, coming back into the room with a fresh pot of tea and Muesli trotting at her heels. My tabby cat seemed to have immediately accepted her new temporary home and was now happily exploring the sitting room.

"The castle might be sending a car to meet guests at the airport tomorrow morning," continued Mabel as she set the teapot down on the table. "I'll speak to my cousin Graeme and suggest that the driver pick you girls up as well."

Which probably means they'll be ordered point blank to take us, I thought, smiling at the mental image of hapless guests watching in bewilderment as Cassie and I were loaded in next to them. With her stentorian voice and bossy manner, Mabel had little trouble getting most people to do her bidding. Still, I was confused as to how her influence had extended all the way to Scotland in this case.

Leaning over to Cassie, I hissed, "What's Mabel's cousin got to do with anything?"

She turned to look at me. "Oh, didn't I tell you? Sorry, I must have forgotten. It was through Mabel that I got this job. Her cousin's one of the gardeners at the Aberglinn Castle Hotel, and he mentioned that the management was interested in providing more activities for the guests. So Mabel rang them up and told them that they should offer a painting workshop—you know, 'take home your own watercolour of the Highlands', that kind of thing— and she nominated me to run it." Cassie chuckled. "She even told them what they should pay me and insisted that room and board be included. I don't think they knew what had hit them."

"You need to haggle hard with the Scots," said Mabel firmly. "I know there are jokes about the Scottish being stingy but that's just an ignorant stereotype. The truth is, Scottish people are frugal and careful with their finances—which is no bad thing—and they have a healthy respect for those who demand value for money too. As my grandfather used to say: *mony a mickle maks a muckle*—it's an old Scottish proverb which means 'if you look after the pennies then the pounds will look after themselves'."

I turned to her. "Your family is Scottish, Mabel?"

She nodded. "Ooh yes. My maiden name was Duncan. Of course, my grandparents moved to England soon after getting married, and my family have lived down south ever since. But I still have relatives all over Inverness-shire—like my cousin, Graeme. That's his wife's recipe for the whisky fruit cake we're having," she added, nodding at the fruit cake sitting in pride of place beside the tea tray. "Sit down and I'll cut you girls each a slice."

Cassie and I dutifully obeyed, and a few minutes later I was placing a piece of the rich, moist cake in my mouth. *Mmm...* I closed my eyes for a second. Even for someone used to being surrounded by delicious baking, this cake was heavenly: dense and sweet, with the wonderful flavours of dried fruit, mixed spices, orange zest, and almonds overlaid by the heady fumes from the whisky.

"This is delicious—" I started to say with my

mouth full, then paused and hastily swallowed as I saw my mother's disapproving eye on me. "If this is an example of Scottish baking, I can't wait to sample more!"

Florence beamed at me. "Oh, I'm glad you like it, dear. I was the one who baked the cake today, although I did use Mabel's recipe." Plump and homely, Florence loved her food and spent most of her time worrying that others weren't eating enough. So she was delighted now to see us tucking into her baking.

"It's very simple to make," she continued eagerly. "You just mix the dried fruit with the zest and juice of an orange and a lemon in a pan, then heat it together with Scotch whisky, butter, and brown sugar. Then you cool the mixture and combine it with the flour, flaked almonds, spices, and baking powder."

"And eggs," Ethel piped up. "Don't forget the eggs, Florence."

"Yes, that's right. It takes quite a lot of eggs. Then you bake it in a cake tin for two hours and it's ready to serve."

"Is this what they call a Dundee cake?" asked Cassie, forking another piece into her mouth. "That's the famous Scottish fruit cake, isn't it?"

"Oh no, this isn't quite the authentic recipe," Ethel said quickly.

As the shyest of the Old Biddies, Ethel was usually the quietest, but being an ex-librarian meant that old habits were hard to ignore, and she rushed now to provide the right information, just as she used to when I was a little girl. "There are so many varieties calling themselves 'Dundee cake' nowadays, but the original recipe didn't have glacé cherries or whisky or even mixed spice. Aside from the flour, butter, sugar, eggs, and baking powder, it only contained a touch of salt, some raisins or sultanas, a bit of orange zest, some almonds, and—most important of all—Seville orange marmalade."

"Marmalade?"

Ethel nodded. "Yes, and not just any marmalade. A proper Dundee cake is made with marmalade from Seville oranges. It's what gives it that subtle bittersweet flavour. I read a book by a food historian once and he speculated that the Dundee cake was actually created for Mary, Queen of Scots who hated the traditional style of fruit cakes. So the royal cook made her a special one with just almonds, raisins, and Seville oranges, which were being imported to Dundee by Spanish merchants at the time."

"Well, authentic or not, I think Graeme's recipe is a nice variation," declared Mabel. "And adding the whisky helps the cake keep for longer."

Glenda gave a girlish giggle, sounding more eighteen than eighty. "Most things are better with a bit of Scotch added," she tittered.

"I quite agree," said my father with a wink.

I gave him a startled look. My father was a semi-retired professor at Oxford University and a classic "absent-minded academic" who spent most of his time with his nose buried in his textbooks. I'd rarely seen him show a playful side and certainly never thought I'd catch him winking!

"I never knew you liked whisky, Dad," I said. To my knowledge, my parents only drank wine and strictly in moderation.

He darted a look at my mother, then gave me a conspiratorial smile. "Oh, I've been to a few whisky bars in my 'wild youth', and I'm still very partial to a nice single malt once in a while. The University has a Whisky Society which holds regular events, you know, and one of their patrons, Professor Tom Wallace, is a good friend of mine. We sometimes meet for a drink. In fact, I was just speaking to Tom last week—he'd heard about a whisky investment opportunity and was keen to tell me all about it."

"Whisky investment?" I looked at him. "What's that?"

"Ah... you see, in recent years, whisky has become a collectable luxury asset—much like antiques or art or watches—and it is now being mooted as an additional option for those who want to diversify their investment portfolios."

"You mean, like buying bottles of whisky and waiting for them to go up in value?" asked Cassie.

"Yes, although investing in casks is more common. Unlike wine, whisky doesn't age once it is bottled, you see," my father explained. "So there is more growth in purchasing casks of new-make whisky, which increases in value as it matures. The idea is that you make a profit when it is finally bottled and released to the market—and those profits can be significant! According to Tom, the price of rare Scotch whiskies has risen over five hundred percent in the last decade."

"Wow. Are you thinking of investing, Dad?" I asked.

"Certainly not," said my mother before my father could answer. "I told your father that we shall adhere to the tried-and-true traditional methods for our investment plans."

"And quite right too," said Mabel with an emphatic nod. "These newfangled ideas sound like a lot of nonsense to me. Investing in whisky? Whoever heard of such a thing? Whisky is for drinking. Or cooking with." She turned briskly to me and said with a change of tone: "Speaking of nonsense, Gemma, what's this we've been hearing about your love life?"

I leaned back nervously as I suddenly found all four Old Biddies peering intently at me. "Wh-what do you mean?"

"Well, your mother was just telling us that you and your young man are broken."

"We're not 'broken'—we're 'on a break'," I said in exasperated tones.

"On a break? You mean, on holiday? Is Devlin going to Scotland with you as well? Oh, I do hope you get a photograph of him wearing a kilt," said Glenda, giggling like a teenage girl talking about her latest celebrity crush. As usual, she was dressed more like a teenager too, with her skinny legs encased in rainbow-coloured leggings and bright blue shadow on her eyelids. "Men look so handsome in kilts," she continued with a sigh. "I once had a dalliance with a Scottish laird—did I ever tell you? He only ever wore kilts, which was not very sensible, really, when you consider the Scottish weather, but it did come in very handy when he was feeling fruity and wanted to quickly—"

"Er, no, no, not that kind of break," I cut in hastily, trying in vain to push the image of Glenda and her Scottish laird out of my mind. I took a deep breath and addressed the four wrinkled faces around me. "We're 'on a break' from our relationship. It means we're spending some time away from each other to... to think about things."

"What do you need to think about?" asked Florence, looking puzzled.

"Well, I..." I stammered, flushing as I realised that everyone in the room was looking at me. "Just... you know... whether we can work through our issues."

"Bah!" Mabel waved a contemptuous hand. "Young people these days... you have no staying power, just like your hair. In my time, we didn't jump ship as soon as things got trying. Take my Henry, for example. When we first got married, he was remarkably flatulent. It was quite off-putting, I can tell you, especially in the bedroom. But I persevered with high-fibre meals and probiotic supplements, and he is now the model of mellifluent digestion."

I groaned internally. I might have known that we'd get round to Mabel's favourite topic of "the bowels" at some point. "Er... well, our situation is a bit different—" I started to say.

"Nonsense. Most men need more fibre in their diet," said Mabel. "Constipation leads to all sorts of problems, you know, and makes you feel exhausted and irritable. I'm sure if you just give your young man a spoonful of psyllium husk with his breakfast—"

"Devlin doesn't need more fibre in his diet! I'm sure he goes regul—I mean—" I broke off, horrified. *AAAGHH! How on earth had I ended up discussing my (possibly ex) boyfriend's bowel movements with the Old Biddies and my parents?* I took a deep breath. "Look, we're just taking a bit of time apart, okay?"

Obviously feeling sorry for me, Cassie spoke up. "Um... anyway, I think we should probably head off soon. We still need to pack."

"Ooh yes, that reminds me—I've purchased some things for your trip, darling," said my mother, turning to rummage in a glossy gift bag next to her feet. She pulled out two spray cans, two clumps of green netting, and what looked incongruously like two giant tubes of lipstick.

"Here you are," she said, handing me and Cassie a clump of netting each.

"What's this?" I asked, frowning down at my hands.

"It's a midge net, darling! For you to wear over your head whenever you're outdoors in Scotland." She demonstrated by taking my clump and shaking it out to reveal a crumpled tube made of fine mesh, which she attempted to slip over my head.

"I'm not wearing that!" I cried, leaning away from her. "I'll look like a complete plonker!"

"Oh, but you must, darling," said my mother. "I read an article which said that the Highlands are plagued by midges! And July and August are the worst times for them. Apparently, they can devour any exposed parts of your body, and they've been known to reduce grown men to tears."

"I'm sure that's an exaggeration, Mother," I said impatiently. "It can't be that bad, otherwise nobody would ever go to Scotland."

"Midges *can* get quite unpleasant," my father spoke up in his gentle voice.

"Yes, they can attack in swarms and cause lots of itchy bites," agreed Mabel, nodding emphatically.

"Maybe we can get away with just using these?" said Cassie hopefully, holding up one of the cannisters. I saw that they were cans of midge repellent spray.

"Oh yes, I bought those for you as extra protection," said my mother distractedly, her attention on the two giant tubes of lipstick now. She picked them up and thrust them at us. "But these are the *most* important things of all. Make sure you keep these with you at all times, wherever you go.

Remember, a lady is always poised and prepared."

Cassie uncapped her lipstick, looked at the lurid pink colour, and blanched. I gave an impatient sigh. I knew my mother adhered fervently to the 1950's attitude that a woman should always look her best at all times, but this seemed to be taking it to extremes.

"Mother, you're not suggesting that we scare midges away with the hideous colour, are you?" I asked sarcastically.

"Oh no, darling, that isn't for the midges. It's a 'Lost Lips Swipe 'n' Glow'."

"A what?" I caught the look my mother gave me. "I mean, pardon?"

"It's a dual-purpose lipstick and flare gun," my mother explained.

Cassie and I gaped at her.

"You see, you twist it this way to pop out the lipstick part—hmm, it *is* rather a bright colour, isn't it?—and you twist it the other way to activate the flare. Apparently, it can shoot out quite a distance and be seen from miles away."

"Mother, why on earth would we need a flare gun?" I asked, exasperated.

"Well, people are always getting lost in the mountains, aren't they? Helen Green told me that the Scottish Mountain Rescue had to search for hundreds of people last year!" My mother indicated the giant lipstick in my hand. "This would direct them to your exact location—and you'd be able to touch up your make-up before they arrived too. Isn't that marvellous?"

I sighed. Suddenly, I couldn't get to Scotland fast enough.

CHAPTER THREE

I took a deep breath as I stepped off the mobile stairway leading down from the plane onto the airfield tarmac at Inverness Airport. The sky rose high above us, framed by wisps of cloud and washed clean by recent rain, and the air was fresh, with a crispness that was somehow different to the mellow country air of the Cotswolds.

I laughed to myself. I was only at the airport, and already I was waxing lyrical about the Scottish Highlands! Still, there was something wonderfully uplifting about the wide-open expanses around me, the sense of space stretching to the horizon, and the view of the misty mountains in the distance. For the first time in a long time, I felt a sense of peace. I wasn't worrying about my tearoom or family or

Devlin or anything else from "real life"... I was just enjoying this moment and revelling in the feeling of pleasant anticipation that filled me.

And Cassie seemed even more ebullient. As we navigated through the airport terminal and out into the Arrivals hall, I could hear her singing a happy tune. In fact, she had been chattering non-stop the whole flight and now seemed to be brimming with repressed excitement.

My best friend paused as she felt my eyes on her and turned to look at me. "What?"

"Cass, what are you not telling me?" I asked.

"What do you mean?"

"You just seem to be so... so happy! Like the way someone is when they're hiding some exciting secret." I gave her a suspicious look. "Are you planning some kind of surprise?"

"What? I... no... I don't know what you're talking about! Look, I'm just happy that we're here, okay? It's been ages since we've done anything together—I mean anything *fun*. It'll be nice to spend time with each other and *not* talk about the tearoom for once."

I felt a stab of guilt. "Sorry. I've been an awful friend lately, haven't I?"

"You know I didn't mean it like that. But it's true that we haven't had much time to have a laugh together, like we used to in our student days. So I'm just really looking forward to that, okay?"

I held up my hands, palms out. "Okay, okay, I'll drop it now. And I promise not to mention anything to do with the tearoom while we're in Scotland."

"Well, I give you permission to check out the local baking for work purposes. In fact, I might even join you in some hands-on—or rather, mouth-on—research," said Cassie, grinning. Then she turned and looked around. "Do you think Mabel managed to wangle a lift for us?"

We scanned the area. Despite handling more than a million passengers a year, Inverness Airport was small by modern standards, with a single low-slung building that housed both the Arrivals and Departures areas. There was a homely, intimate feel to the place—nothing like the big, sleek, but often impersonal international airports that I frequented when I worked as a high-flying executive before giving it all up to open my tearoom.

"I can't see anyone holding a sign with 'Aberglinn Castle Hotel', you?" said Cassie, squinting. "Listen, you stay here and keep looking. I'm going to pop over to the café and see if they might be hanging around there."

Left on my own, I turned to check the crowds of people milling around me again. Then I froze as a group of backpackers parted and a young man standing behind them turned into view. Dark hair, brilliant blue eyes, strong, handsome profile...

The breath caught in my throat. *No, surely he can't be here—?*

The next moment, the man stepped out from behind the group and, as the light fell fully on his features, I let out the breath I had been holding. The resemblance was strong, but this man was definitely a stranger. His eyes met mine and I began to look away, embarrassed to be caught staring. To my surprise, though, his face brightened and he hurried towards me.

"Are you Cassie Jenkins, by any chance?" he asked.

He had a rich baritone, with the kind of Scottish burr that romantic novelists raved about. In fact, with his good looks, tall, athletic figure, and sexy accent, the man was a Highland romantic hero come to life. The only thing missing was a kilt and sporran, although I noticed that he *was* dressed in a distinctive outfit that somehow combined rugged outdoor wear with traditional sartorial elegance: a jacket and waistcoat in a subtle tweed pattern, combined with wool breeches and checked shirt, and accessorised with a forest-green tie and mud-flecked gaiters over leather boots.

I realised that I was staring again and hastily dropped my gaze. "Um, no... but I'm Cassie's friend," I said. "Are you from Aberglinn Castle?"

He flashed me a smile. "Yes, my name's Ewan— Ewan Campbell. I was supposed to collect a couple of guests, actually, but they've cancelled at the very last minute. Still, I suppose it was good that I was here, as I got a message saying that you girls were arriving and I should pick you up as well, if there was room."

Good old Mabel, I thought. "That would be brilliant if you could give us a lift," I said warmly. "Let me just find Cassie. She'll be delighted to see you."

To my surprise, though, Cassie looked less than pleased when she was introduced to Ewan. She treated him with a reserve bordering on hostility as he helped us with our bags and led us out to a weathered Land Rover.

"Is it a long drive to the castle?" I asked, feeling the need to make some polite conversation to make up for Cassie's stony silence. I had climbed into the front seat beside Ewan and watched now as he expertly manoeuvred the Land Rover out of the airport car park and onto the main road.

"A couple of hours," said Ewan with a shrug. "It's not too bad."

"I suppose if you're doing the route often, it'll be very familiar—"

"Actually, I don't usually pick up guests," said Ewan, then he added with a grin and a sideways look at me: "—although I'm glad I did today."

I felt my cheeks warming. Was he flirting with me?

"So how come you're here then?" said Cassie from the back seat. I glanced over my shoulder uncomfortably. My best friend had been uncharacteristically quiet on the drive so far, and now her question sounded so sharp as to be almost rude.

Ewan, however, seemed unfazed and answered equably, "Well, we're a bit short-staffed at the moment, so I'm just helping out."

"So what do you do?" I asked in a friendly tone, trying to make up for Cassie's asperity.

"I'm the ghillie."

"The what?"

"The ghillie. It's a sort of gamekeeper-cum-hunting guide-cum-land manager... and a million other things these days," said Ewan with a dry laugh. "The word comes from Gaelic, and it means 'manservant' or 'attendant'. Ghillies were basically the personal menservants of the Highland chiefs in the old days. They knew the best places to fish, the best ways to stalk deer, the character of the local rivers, the seasonal weather conditions... and in recent decades, they've also helped to manage the game on the estates, monitor the wildlife populations, maintain the woodlands and forests. Nowadays, they even get involved in things like sustainable eco-tourism."

"Bloody hell," I said, impressed. "You do all that?

Ewan gave a slightly embarrassed laugh. "Well, to be honest, I spend most of my time taking guests and visitors on wildlife walks and 'ghillie experiences', like letting them try their hand at fly fishing or stalking deer with a camera. Oh, we still get proper shooting parties now and then, especially in deer rutting season in the autumn, but Aberglinn isn't really much of a hunting estate anymore. Its income mainly comes from the hotel now, and most of the guests are just tourists—you know, honeymooners, retired couples, families, Americans tracing their Scottish ancestry..." He indicated his clothes ruefully. "So in spite of wearing the traditional 'ghillie suit', you could say that I don't do much *real* ghillie work anymore, at least in the traditional sense."

He paused, then—perhaps feeling that he might have sounded too negative—added hastily, "Not that I'm complaining. It's great to see people learn about Highland country pursuits and give them the chance to experience it." He glanced sideways at me again. "Maybe I'll get the chance to show you some of these experiences during your stay?"

"Oh, I'm not a proper guest at the hotel," I said quickly.

"You're still welcome to tag along on any of my 'ghillie experiences'," said Ewan with a warm smile. "In fact, I could take you out when my shift is over and give you a private lesson in fly fishing or—"

"Gemma's going to be too busy to have time for that," Cassie cut in. She scowled at the back of Ewan's head, then turned to me and said, "You're going to be tied up researching Scottish baking, remember?"

"Well, not all the time," I protested.

"I'm sure Ewan wouldn't want to distract you from your professional obligations," said Cassie primly.

I glanced at her. What was wrong with her? Why was she speaking like that?

"Your 'professional obligations'? Are you a baker?" said Ewan, throwing me a curious look.

I laughed. "God, no. I mean, I've tried but I'm not very good... no, Cassie's referring to my work. I run a tearoom back in the Cotswolds, you see, and thankfully I have a lovely baking chef who produces all sorts of delicious treats for our menu. But Dora did ask me to pick up some tips from local bakers here in the Highlands if I can." I hesitated. "Do you think one of the chefs in the castle kitchen would be willing to chat to me and let me watch them work?"

"I'm sure they would. They're a nice bunch in the kitchen. We don't have any of that 'temperamental chefs' rubbish. In fact, Morag—that's the head cook and our main pastry chef—she'd probably love to be interviewed. Once you get her talking, you won't be able to shut her up," said Ewan, chuckling affectionately. "And Mairi and Rhona are really nice too. They're the sous-chefs and you won't find anyone who works harder than them at the castle. But they've always got time for you, no matter how busy they are. Then there's Izzy. She's the new girl— she helps to serve in the dining room, along with Jenny. They're a great laugh, especially if you get them down to the pub. Silly daft cows, the pair of 'em, but good company, you know? Anyway, yeah, I'm sure they'd be more than happy to show you some traditional Scottish baking." He paused, then said in a different voice: "But you probably need to check with Aileen first."

"Who's Aileen?"

"She's the castle manager."

I waited for Ewan to say more, and when he didn't, I looked at him curiously. After his loquaciousness in describing the other castle staff, his sudden reticence about its most senior member was slightly odd.

As if sensing my scrutiny, Ewan cleared his throat and said, looking at Cassie through the rear-view mirror: "You'll likely have dealt with Aileen when you were organising your gig?"

"Yeah, I spoke to her when I was sorting out the details of my workshop. She seemed very brisk and efficient," said Cassie.

"Aye. She runs the castle very well," said Ewan in a neutral voice. Then he pointed ahead, changing the subject. "You see those mountains? That's the start of the Grampians. They're the largest mountain range in the Highlands—they occupy nearly half of the land area of Scotland, in fact."

I leaned forwards to peer through the windscreen. "Isn't Ben Nevis a part of the range?"

Ewan grinned at me. "You remember your school geography, eh? Yes, Ben Nevis—Britain's highest mountain—is part of the Grampians, and that's the one most people know. But there are several other peaks that are worthy too, which many tourists never appreciate... like Ben Macdui in the Cairngorms, which has some of the best climbing in the area... and Braeriach, if you really want an epic hike... and Ben Lomond, which is a great place to get fantastic views of Loch Lomond—" He broke off and gave me a slightly sheepish look. "Sorry, I get a bit carried away."

"Oh no, it's all really interesting," I assured him. "They all seem to be called 'Ben Something'—is that like another name for a mountain?"

"Aye, Gaelic has a lot of different names for features in the landscape. 'Ben' comes from 'Beinn', which is sort of a generic name for hills, especially the big ones."

I smiled to myself as I glanced at the towering peaks in the distance. I would've hardly called them 'hills'!

"Aberglinn Castle is situated in a glen at the foot of the mountains," Ewan continued. "It's a spectacular spot, if I do say so myself. Nothing around but the mountains and open moorlands, deer and gorse and thistle—"

"D'you know, I've never seen a thistle in real life?" I said. "I've seen loads of pictures of them, of course, and drawings on logos and stuff, but I've never seen the actual plant."

"You're not likely to mistake it, especially if you step on it," said Ewan with a wry smile. "There are few things as painful as a thistle thorn. That's the reason Scotland wasn't conquered by the Vikings, did you know?"

I gave a laugh. "No, I've never heard that."

"According to legend, the Norse army tried to invade Scotland in the thirteenth century and arrived in their ships under the cover of night. Their plan was to ambush the sleeping Scots, and so they took their shoes off to be as quiet as possible... but then one of them stepped barefoot on a spiky thistle and his scream of pain woke the Scottish warriors, who then rose up and vanquished the invaders." Ewan grinned at me. "Good story, eh?"

"And is that why the thistle is Scotland's national flower?" I asked,

"Aye, we love the idea of this plant which produces a beautiful flower but is also so tough that it can survive in the harshest of climates, and if anyone tries to cut it, they get a handful of painful barbs! There's even a motto that goes with it: *Nemo me impune lacessit*—which is Latin for 'No one provokes me with impunity'. Some say that's a perfect description of the fiery Scots' temperament." Ewan chuckled. "Don't expect to harm a Scotsman or his clan, without being punished in return. The motto was added to the arms of the King of Scotland, you know, in the seventeenth century, and it's still part of the Royal Arms today."

"It's a really 'cool' motto," I said appreciatively. "It makes you feel all proud and fired up, in a way."

"Yes, I suppose it does. Personally, I think a lot of it is marketing by the Scottish Tourist Board more than anything else," he said with a cynical smile. "I mean, we're not all running around like crazy clan warriors anymore, demanding loyalty and vengeance. Us modern Scots are a lot more laid-back now."

The time on the drive seemed to pass very quickly,

and I had to admit that this was largely because of the pleasure of Ewan's company. By the time we pulled up to the front of the estate, the handsome ghillie and I were talking and laughing like old friends. Cassie, though, didn't seem to share in our camaraderie. She remained mutinously silent in the back seat, despite my best efforts to draw her into the conversation. As we approached the main driveway, however, she seemed to rouse herself at last and looked out of the window with interest.

"Wow, it's gorgeous..." she murmured.

I had to agree as I gazed through the windscreen at the driveway, which led in between two carved stone pillars that flanked the main gate. The winding driveway made its way through beautifully landscaped grounds, backed on one side by a small loch, its waters sparkling in the afternoon sun, and on the other side by mature woodland which stretched up into the foothills of the Grampians. The brilliant yellow of gorse glowed from the undergrowth as we drove past, interspersed with the tall spires of wild foxgloves and pink willowherb swaying in the breeze.

"Summer is probably one of the nicest times to be in the Highlands," said Ewan enthusiastically as he steered around a bend in the drive. "You can—"

He broke off with an exclamation as another car came shooting round the bend from the opposite direction.

"Look out!" Cassie screamed. "It's going to hit us!"

CHAPTER FOUR

Ewan yanked the steering wheel with desperate force, cursing viciously as he swung the car sideways to try and avoid a collision. I clutched frantically at the car door, feeling the seatbelt dig into my chest as I was thrown to one side. The Land Rover veered sharply, almost plunging off the driveway into the ditch alongside, before wheeling around and narrowly missing a stump of moss-covered oak by the roadside.

The other car careened past. It was a cream Rolls-Royce, its powerful engine gunning as it sped by. The driver was a young man, sitting back with one arm draped negligently along the open window frame, his head turned towards his companion, a voluptuous brunette lounging in the front passenger seat. He barely spared us a glance as he drove recklessly by.

"*Ahh... ya f'knbawbag!*" Ewan snarled as the other car roared away and disappeared from sight.

We lurched to a stop and I sagged in my seat, feeling my heart rate slowly return to normal.

In the back, Cassie let out a shaky breath and said: "Bloody hell! I thought we were going to crash for sure." She gave Ewan a look of grudging respect. "Your reflexes are pretty good."

"They shouldn't have to be," said Ewan, his mouth set in a grim line. "Man shouldn't have been driving like a bloody dobber." He glanced at us. "You girls all right?"

We nodded. "Who was that?" I asked.

"One of the guests," said Ewan shortly. "English bastard calling himself Tristan St Clair. Arrived yesterday with his girlfriend. One of those cocky types who thinks money gives them the right to be a total arsepiece—"

He broke off and gave us a shamefaced look. "Sorry. Excuse my language." Taking a deep breath, he seemed to get a hold of himself again. Then he restarted the engine and, as we rounded the bend and came within sight of the castle, he said in a calmer voice: "Anyway... let's try again, eh? Welcome to Aberglinn Castle Hotel."

A minute later, we glided through a carriage arch and slid to a stop in front of a stone façade dominated by a pair of enormous, studded oak doors. I stepped out of the car, the recent frightening incident forgotten as I looked up at the building. Aberglinn Castle might not have been very large, but it more than made up for it with its august grandeur—from the imposing edifice of grey sandstone and looming curtain walls to the romantic turrets rising above the battlements adorned with crenellations. Surrounded by the hills and forests of the wild Highland landscape, it looked like a medieval fantasy come to life.

And the castle was even more impressive on the inside. We were led in, past the antique reception desk in the Gothic-style vestibule, and into the Great Hall—a vast space with soaring ceilings, ornamental wall panels, rich drapery, and sweeping windows topped by golden pelmets, which gave onto a spectacular view of the loch and the surrounding estate. There was a marble fireplace on one side of the hall, adorned with the castle's coat of arms, and scattered around the rest of the room were deeply cushioned sofas and armchairs, upholstered in beautiful plaid fabric.

Leaving Cassie and Ewan by the sweeping wooden staircase that dominated one side of the Great Hall, I wandered across to the windows. There were several guests lounging about the room: a middle-aged couple ensconced in matching armchairs, facing each other over a vintage chess set, a pair of elderly English ladies admiring a vase filled with giant mophead hydrangea blooms, a man sitting by himself, reading the newspaper, and a family with two young children boisterously playing by the fireplace. Next to the bay windows, a young Chinese couple stood together, posing with bright grins as the girl held up her phone. It was attached to a selfie stick, and she waved it wildly as she attempted to get them both into the frame. I jumped hastily back as the selfie stick swung perilously close to my head.

"Oh!" The girl whirled around to look at me, her face filled with dismay. "I am very sorry!"

"That's okay." I smiled at her. Something about their entwined hands and intimate posture made me guess that they were newlyweds, and I was proved right when the girl gave me a shy smile in return and said, as if in apologetic explanation:

"We are on honeymoon. It is so beautiful—so wonderful! We want photos of everything and every place to remember!"

"Oh, I totally understand. Congratulations! Here…" I held out my hands. "Would you like me to take the picture for you?"

She nodded eagerly. "Yes! Thank you. With the window, please?" She indicated the view through the windows behind them. "Can you take some from different angle?"

"Of course, no problem." I took her phone and lined up the shot.

The girl beamed with gratitude when I returned her phone, and I left them poring over the images on the screen. When I returned to Cassie, I found her talking to a matronly woman in an elegant uniform.

"...*och*, I'm sure it'll be fine," the woman was saying as I joined them. "We're not usin' that room anyway, noo that those guests have cancelled, and there's noan else booked in fer this weekend. It's one of oor more modest rooms, o' course, but it's got two proper beds and a nice view oot the side o' the castle."

"It sounds brilliant. Thanks ever so much!" said Cassie. She turned to me, her eyes shining. "Gemma, guess what? We're going to be staying in one of the hotel guest rooms! This is Bridget—she's the head of Housekeeping—and she's organised for us to swap."

"Well, seems daft fer you tae be squeezin' intae that wee room when this one's goan tae stay empty anyway and ye could be so much more comfor'able in there," said Bridget.

Ewan stepped forwards and said with a frown: "You sure about this, Bridget? You know what Aileen can be like—"

Bridget waved a hand. "*Wheesht! Aileen thinks she knoos everything but I can still teach her a thing or two aboot proper Scottish hospitality. Anyway, she's on the phone now, dealing with* that cancellation, so I'm jus' goan tae settle the girls intae this room and that's that." She turned and began leading the way up the grand staircase. "If ye'll follow me, I'll show ye aroond..."

We fell into step beside her as she proudly took us on a tour through the public areas of the castle. We dutifully admired the elegant furnishings, the rich oil paintings on the walls, and the beautiful antiques that adorned every corner. Aside from the magnificent Great Hall, there was an equally magnificent drawing room, resplendent with golden Rococo mirrors and sumptuous sofa suites. Beyond it lay a grand dining room with patterned wallpaper and Murano chandeliers, and around the corner from the Great Hall was an intimate hotel bar—a cosy, wood-panelled room that looked like a cross between a tiny country pub and a gentleman's study.

The room that intrigued me the most, however, was the library. Bridget skimmed over this, leading Cassie eagerly on, but I couldn't help lingering in the doorway and eyeing the room with wonder. It was filled with solid oak bookcases, brimming with leather-bound volumes, and interspersed between them were glass display cases showing hunting trophies and taxidermy mounts of native Scottish game and fowl. On the walls above were mounted numerous stag heads, their glass eyes glaring into the distance and their enormous antlers splayed towards the ceiling.

The far wall of the library was dominated by an expansive bay window, and I itched to cross over and see if the view was as fantastic as the aspects we'd enjoyed from other points in the castle. But I could hear Bridget and Cassie mounting the main staircase and I hurried to catch up.

"...most o' the rooms are named after different tartans and they're decorated in the clan colours," Bridget was saying as I rejoined them.

She gestured to the doors we were passing, and I saw that each had a brass plate etched with names like "Ramsay", "Hamilton", and "Mackenzie".

"So do all Scottish surnames have their own tartan?" asked Cassie curiously.

Bridget shook her head. "Only the clans and their septs. But there're some tartans not linked wi' clans. Aye, 'universal tartans', they're called. Anyone can wear those. Like the 'Black Watch' tartan; that was created fer the famous Scottish army regiment but it's noo used aroond the world—"

"Oh yes, I saw it in all sorts of places when I was travelling for my old job," I exclaimed, thinking of the iconic black, dark blue, and green pattern. "I think it's really beautiful and elegant—and it pretty much screams 'Scotland' or 'Scottish' whenever it's used in branding," I added, laughing.

Bridget beamed, looking as proud as if she'd created the tartan herself. She turned a corner and led us to a room at the end of the corridor. A few minutes later, the bedroom door shut behind her and we were alone.

Cassie and I stood for a moment, admiring our spacious new accommodation with its elegant wainscoting and matching wallpaper, framed watercolours of the Scottish countryside, and an antique writing bureau that occupied pride of place by the window.

"Bloody hell!" said Cassie, flopping onto one of the twin beds with a gleeful whoop. "If this is one of their more 'modest' rooms, can you imagine what their suites look like?"

I walked over to the windows to inspect the view. Bridget was right: it might not have been the prime aspect at the front of the castle, but it was still a stunning vista of the side of the glen, backed by the peaks of the mountains in the distance. *There probably isn't a single window in this place that doesn't look out onto a stunning view!* I thought.

Below me, I could see two figures on the terrace, and I smiled as I recognised the Chinese couple, still wrangling their selfie-stick as they attempted to take photos of themselves against the backdrop from every angle.

"Oh, Cass!" I said, turning back into the room and beaming at my best friend. "I'm so glad you made me come! This place is absolutely gorgeous; it's like stepping into a whole different world. It's just what I needed! And everyone's so nice—ooh, don't you just love the Scottish accent? I could listen to it all day! And they make you feel so welcome, even though we're not real guests. You almost feel like you're old friends and—"

"Yeah, I've noticed," said Cassie with a dark look.

I paused. "What's *that* supposed to mean?"

"Well, you were certainly getting *really* friendly with Ewan Campbell, weren't you? In fact, you were flirting outrageously with him."

"What? Don't be ridiculous. I wasn't flirting!"

"Oh yeah?" Cassie put on a baby voice and

fluttered her eyelashes in an exaggerated manner. "*Ooh, what's a ghillie, Ewan? Ooh, how impressive, Ewan! You do all that? Omigod, you're amazing, Ewan!*"

"I didn't talk like that," I cried indignantly. "I was... I was just being polite! And I really didn't know what a ghillie was—did *you*?" I demanded.

"You could have Googled it," said Cassie sulkily.

I shook my head and laughed. "Cassie, what's got into you? I've never seen you take against someone like this. If anything, most women would be instantly smitten by someone as cute and charming as Ewan."

"He's not *that* attractive," muttered Cassie.

"Aw... come *on!* Are you blind? The man's practically a living, breathing *Outlander* fantasy come to life."

Cassie made a rude noise and didn't answer.

I regarded my best friend in puzzlement. *Was she jealous of the attention that Ewan had given me?* It didn't seem like her, though. Cassie was straightforward and blunt to a fault—if she had really wanted Ewan for herself, she would have come right out and told me. Besides, her hostility seemed to be directed at Ewan personally. It was as if she had met him and instantly decided that she didn't like him.

Maybe it's a different kind of jealousy? Maybe Cassie was resentful of my instant camaraderie with Ewan; maybe she felt that it threatened the bond of our own friendship? But that didn't make sense either. Cassie wasn't the possessive type, and she'd never shown any resentment in the past towards any other friends I'd made. If anything, she was quick to embrace them herself and include them in any activity. Cassie's warm, generous nature was one of the things I admired and loved most about her. I shook my head. None of this made sense.

"What?" said Cassie as I continued to stare at her.

"Cassie—you're not jealous, are you?" I asked tentatively.

"Jealous? Over Ewan?" she said, with so much scorn that I hastily backtracked.

"Well, I just thought..."

"I'm going to unpack," she said, getting up off the bed. She opened her case, grabbed some toiletries, and stomped into the ensuite bathroom.

"Er... I think I might pop out and explore the castle for a bit," I called after her. Long experience had taught me that the best thing to do when my best friend was in a strop was to let her cool down.

Cassie grunted in reply. With a last troubled look in the direction of the bathroom, I turned and let myself quietly out of the room.

CHAPTER FIVE

I descended the sweeping staircase and stood for a moment in the Great Hall, feeling slightly at a loss, my mind still on Cassie's strange bad temper. Then I caught sight of the doorway to the library and remembered how fascinating it had seemed from my quick glimpse during our castle tour. Pleased to have a distraction, I headed over. At the doorway, I paused again, my eyes instantly drawn to the enormous stag heads mounted on the walls around the room. Perhaps it was because taxidermy was so rarely encountered in modern life, but there was something incredibly creepy yet mesmerising about the dead creatures.

Slowly, I walked into the room, and as my gaze dropped, I took in, for the first time, the eclectic mix of furniture. There were Chesterfield sofas in butter-soft leather, deep velvet-upholstered settees, and quaint club sofas with rolled arms and wooden legs, all accompanied by vintage side tables exuding "country charm". Although in a variety of different styles, all the seats seemed to invite you to curl up with a title from one of the bookcases lining the walls—if you didn't mind reading under the glassy stares of dead deer, that is!

Then I remembered the big bay window and I turned quickly towards it, keen to see if this view would live up to the others. I wasn't disappointed—if anything, it was probably the most breathtaking vista I'd seen so far. While it didn't have the grand formality of the prospect from the Great Hall, it provided a sweeping—almost panoramic—view of the surrounding countryside. Days were long at the moment, but even so, the afternoon light was deepening, becoming rich and mellow, and the lengthening shadows on the sides of the mountains, coupled with the golden glow on the low-lying clouds, gave a wonderful luminous quality to the landscape. It was like a Horatio McCulloch painting come to life, filled with all the dramatic grandeur and romance of the Scottish Highlands.

I groped in my pocket for my phone and eagerly snapped several shots, laughing to myself as I thought of how the Chinese couple would have been proud of me. Then, with my eyes still on the view, I sank into a Victorian leather armchair that had been placed in a perfect position by the windows and gave a dreamy sigh.

My God, this chair is an experience in itself! I thought as I wriggled deeper into the seat and leaned back against the button-tufted, high-rolled back. Flanked on either side by wide wings which merged into thick scroll arms, the armchair seemed to enclose you completely in a cosy leather cubby, hidden from the rest of the room—and even the rest of the world.

I'm going to come here tomorrow and stake out this seat, I thought with a smile. *With that view in front of me, a good book on my lap, and a hot drink at my elbow, it'll be absolute heaven!*

Slightly regretfully, I pushed myself upright again. It would be dinnertime soon and I knew I should probably return to the room to find out what Cassie's plans were. Before I could rise from the armchair, however, I heard voices behind me. Squirming, I peeked around the side of the armchair and saw that two people had come into the library.

One was a thin middle-aged woman dressed conservatively in a high turtleneck sweater and wool pencil skirt. She wore a pair of wire spectacles dangling from a gold chain around her neck and her hair was grey, cropped in a severe, almost masculine style. She was speaking in sharp tones to the man next to her, in an accent that marked her as definitely Scottish. The man, on the other hand, sounded American, but as he was standing with his back to me, slightly out of my line of sight, I wasn't able to make out much more about him. Twisting in my seat, I leaned surreptitiously out the side of the armchair to try and get a better view—but all I could see was that he seemed to be a large, tall man who was (incongruously) wearing what looked like a cowboy hat.

I hesitated, realising that they couldn't see me due to the high back of the armchair and wondering if I should show myself in case they were discussing something confidential. I started to rise, then paused as I realised that they seemed to be arguing.

"...don't want to have to repeat our whole discussion earlier," the woman was saying impatiently. "I need the full payment by the end of today."

I saw the skin on the back of the man's neck turn red. "Today? You gotta be kidding me!"

"I apologise for any inconvenience," said the woman in mocking tones. "You were aware of the terms and conditions." She paused, then added, "If you're not happy with the quote I provided, I can approach the other interested party—"

"No!" snapped the man. He fumbled at his neck, as if adjusting a tight collar. "No, you'll get the damned payment. I told you that I just need a bit of time—"

"You've had more than enough time, Mr Hudson. In fact, now that I think about it, an additional fee for the extra effort I've had to expend on your behalf would be appropriate."

"What? You greedy bitc—"

Hastily, I stood up, wanting to reveal my presence before things got any more heated, and walked quickly towards them. Instantly, they ceased talking.

The woman eyed me coldly. "What are you doing here? Are you a guest? I don't recognise you."

"Oh, I'm... er... I'm not an official guest," I said, annoyed to find myself stammering under her frosty gaze. "I... um... came with my friend Cassie. Cassandra Jenkins, I mean. She's teaching the painting workshop this weekend."

"Ah." The woman regarded me contemptuously, then said, in a clipped voice that managed to strip the Scottish accent of all its warmth and charm, "I'm Aileen Fergusson, the Manager here at Aberglinn Castle Hotel. I didn't see you arrive, but I assume that the staff have settled you in?"

"Yes, Bridget showed us to our room," I said, trying not to be put off by her manner. "Um... thank you for putting us up. It's really kind and generous of you—"

"I wasn't the one who approved that," she said. "It was Mr Mackay, the owner of the castle, who spoke to the lady making the arrangements. I'm not sure how he got steamrollered into offering room and board with the contract, but I can assure you that it's not the norm. It certainly wouldn't have happened if I had been involved."

I could feel myself flushing. "Oh. Um... well, we're

very grateful," I said awkwardly. "Our room is absolutely beautiful and—"

"Yes, well, you should never have been put in *there*," said Aileen, her mouth tightening. "I don't know what Bridget was thinking! Anyway, it's too late now, but I hope you realise that you're essentially trespassing on the hotel's hospitality. And don't get any ideas about the toiletries," she added crisply. "Those are premium luxury brands and strictly for paying guests. I know what you girls are like, thinking you can pilfer bottles and tubes to take home, but—"

"Cassie and I would never dream of doing that!" I cried, stung. "Look, you seem to have got the wrong idea. We're not trying to sponge off the hotel. I'm happy to pay towards the room if you think—"

"It's done now." Aileen waved a hand, already turning away and dismissing me. "As long as you remember your place."

I gasped at her rudeness, and irritation made me call out, on an impulse:

"Actually, wait—I wanted to ask you something, Ms Fergusson."

She turned back, looking annoyed. "Yes?"

"I was wondering... would it be okay for me to spend a bit of time in the castle kitchen? I just wanted to watch the chefs at work, perhaps ask them some questions about traditional Scottish baking—"

"Absolutely not," she cut me off. "I can't have you disturbing the staff and wasting their time. They need to be focused on their work. We have an award-winning dining room here at Aberglinn Castle Hotel; we are a professional commercial kitchen in a five-star establishment, not a community college for wannabe bakers."

Before I could think of how to reply, she turned and strode from the room, leaving me speechless with angry indignation. Now I understood why Ewan had been so terse when he mentioned the castle manager: unless he'd wanted to badmouth her behind her back, there was really nothing good to say!

A sound beside me made me look around, and I realised suddenly that the American was still standing there. My cheeks reddened even more as I realised that he'd just witnessed the whole humiliating scene.

There was a strained silence for a moment, then he cleared his throat and said, gesturing to the stag heads on the walls above us:

"Some mighty fine trophies here, huh?"

I gave him a wan smile, grateful for his attempt to smooth over the awkward moment. As I looked at him properly for the first time, I found myself trying not to stare. I had been right about the cowboy hat—it was a black Stetson, to be exact. Coupled with a jacket showing yoke detailing across the shoulders, a leather belt with the most enormous gold buckle I'd ever seen, and cowboy boots peeking out from beneath his jeans, the man looked like a character from a Wild West theme park.

He completed the cliché by hooking his thumbs into his jeans pockets and saying loftily, "'Course we got much bigger game in America. You ain't really done hunting 'til you've taken down a Rocky Mountain elk with a rack that's over four feet wide. Or a bison—man, we have bulls that weigh over two thousand pounds. Even the wild hogs down in my neck of the woods are probably bigger than these Scotch deer."

"They do sound very impressive," I said politely. "Are you a hunter?"

"Nah, not really. I mean, I've been out on game hunts and all that, but it's not really my thing. I'm more of a bourbon-and-cigar kinda guy—more cultured, you know?" he said, giving me a wink and a leer.

I shifted slightly back, putting more space between us. "Oh. Um... so are you visiting Scotland for the whisky distilleries?"

"Yeah, kinda. Got here earlier last week, but I haven't done much exploring yet." He stuck out a big, beefy hand. "Name's Jerry Hudson."

I shook his hand gingerly. I didn't particularly want to exchange names with this man, but it felt rude not to respond in kind. "Um... I'm Gemma... Gemma Rose."

"Rose? Ah, so you're from Clan Rose?"

"I beg your pardon?"

"You know, the Rose clan of Kilravock." He gave

me a smug look. "I know all about clan history, see, cos I'm Scottish myself."

"You... you are?" I blinked at him.

"Yeah. My great-great-great-grandfather came from round these parts," he said, waving a hand towards the view through the window. "Might even be a descendant of Robert the Bruce, you know... although I think I'm probably more Clan MacGregor. So what clan *are* you from?"

"Oh, I'm not Scottish."

"Is that right? But you've got that cute accent." He gave me another wink and salacious smile.

I shifted my weight. "Er... thank you. My accent isn't Scottish, though. I'm from Oxford, which is down south. Close to London."

"But it's all kinda the same, right? You're all part of England—"

"Oh God, don't let the Scots hear you say that!" I cried with a horrified laugh. "You'll get lynched! Scotland is part of *Great Britain*, together with England and Wales, but they're all separate countries and they've each got their own... well, personalities, if you like. Their own cultures."

"Oh sure. I'm big into Scotch culture. I know all about tartans and bagpipes. I know Scottish 'whisky' is spelled without an 'e'. And I know you say it 'Edin-BRUH'." He gave me a challenging look. "You think just because I dress like this, I must be a dumb American?"

"No, of course not," I said quickly. "I'm sorry. I

didn't mean..." I broke off, annoyed at my own very English habit of offering apology instantly. Raising my chin, I looked at Jerry Hudson levelly and said: "I wasn't trying to be offensive, and I think you know that. You were baiting me. And you must know that by dressing like that, you're deliberately inviting people to see you as a cliché."

He grinned at me. "Huh. I like a girl with a bit of spunk. And hey, I'm no cliché. I wear this stuff 'cos I like it. Back in Texas, we're proud of our Midwestern traditions and you see regular folk out wearing boots and hats anywhere in the state." He stepped closer and leaned towards me, wagging a stubby finger in my face. "In fact, you go out to a dance hall or bar or restaurant without boots and a hat, and *you're* likely to be the odd one out. 'Course, a pretty gal like you would stick out anyway, so maybe it don't matter."

I could feel his breath on my face and his eyes skimming over my body in a way that made my skin crawl. But given that he hadn't actually touched me, I didn't feel that I could say anything. Instead, I took another step back, trying to put more distance between us again, and said at random:

"That's... er... unusual, what you're wearing around your neck... What is it?"

"This? It's a bolo tie," said Hudson, fingering the loop of braided leather which encircled his shirt collar and was secured at the front by an ornamental silver clasp, so that the two long ends were left hanging.

"This here's the official tie of Texas, you know. All the cowboys wear 'em. They come with different slides—" He held up the silver clasp on his tie. "—this one's from an antique dealer. It was carved by a Navajo silversmith; see the marks between the turquoise stones? That's a traditional eagle feather pattern." He raised the clasp to his lips and gave it a kiss. "It's my lucky piece. I wear it every day—never go anywhere without it. I like to call it my trademark look."

He tipped his hat at me and smirked, stepping closer to me again. "I think I look pretty good as a cowboy. Whaddya think?" he asked in a deliberately husky voice.

Suddenly, I had had enough of his heavy-handed leching. "I think you have to be pretty desperate to come up with cheesy chat-up lines like that," I said, crisply.

He flushed bright red. "I... I wasn't... You got the wrong end of the stick, ma'am! I was just being friendly," he spluttered. "What makes you think I was trying to chat you up?"

I gave him a sweet smile. "Well, this ain't my first rodeo".

CHAPTER SIX

When I got back to the room, I found Cassie frantically rifling through the contents of her case.

"Guess what, Gemma?" She looked up, her eyes bright with excitement. "Aberglinn Castle holds a six-course 'tasting menu' dinner once a week on Friday nights, and I've just been told that the guests who were supposed to stay in this room had a table booked. That's cancelled now, of course, but the food's all prepared, and with all the focus on 'sustainability' now, they don't want to let anything go to waste, so... they've offered us the table for free!"

"Wow, really?" I said, thinking that this obviously hadn't been run past Aileen Fergusson either, otherwise there was no way Cassie and I would have been allowed to sample a Michelin-starred degustation menu instead of the plain gruel she had probably planned for us!

"Yeah, it starts with pre-dinner drinks downstairs in the Great Hall." Cassie made a rueful face. "The only problem is, it's formal. Jacket and tie for men, and something posh for the ladies. No jeans allowed. I didn't bring anything dressy—did you?"

I shook my head. "I thought we were just going to hang around the castle or go out hiking, so I only brought casual stuff. Oh, wait... I think I did bring a black skirt. I suppose that'll do?"

Cassie sighed and looked down at her case. "I didn't bring a single skirt or pair of smart trousers or anything. The only thing I've brought are extra painting smocks!" She reached down and lifted an item out of her case. "Hmm... this one is completely new though, and it's quite a pretty colour. Maybe I could turn it into a makeshift dress?" She went over to the mirror and held the pinafore-style garment up against her chest, eyeing it critically. "What do you think?"

I looked enviously at my friend. To be honest, Cassie had the kind of hourglass figure that would look good in a black rubbish sack. I was sure she could make a cheap artist's smock look like designer wear—and I was proved right half an hour later when she came out of the bathroom, all dressed and made-up.

"Well... what d'you think?" she asked, twirling on the spot.

"You look incredible!" I said. "Honestly, Cass, anyone would think you're wearing some trendy bohemian dress! It's got a sort of Sixties vibe... and I like how you've done your hair to go with it," I added, admiring the way my best friend had pulled back her dark tresses at the sides and pinned them so that they cascaded around her shoulders.

"Thanks!" Cassie plucked at the hem of the smock, which ended several inches above her knee. "Do you think it's too short though? I can't really do anything about the length and I didn't bring any tights or leggings."

"People will just think it's a minidress," I assured her. "Anyway, the rest of it is quite loose and baggy, so it's not like it's clinging to your body in a vulgar way as well. I'm sure it's fine." I indicated my own ensemble and asked worriedly, "What about me? Will I pass muster?"

"Mm..." Cassie tilted her head to one side and examined me.

I had opted for the ubiquitous "little black dress"—or little black skirt and top, in this case. It was safe but boring, and I wished wistfully that I had a bit of Cassie's creative flair when it came to fashion.

"It's a bit *black*, isn't it? Especially with your dark hair as well—you look like you're going to a funeral," she said with a best friend's merciless honesty. Then she brightened. "I know! You just need to put on some bright lipstick and add some colour with accessories—I've got the perfect thing!"

She hurried over to where she had tossed her tote bag on a chair and rummaged in its depths, emerging a few minutes later with a crumpled bundle. When she untangled it, I saw that it was a long silk scarf in a mix of vivid colours that was reminiscent of the rich gold-and-ruby glow of autumn foliage.

"I usually have this to tie my hair up," Cassie explained. "But you can wear it around your neck or draped over your shoulder..." She arranged the scarf on me and turned me back to face the mirror. "Ta-da!"

She was right, and when I left the room a few minutes later, with a dash of vivid lipstick on my lips and the silk scarf around my neck, I felt more than ready to face the world.

We swept down the grand staircase and arrived in the Great Hall to find it filled with guests milling about, sipping glasses of sherry and champagne. Those who had booked ahead for the dinner had obviously known about the formal dress code and brought appropriate wear—although as usual, the women had made more effort than the men. There was an elegant middle-aged woman in a black, sequinned gown accompanied by a man in a sombre grey suit—I recognised them as the couple who had been playing chess in the Great Hall earlier. Two elderly English ladies—the ones who had been admiring the vase of hydrangeas—were standing shyly together, wearing floral summer dresses and carrying matching handbags. A young blonde woman wearing a sleek minimalist sheath stood by the fireplace, toying with a glass of champagne. Her companion leaned nonchalantly against the mantelpiece next to her, his blond good looks matching hers and the two of them looking like models in a fashion shoot.

At the foot of the stairs stood two men; I recognised one as the man who had been sitting by himself, reading the newspaper earlier, and I guessed that the other—younger—man was his partner. The former was conservatively dressed in a simple jacket and tie, but the younger man wore a flamboyant silk shirt paired with denim trousers, which would have flouted the dress code had it not been for the fact that they were obviously so expensive and *avant-garde*, they could never be called anything as plebeian as "jeans".

Next to them stood Jerry Hudson, talking loudly and gesticulating with his hands. He was still wearing his Western-style suit, complete with bolo tie, but he had dispensed with the cowboy hat, and his balding head gleamed in the light from the chandeliers above.

"Come on," I said to Cassie, steering her away from them.

"Hey... that's Shane and Luke from Sydney," Cassie protested as I tugged her arm. "They're really nice. I bumped into them earlier and we got chatting. Shane's an engineer and Luke is in fashion. You'd like them—"

"Yes, but they're with Jerry Hudson and I promise you, you *wouldn't* like chatting to him," I said firmly, leading her to the other side of the room.

We came across the young Chinese couple I'd met earlier—the girl in a pretty cocktail dress and her husband sporting a bow tie. They were eagerly taking photos of an enormous harp, which had been brought into a corner of the Great Hall. A red-haired girl sat at the harp, moving her arms gracefully across the strings, but any music produced was drowned out by the shrieks of two children who were running around the hall, chasing each other, whilst their parents watched indulgently.

I realised that it was the family I'd seen by the fireplace earlier. The father was dark and bearded, dressed in an expensive Italian suit, and the wife was heavily made-up, with a diamond-encrusted watch sparkling on her wrist and gold jewellery dripping from her neck and ears. She flicked the skirt of her haute couture dress to one side to prevent her son stepping on it but made no attempt to stop him as he ran past her.

"You can't catch me! You can't catch me!" the little boy chanted as he dodged around an antique side table, knocking against the ceramic figurine on display.

"Hey!" cried Cassie, lunging to grab the figurine before it toppled over. She set it carefully right again and turned to frown at the little boy. "Be careful. You might break something."

"So what?" said the boy's older sister, who looked about seven. "My father can pay for it. He's the richest man in Dubai!"

Cassie looked taken aback. She glanced at the parents, obviously expecting them to reprimand the child, but the father just roared with laughter, as if the little girl had said something very clever.

"Maybe not the richest... *yet*, Safa," he said with a smug smile. "Now take your brother and go see that lady at the harp."

The girl turned and called: "Hamid! Come here!"

"No!" the little boy yelled back.

"Baba said you have to listen to me!" she hissed.

"No!" her brother said, unimpressed. Then he started chanting "*You can't catch me! You can't catch me!*" again as he skipped away.

"YOU LISTEN TO ME!" shrieked his older sister, chasing after him. "*HAMID!* COME HERE!"

They began chasing each other around the room again, both yelling at the top of their voices. The din was deafening, and I saw several of the other guests frown as the children raced past them, chanting and shouting. I glanced at the parents, sure that they would do something at last to check their offspring's behaviour, but the wife just giggled as her son collided with one of the elderly ladies, nearly knocking her off her feet.

The father chuckled and glanced at us. "*Wallah...* they're cute, huh?" he said with indulgent pride.

"No, they're bloody rude, spoilt brats," Cassie

muttered under her breath. "Honestly, if the parents don't do something, I'm going to—"

The yelling ceased abruptly, and I looked up in surprise to see both children standing frozen. Looming over them was Aileen Fergusson, who had come quietly into the Great Hall. She was looking at the children like they were bugs she was about to squash underfoot.

"That is *enough*," she said in a deadly quiet voice.

The children stumbled backwards, then turned and ran back to their parents. I saw the father frown at Aileen and make as if to stand up, but he was distracted by his daughter flinging herself sulkily into his lap. The rest of the guests, though, breathed a sigh of relief and I saw several people look over at Aileen with new respect.

"It's a shame she can't shut the adults up as well," said an American voice behind me, and I turned in surprise to see the elegant middle-aged couple who had been playing chess earlier.

The husband caught me looking at them and said quickly in embarrassment, "Sorry, didn't mean for you to hear that! It's just that *that* guy..." He shot a disgusted look across the room at Jerry Hudson, who was talking loudly once more.

I gave him a sympathetic smile. "It's all right. I met him earlier so I... um... know what you mean."

"I hope you don't think all Americans are like him!" said the husband quickly. "Some of us do have manners, you know."

I laughed. "Don't worry. I run a tearoom so I've met lots of American tourists. Many are lovely, modest people."

"Yes, but it's always the ones like *him* who are the loudest and who people remember," said the husband ruefully. Then he looked at me with interest. "A tearoom, huh? Here in Scotland?"

"No, actually, it's down south, in a little village just outside Oxford," I explained. "I'm here on holiday. Well, sort of. My friend—" I indicated Cassie, who was chatting with the Chinese couple. "—is teaching the painting workshop this weekend and I've sort of tagged along."

"Oh, I'm booked on that workshop," said the wife brightly. "Not that I'm much of an artist," she added with a self-conscious laugh. "But it'll be real nice to take home a souvenir that I've painted myself."

"Will you be doing the workshop too?" I asked the husband politely.

He shook his head. "I'm gonna do the 'Ghillie Experience'. Really looking forward to that! Especially how to forage for mushrooms—apparently there are lots of wild chanterelle mushrooms growing on the estate. I'm hoping we'll also get to try out fly fishing. Well, actually, I've tried it back in Texas, but nothing beats doing it in Scotland, right?"

"You're from Texas?" I blurted. "But you're nothing like—" I broke off, embarrassed.

The husband gave me a wry look. "Nothing like Jerry Hudson? Yeah, like I said, it's people like him who give Americans—and Texans—a bad name. And here's the kicker: Hudson isn't even *from* Texas. That's right; he acts like he's some big Texas oil tycoon but he's originally from Southern California. He just married a local girl and now he's swaggering around like the original cowboy or something." He shook his head in disgust.

"I'm Connie, by the way," said the wife, smiling at me and extending a hand. "And this is my husband, Bruce."

I shook her hand, returning the smile. "I'm Gemma. And it's lovely to meet you both. Is this your first time in Scotland?"

"Oh no, we have visited before but just Edinburgh," said Bruce. "So this time we wanted to stay longer and see a bit of the Highlands." He grinned at me. "One of the perks of being retired: you can vacation for as long as you want. We're planning to head down to England after this—actually, Oxford is on our itinerary. We must look you up. What's your tearoom called?"

"Oh, it'll be lovely to have you," I said warmly. "My tearoom is called The Little Stables and it's in a village called Meadowford-on-Smythe, which is just on the edge of the Cotswolds."

"It sounds delightful," said Connie. "I love your traditional English tearooms. We've got a few back in the States, of course, but it's just not the same."

At that moment, a couple appeared at the top of the stairs and everyone looked up. It was the young man who had been driving the Rolls-Royce that had nearly crashed into Ewan's car. He swaggered down the steps with his voluptuous companion from earlier sashaying next to him. She was wearing an excess of jewellery and a dress so tight that it looked like it had been spray-painted onto her body—the hem barely coming down low enough to cover her derrière.

"My God, I can't believe I was worried about *my* dress," said Cassie, rejoining me.

"We haven't got any of those either, back in America," Connie said to me with a wink as she nodded at the young man descending the stairs. "He's some kind of lord, I think?"

"No, honey, he hasn't got a title, but he *is* a member of the landed gentry," said her husband. "I was talking to him at breakfast this morning—his name's Tristan St Clair, and apparently his father owns estates across half of England."

"Great. Another arrogant, rich plonker," muttered Cassie to me. "I just hope he's not enrolled in my workshop tomorrow—or that tart on his arm."

Before I could reply, a large, rotund man walked into the Great Hall and called out to the gathered crowd. He was magnificently attired in formal Highland dress: a black Prince Charlie jacket and three-buttoned waistcoat paired with a pleated tartan kilt, white hose socks, a calfskin sporran, and ghillie brogues. He looked to be in his sixties and had a rather florid complexion, with the kind of flushed skin and broken veins of someone who enjoyed his drink frequently.

"Welcome, welcome! Hoo are ye?" he said in a booming, jovial voice. "My name is Angus MacKay and I'm yer host. Aberglinn Castle has been in my family fer generations, and I'm delighted tae welcome ye tae my home." He beamed at us. "We're looking forward tae shoon ye the famous Scottish hospitality. My staff and I will do everything tae make yer stay as comfortable as possible. Feel free tae wander aroond the castle and if ye have any questions, just ask—"

"Yeah, I got a question," yelled Jerry Hudson. "You wearing anything under that kilt?" He guffawed loudly and there was a twitter of nervous laughter from a few others, but I also saw several people roll their eyes. Next to me, Connie and Bruce grimaced.

Angus Mackay gave a forced laugh. "Ahh... a better question would be where that idea came from! There's no documented evidence tae say a true Scotsman shouldnae wear underpants under his kilt—'twas probably a joke that's goan tae become urban myth. Mind ye, Scottish culture is full o' myths and traditions which have spread all over the world. Aye, ye be surprised hoo many common beliefs and customs originated from Scotland."

He pointed at the American guests. "Fer example, did ye know that one o' yer biggest holidays started here in Scotland? Aye, Hallowe'en is rooted in the Celtic festival o' *Samhain*. 'Twas believed that this was a time when the veil that protected us from the

Otherworld became thin, alloon spirits and demons tae pass through. So people started 'guising'—that is, puttin' on disguises when they had tae venture oot, so that demons wouldnae recognise them and do them harm. And that's become the modern tradition o' Hallowe'en costumes. Even 'trick or treat', ye know, comes from the old Celtic beliefs that ye had tae leave tokens o' food tae appease the spirits."

"No way!" said Jerry Hudson, grinning. "So you Scotch gave us Hallowe'en, huh?"

Bruce winced next to me and muttered, "It's 'Scots', you idiot."

Angus Mackay, however, was continuing unperturbed: "...aye, we love oor myths and legends here in Scotland. Most places have a story attached. In fact, Aberglinn Castle itself has a legend—the legend o' the phantom piper."

"What's a piper?" cried the little girl, Safa.

"Ahh... a piper is someone who plays the bagpipes, and it's a very respected and honoured position in Scottish history. Because he wasnae just a musician, ye see. He was also the one who led the Highland warriors intae battle. He'd walk at the front o' the army and play tunes tae inspire the clans—so there's noan braver than the piper," said Mackay, running his eye over his audience.

There was a hushed silence in the Great Hall, everyone rapt as they waited for him to continue his story. Even the children were sitting quiet and wide-eyed.

Mackay smiled, looking pleased. "Well, legend says there was once a ghostly presence in the mountains aroond Aberglinn Castle, and the people o' the village were terrified. So they came tae the laird and asked him fer help, and he sent his best piper oot tae the hills. Noo, this piper had a cat—a wee black creature with yellow eyes, who followed him everywhere he went, just like a shadow—and so when the piper went oot intae the mountains, the cat went too. And all the village could hear the music o' the pipes as they got fainter and fainter..." Mackay dropped his voice. "Until at last, it stopped altogether and the villagers couldnae hear no more. They searched fer the piper fer days and days, but they never saw 'im agin."

"What happened to him?" asked Safa in a loud whisper.

Mackay shrugged. "Who knows? P'haps he was spirited away by the faerie folk... or p'haps he found his way oot o' the mountains, on the other side o' the Highlands... or mebbe he's oot there still..."

He turned his eyes towards the windows and all the guests turned their heads too, to stare out at the mountainous landscape.

"But they do say that if ye walk oot in the mountains aroond Aberglinn on a dark night, ye might see a wee black cat with yellow eyes and ye might hear the piper playin' nearby..." Mackay paused dramatically, a twinkle in his eye. "Aye, there are some who even say that when ye hear the music o' the pipes up in the mountains, it's a sign that someone at the castle is goin' tae die."

There was a collective indrawn breath from the guests and the children whimpered. It was silly and melodramatic—and probably due to nothing more than the setting of the castle, with the brooding landscape all around—but Mackay's words made a shiver go down my spine in spite of myself.

Then a voice said crisply: "That's enough with the havering, sir. The guests might not know you're talking mince"

I turned back to see Aileen Fergusson giving her boss a pointed look, obviously reminding him of the importance of providing a welcoming and positive ambience.

Angus Mackay looked sheepish. "Oh... aye... aye... these are all jus' stories, o' course. Don't worry, noan is going tae die." He gave a hearty laugh and hastily changed the subject. "Speakin' o' life and death, did ye know that whisky is known as the 'water o' life' in Scotland? Aye, there's nothin' like whisky tae reinvigorate ye, especially if yer cold or ill. And if any o' ye would like tae taste some famous 'water o' life', I can take ye over tae the bar right noo..."

He began leading the way out of the Great Hall, with several of the guests eagerly following. I saw the children's father stride out after Mackay and—after a hasty "You stay here and play" to Safa and Hamid— his wife followed. The rest of the guests began mingling again, and the hum of conversation filled the hall once more. Cassie drifted over to the two elderly ladies and began chatting to them animatedly. I was just about to join them when I was halted in my tracks by a scream.

Whirling, I saw the little girl, Safa, staring at something behind an armchair. She pointed a shaking finger and cried, her eyes round with fear:

"It's the cat! The black cat from the story!" She looked wildly around. "Somebody in the castle is going to die!"

CHAPTER SEVEN

Behind me, the harp twanged suddenly as the harpist hit a discordant note. There was a hubbub of concern as everyone turned to see what Safa was pointing at. I leaned over and saw that there was indeed a small black cat skulking behind the armchair. It didn't seem to be doing anything particularly threatening, but the little girl was working herself into a state, sobbing and screaming hysterically. Her brother began to look scared too, his mouth wobbling as he thought about joining in the outcry.

"That's enough of that," said Aileen sternly, hurrying over to the children. "*Wheesht!* Stop your carrying on! It's nothing but a stray that's got in by mistake. There are always cats hanging around the kitchen—this one must have slipped into the castle when no one was looking."

Safa ignored the words. In fact, the little girl shot a gleeful look around the circle of grown-ups, all watching her in concern, and—with a deep breath, like a prima donna gearing up for her great solo—she launched into fresh wails.

"I said that's *enough!*" snapped Aileen, swinging her arm.

There was a loud *SMACK!* and, for a shocked moment, I thought the castle manager had slapped the child. Then I realised that what she had actually slapped was the top of the side table next to the armchair. The noise was explosive, startling the girl into silence and causing the cat to shoot away in fright.

Safa gave a gulping sob, her chest heaving, as she stared at Aileen. Then her little face flushed in fury and she opened her mouth again. Before she could make a sound, however, the harpist rushed across the room and threw her arms around the little girl.

"Can't you see that she's terrified?" cried the harpist, giving Aileen an anguished look. "This will traumatise her for life!"

Aileen made a noise of scorn. "Och, don't be ridiculous! She's just being a drama queen. She knows the cat is harmless and she's still carrying on, just for the attention—"

"No, no, some people really *are* scared of cats!" said the harpist. "Some people have a cat phobia and can't help it—"

Aileen gave a jeering laugh. "Cat phobia? Whoever heard of such a stupid thing?"

The harpist flushed bright red and looked on the verge of tears herself. Safa had been listening wide-eyed, her head swinging back and forth between the two women. Now, she wriggled free of the harpist's arms and backed away.

"I'm going to tell my father!" she said, glaring at Aileen, then she turned to run out of the Great Hall with her brother following.

They took a zigzag path, shoving things out of their way as they darted between the various pieces of furniture. I gasped as they shot past me and knocked against the harp. The huge instrument began toppling over sideways. The harpist cried out in dismay and rushed across the room, but she was too far away—she would never catch it in time. Without thinking, I lunged forwards and grabbed the harp, staggering under its weight.

"Oh my God! Thank you!" cried the harpist, arriving at my elbow and taking hold of the harp as well.

She helped me set the instrument back upright, then turned and gave me a grateful look. "Th-thank you so much. I can't imagine what would have happened if it had fallen on this," she said, indicating the hard flagstone flooring of the castle. "It cost a fortune to buy the harp. I don't know what I would have done if it was damaged!"

"That's okay," I said, smiling at her reassuringly. "I'm just glad I caught it in time. It's a gorgeous instrument—and you play it beautifully."

She flushed with pleasure and some of the panic left her green eyes. I noticed for the first time how pretty she was, with milky white skin and a smattering of freckles across her nose that complemented the vivid red locks tumbling around her face. She was also a lot taller than she had looked sitting down at the harp, with a slim figure that I guessed was more the result of nerves than any excessive dieting.

"Thanks," she said shyly. "I'm still a fairly novice player, but I work really hard at it. I'm Lilian, by the way. Lilian Monaghan. And I overheard you introducing yourself to that American couple earlier—Gemma, isn't it?"

"Yes, that's right. Do you come to play at the castle often?"

"No, actually, this is my first time. I was really lucky to get this gig. The lady who normally plays on these formal dinner evenings had to go down south suddenly—some family emergency, I think—and so they needed someone at the last moment. Uncle Angus—I mean, Mr Mackay—knows my parents, and so they suggested me and he gave me the job."

"Well, I think they're lucky to have you," I told her warmly. "Honestly, the music was wonderful, and I would never have guessed that you were new at the instrument."

"Oh, thank you!" she said, her eyes shining. "That's really nice of you to say! It's made the whole evening worth it—especially as I'm not getting paid," she confided.

"You're not getting paid?"

"No, you see, Mrs Fergusson said that since I'm new and not as experienced, she would only take me as a trial, and she's only paying for my train tickets to get here. But anyway, it's good experience—and it'll go on my CV and hopefully get me more gigs," she said cheerfully.

"I hope they're at least providing you with a nice dinner," I said.

"Oh... not really. Mrs Fergusson wanted me to keep playing while the guests are eating in the dining room. You know, to provide background music and maintain the ambience."

Bloody hell, Aileen Fergusson sounds like a slave driver. "I still think they should give you some food," I said indignantly.

"It's okay," said Lilian, smiling at me. "I had quite a large tea before I came, so I'm not that hungry. I can have a late-night snack when I get home."

We were interrupted by a commotion, and I looked up to see that Safa and Hamid had come back into the Great Hall, towing their father behind them.

"That's her!" said Safa with a spiteful look, pointing to Aileen Fergusson.

The little girl's father approached Aileen, scowling. "My daughter told me you shout at her. You bully her!"

"Oh, don't be so melodramatic," said Aileen impatiently. "The child was making a fuss over nothing and carrying on just to get attention. I simply showed her a bit of tough love. Children need discipline and boundaries, not endless fussing and spoiling, and all that modern 'helicopter parenting' nonsense."

"What do you know about teaching children?" demanded the father.

"Quite a lot, actually, considering that I used to be a professional nanny," said Aileen crisply. "Furthermore, as manager of the hotel, I also know that the other guests have a right to enjoy the castle without your spoilt brats disturbing them. So if you can't control their behaviour, I'll have to ask you to remove them from the public areas."

The father spluttered angrily. "You are a servant! You don't talk to me like that!" He shoved a finger in her face. "I will go speak to your boss. I will make him fire you!"

If he had hoped to scare Aileen, he failed miserably. The castle manager simply shrugged and turned away. She addressed the rest of the guests, saying calmly: "Dinner will be served in five minutes. Please start to make your way into the dining room." Then she left the hall without a backward glance.

The father stared furiously after her retreating back, then he spun on his heel and stalked back towards the hotel bar. There was an awkward silence, then Lilian hurriedly sat down at the harp again and began playing a Celtic tune. After another uncomfortable pause, everyone started making their way out of the Great Hall and into the dining room. I followed suit, although I loitered at the rear of the crowd, curious to see if Safa's father would return with Angus Mackay.

Just as I was about to step into the dining room, I saw the castle owner come back into the Great Hall, accompanied by Safa's father. The latter was talking rapidly, with aggressive motions of his hands, whilst Mackay seemed to be trying to soothe him. I slowed my steps, wishing that I could make out what was being said, but it would have been hard to listen to their conversation without making it obvious that I was hanging back and eavesdropping.

"Miss Rose, are you coming in?"

I turned to see Aileen herself standing in the doorway to the dining room, waiting impatiently for me. Then her eyes went beyond me to the two men on the other side of the Hall. The father was gesticulating furiously now, his voice rising, and this time I didn't have to strain to hear the words:

"...want you to fire her immediately!"

I glanced at Aileen and was surprised to see that she didn't look remotely worried. Instead, a smug smile played around the corners of her lips, almost as if she was enjoying the scene. Mackay glanced across the hall and saw us. He shifted uneasily and there was a trapped look in his eyes. Aileen raised an expectant eyebrow and Mackay flushed, then he turned back to the father and said in effusive tones:

"Please accept my apologies, Mr Al-Mansouri! I know yer upset but I'm sure it was jus' a misunderstandin'. Aye, Mrs Fergusson is very experienced, especially wi' children, and she was jus' lookin' oot fer yer wee girl. I'm sure she didnae mean tae offend ye in any way..."

Aileen turned and went back into the dining room, and I felt obliged to follow her. I found Cassie already seated at our table, which—like all the furniture in the dining room—was a dark oak affair with carved legs and matching high-backed chairs. My friend was staring at the myriad types of crockery, glassware, and cutlery laid out on the snowy white tablecloth in front of her.

"Bloody hell, this reminds me of Guest Dinners at Oxford," she said in a hushed voice as I sat down. "All these fish knives and bouillon spoons and trying to remember which one to use first..."

"Isn't there some simple rule? Start from the outside and work your way in, isn't that it?" I replied. Then I glanced across the room at Jerry Hudson, who had seated himself at a table with the two elderly English ladies. He was talking loudly and pointing with his butter knife as he illustrated a point. "Honestly, as long as you don't wave your knife around like *him*, you're probably okay."

Cassie followed my gaze. "Ugh, that sleazy git. I walked past him out in the Hall just now and he started trying to chat me up. He was standing next to me and started sliding his hand behind me and pretending to 'brush against' my bum by mistake. Can you believe it?"

"Sadly, I can. I met him earlier when I was in the library," I said ruefully. "I'm hoping to avoid him for the rest of our time here—"

I broke off as the waiting staff came out of the kitchen bearing the first course. It was a plate of grilled langoustine accompanied by smoked-seaweed butter, Oscietra caviar, and a pear, celeriac, and hazelnut salad—all arranged so beautifully that it looked like a work of art. But it wasn't so much the gourmet food that made me break into a smile as the sight of the familiar figure bearing the plate.

"Ewan!" I cried in delight as he came over to our table. "What are you doing here? Don't tell me serving dinner is part of a ghillie's duties too?"

"No," said Ewan, chuckling. "They're a bit short-staffed in the kitchen tonight so I offered to help out."

"You seem very experienced for someone who's just 'helping out'," said Cassie sarcastically, watching as Ewan expertly laid the dishes down in front us, flicked out our napkins to lay over our laps, and poured the accompanying wine.

"Well, you could say that this is my old stomping ground. My aunt used to work at Aberglinn Castle, so I used to come and do part-time jobs when I was in my teens—you know, just helping out wherever they needed me. I got to know the ropes pretty well."

He indicated the wine glasses by our plates. "A glass of wine comes complimentary with the meal, but if you'd like more, just let me know."

"One glass is fine. I don't think we can afford any of the wines in this place," said Cassie with a wry look. "Besides, Gemma's a lightweight—she hardly drinks at all."

"You don't drink?" said Ewan, looking at me with surprise.

"I do a bit... sometimes," I said, slightly embarrassed by his incredulity. "I just... I'm not very into alcohol."

"Ahh, that's because you haven't tasted the right kind," said Ewan, grinning. "Well, drinker or not, you've *got* to try some proper Scotch whisky while you're here. You can't come to the Highlands and not taste one of our famous single malts. In fact, there's a small distillery not far from here. I know the owners really well and I'd be happy to take you over for a tour and private whisky tasting sometime, if you like."

"Er... thanks, that sounds nice," I said, trying to ignore Cassie scowling from across the table.

Her stormy expression put a strain on the atmosphere and I was glad when Ewan finally left us to go and serve other tables. I half expected my best friend to launch into another tirade about him as soon as he'd gone, but to my relief, she seemed too intent on prising her langoustine out of its shell to have much energy left for conversation. In fact, the succession of courses, each more delicious than the last, demanded our full attention for the rest of the meal. There was roast Orkney scallop with cashew nuts and purple broccoli, pan-fried duck liver with poached rhubarb, a beautiful smoked salmon terrine accompanied by dainty quail eggs, herb-crusted lamb with minted peas and crispy kipfler potatoes... and for dessert, a crowdie cheesecake with macerated strawberries or a hot chocolate fondant with honeycomb and caramel ice cream. By the time we'd finished the "after-dinner" tea and coffees, accompanied by a selection of rich chocolate truffles, we were groaning about our distended bellies and swearing to each other that we weren't going to eat again for a week!

It was late—the grandfather clock at the base of the stairs was striking ten thirty as we ascended the steps—and once in our room, we lost no time in getting ready for bed. But to my annoyance, I found myself wide awake half an hour later, lying in bed and staring at the ceiling. After the long day of travelling and the big meal we'd had, it should have been easy to fall asleep. I was exhausted and yet my mind was buzzing, too busy to allow me to relax enough to drift off.

Tired but wired—isn't that the phrase? I thought as I sighed and turned over once more.

My eyes had acclimatised to the darkness and I could make out the faint shapes of the furniture in the room. The pale light that seeped in between the edges of the heavy drapes at the windows seemed unusually bright and I wondered if there was a full moon tonight. I listened enviously to Cassie's deep breathing as she slept peacefully in the twin bed next to me and tried to match my own breathing to hers. But to no avail.

Finally, I sat up and flung back the bedclothes in frustration. Getting out of bed, I padded across to the windows and gently parted the drapes. Despite the warmth of the day, temperatures had dropped since the sun had set, and my breath fogged the cold glass as I peered out at the moonlit landscape. There *was* a full moon tonight, although it was partially obscured by clouds. But the pale light was reflected and amplified by the white mist that swirled in ghostly shapes around the base of the mountains. It looked like something straight out of a fantasy or fairy tale, and I could see how the Scots ould have believed so readily in myths and superstitions. Who wouldn't, living in a setting like this?

I started to turn away from the window, then froze, the hair prickling on the back of my neck. Was that the mournful wail of the wind? Or was it the plaintive drone of a bagpipe?

Yes... there... above the sound of the wind... I was sure I could hear an eerie wailing tune that rose and fell in rhythmic succession, the haunting echo of an ancient highland melody.

Angus Mackay's voice reverberated in my mind: *"Aye, there are some who even say that when ye hear the music o' the pipes up in the mountains, it's a sign that someone at the castle is goin' tae die."*

Stop being ridiculous, I berated myself silently. *Your imagination is just going into overdrive because of that story Mackay told before dinner.*

Turning away from the window, I decided that the best thing to do was try and read a bit. Perhaps that would distract my busy mind and tire me enough to fall asleep. I hadn't brought a book along but, like many people nowadays, I had an e-book reading app on my phone and a virtual library full of volumes to be sampled. Trying to move quietly so as not to wake Cassie, I began to search the room for my mobile. A few minutes later, I straightened with a frustrated sigh. Where on earth was my phone? Had I not brought it back up to the room with me? I tried to think back to when I'd last had it. I couldn't remember having it with me at dinner. Had I left it somewhere during my exploration of the castle earlier?

The library, I thought suddenly. *Yes, that's where it probably is!* I remembered now: I had been using my phone to photograph that amazing panoramic view from the library windows. I must have put it down on the side table by that Victorian leather armchair and then completely forgot about it.

Hurriedly, I pulled on a cardigan over my pyjamas and slid my feet into a pair of shoes, then quietly stepped out of the room, pulling the door firmly shut behind me. Trying to avoid the creaking floorboards, I made my way softly down the corridor and along the upper gallery to the main staircase that swept down into the Great Hall. All was quiet behind the bedroom doors that I passed. It must have been nearly midnight, and it looked like all the guests had gone to bed.

As I arrived at the landing at the top of the staircase, however, I heard masculine laughter drifting up from downstairs. I leaned over the banister and looked down. It was dark in the Great Hall—the chandeliers had been dimmed and the only illumination came from a few table lamps which had been left on in the corners of the room. At the far end, though, I could see light spilling out of the doorway that led to the hotel bar, and that was also where the roars of mirth were coming from. I guessed that several of the male guests had lingered after dinner, and it sounded like they were making good use of the castle's alcoholic resources!

Padding quietly down the stairs, I made my way around the large carved newel post at the bottom to head to the library. It was situated at the end of a short hallway opposite the doorway to the hotel bar. It was even dimmer here and I had to rely on my memory of my earlier wanderings to find my way— past a couple of rooms which seemed to have been converted into offices, a guest toilet, and a side door which led to the fire exit and the back staircase.

At last, I found the library and stepped inside. The lights had been dimmed here too, and I made my way carefully forwards in the semi-darkness. The stag heads on the walls appeared creepier than ever, their eyes seeming to follow me as I moved slowly across the room. I tried not to look at them as I weaved between the various sofas and other furniture until I reached the bay windows. Reaching the tall Victorian armchair, I bent to search the small table next to it for my phone.

But my hands met air when I reached down, and I soon realised why: the table had been knocked over. Carefully, I set it upright and, as I did so, I was surprised to hear the crunch of glass. I glanced down to see that I was standing on what looked like the smashed remains of a glass tumbler. And suddenly I realised that there was a strong smell of whisky in the air.

What on earth happened here? I wondered. Thankful that I had taken the trouble to put on proper shoes before coming downstairs, I stepped gingerly away from the area of broken glass and paused, hesitating. My phone was probably somewhere down in the shadows by the side of the armchair, as it had probably fallen to the floor when the table got knocked over. But I was nervous about reaching down and groping around on the floor for my phone. It would be so easy to cut my fingers on a piece of broken glass, especially as it was so dark in this corner. I straightened again and looked around, wondering if there was a light switch...

Suddenly, I realised that someone was sitting in the armchair. They had been so still that I hadn't even been aware of their presence.

"Oh! Sorry, I didn't realise that you were there—"

I broke off. A chill ran up my spine, but this time it was not due to some ghostly bagpipe music. No, it was the glassy stare of the person sitting in the Victorian armchair, their head lolling sideways at an unnatural angle.

It was Aileen Fergusson, and she was dead.

CHAPTER EIGHT

"Now, let me see if I have it right, lassie: you said that you couldn't sleep so you came downstairs to get a book, aye?"

I looked at the grey-haired detective sitting opposite me. Inspector Monroe was a tall Scotsman with a grave face and the stoop of a man who spent a large part of his life bending over to listen to those much shorter than him. He spoke with a lovely soft burr and had such a courteous, almost old-fashioned manner that being questioned by him felt more like afternoon tea with a friendly uncle than a police interview.

"Yes, Inspector, although I wasn't getting a physical book but rather my phone. You know, to read an ebook," I explained.

"Ahh... and your phone was in the library?"

"Well, I was in there earlier yesterday, you see, and I remembered using my phone to take some pictures of the view out the window. So I realised that I had left it there by mistake."

"And did you see anybody on your way to the library?"

I shook my head. "Not a soul. I *heard* some people though. There were voices, talking and laughing, coming from the hotel bar." I looked at him enquiringly. "It was some of the male guests, wasn't it?"

Inspector Monroe glanced down at his notes. "Aye. There were four of them having a late-night drink: Jerry Hudson, Tristan St Clair, Tariq Al-Mansouri, and the owner of the castle, Angus Mackay. They tell me that they heard you shouting and rushed out together to see what the commotion was. They must have been the first on the scene?"

I gave him a sheepish look. "To be perfectly honest with you, sir, lots of people rushed into the library after I started calling for help and I wasn't really paying attention to who came in first. Are you thinking that the murderer was someone in the castle?"

"Well now... Mr Mackay is convinced that it was an intruder who sneaked in from the outside. He thinks that Aileen caught the thief trying to steal something from the library. There are certainly some very valuable antiques and ornamental pieces here at Aberglinn—"

"Yes, but if that was the case, how come Aileen was sitting in the armchair?" I asked. "If she surprised someone and they attacked her, wouldn't she have been lying on the floor somewhere? Maybe next to some overturned furniture or something?"

"The side table next to the armchair *was* knocked over," Inspector Monroe pointed out. "And there was a smashed glass on the floor. Once they've completed their analysis, Forensics will be able to confirm what had been in it—my nose says it was whisky. Also, there's a crack in the glass door of the display case by the window, as if someone or something had knocked against it. So it's very likely that Aileen was sitting in the library, enjoying a wee dram, when the intruder entered. Maybe she challenged them, they subdued her, and then they placed her body in that chair *after* they'd killed her."

"I suppose so," I said doubtfully.

He regarded me kindly. "All right, lassie. If you dinnae think it was an intruder, then who do you think killed her? A guest at the hotel?"

"Well, don't you think that's just as likely—or even *more* likely—than some random person coming in from the outside?"

"Not necessarily. After all, it is well known that this is a luxury hotel and that the guests here are wealthy, with valuable possessions. It would not be surprising if a local criminal decided to chance his luck." He leaned forwards. "Is there a particular guest that you suspect? Is that why you think the murderer was someone in the castle?"

"N-no..." I demurred, reluctant to name names.

"Did you see anyone behaving strangely towards Aileen last night?"

"It depends on what you mean by 'strangely'," I said.

"Threatening her, intimidating her—"

"No, not really. I mean..." I thought of the conversation I had overheard in the library between Jerry Hudson and Aileen, but surely that didn't have a sinister interpretation? Then I thought of Aileen's showdown with Tariq Al-Mansouri. The businessman *had* been trying to intimidate Aileen, that was true, but it didn't feel serious because she hadn't seemed remotely bothered.

"Ah, but there *is* something bothering you," Inspector Monroe said with a shrewd look.

"It was just one or two slightly odd things..."

"Such as?"

"Well, I don't know if they'd be motives for murder..."

Inspector Monroe pulled a face. "Ah, lassie, you'd be surprised. In my time working as a detective, I have seen some very strange and silly reasons for murder."

I hesitated, then said in a rush: "Well, okay—the first thing is something I overheard. As I said, I was in the library earlier yesterday, and while I was sitting in the armchair by the window, Aileen came in with one of the guests, the American Jerry Hudson."

"Aye?" Inspector Monroe looked at me expectantly.

"Well, they were sort of arguing—I mean, not like fighting or anything, but Aileen was asking Hudson for payment for something and he was complaining that he needed more time to get hold of the money."

Inspector Monroe raised his eyebrows. "Payment for what?"

I shrugged. "I don't know. Aileen talked about 'terms and conditions' and mentioned a quote... so I suppose it might have been a service or something offered by the hotel? Like maybe arranging a private excursion or... or helping Hudson purchase something? Aileen did mention approaching another 'interested party'," I said thoughtfully. "Don't rich people have agents who help organise private sales of antiques or boats or whatever?"

Inspector Monroe didn't answer. Instead, he said, "Did you feel that Hudson was threatening Fergusson in any way?"

"No, not really. If anything, it was the reverse. She was really hounding him to provide the payment by the end of the day."

"So what was 'odd'?"

"Nothing really," I admitted with a sheepish smile. "I just thought I should mention it. But actually, thinking about it, the more interesting interaction was the confrontation between Aileen and that businessman from Dubai."

"Tariq Al-Mansouri?"

"Yes. He has two children—a boy and a girl— who are quite... um... spoilt and badly behaved. They were left alone in the Great Hall when Mr Al-Mansouri and his wife went off to the hotel bar with Angus Mackay during the pre-dinner drinks last night. The little girl freaked out when she saw a cat— Mr Mackay was telling us a story earlier, you see," I explained. "It was the legend of the phantom piper of Aberglinn Castle and—"

"*Och*, has Aberglinn got one too?" said the inspector with a chuckle. "Seems like there isn't a place in Scotland that doesn't have its own phantom piper. There's one at Culzean Castle in Ayrshire, another who was lost to the fairy caves at Clanyard Bay, and an especially grisly one at Duntrune Castle who has no hands. Of course, the most famous one is probably the ghostly piper boy at Edinburgh Castle." He winked at me. "I might even have heard that one myself after one too many whiskies in a pub on the Royal Mile."

I laughed self-consciously. It seemed a bit wrong to be laughing when we were discussing a murder, but after the strain of a long night waiting for the police to arrive, watching Aileen's body being removed and the CID team securing the crime scene, followed by the interminable morning waiting to be questioned, it felt good to release the tension a bit.

"The Aberglinn version has a little black cat who

used to follow the piper everywhere," I said to Inspector Monroe. "And after he disappeared, supposedly the cat would appear when you heard ghostly pipe music in the mountains and it was an omen that someone at the castle was going to die..."

I faltered, remembering that moment last night when I'd been sure I'd heard eerie bagpipe music drifting across the night air. Hurriedly, I pushed the thought away and continued:

"Well, Safa—Mr Al-Mansouri's daughter—saw a black cat in the Great Hall and she started having hysterics. Or maybe she was *acting* like she was having hysterics," I amended, remembering the little girl's sly look as she enjoyed everyone's attention on her. "Anyway, Aileen got impatient with the girl; told her it was just a stray cat that had sneaked into the castle and to stop being silly. But Safa didn't like being told off and she ran off to tell tales to her father... and next thing you know, he came charging back into the hall and started yelling at Aileen."

"Oh aye?" said Inspector Monroe, looking interested. "And was she upset?"

"Oh no! She wasn't fazed by him at all, which just seemed to make him even more furious. She started giving him a lecture about parenting and was being quite rude to his face—"

"Are you saying that you think Mr Al-Mansouri may have murdered Aileen in revenge for her impudence?" said Inspector Monroe sceptically.

I flushed. "No... I know that sounds crazy. But you

did ask if there was anything that I'd noticed."

"Aye, I did. I'm sorry, lassie," said Inspector Monroe, waving a contrite hand. "Please continue."

"Well, that's it, really... Oh, I suppose there was one other thing: Mr Al-Mansouri threatened to have Aileen fired and he even went to Angus Mackay and demanded it, but I noticed that... well, Mr Mackay seemed almost scared to punish Aileen."

"Scared? That's a strange choice of word," said Inspector Monroe.

"Maybe not 'scared'," I said, backtracking slightly. "But he seemed very reluctant to cross her in any way."

"Could it not just be that Mackay valued his manager and didnae want to lose her?" said Inspector Monroe. "After all, it seems that she ran the hotel for him very efficiently. Good staff are hard to come by. He would not want to lose her just because of one complaint from a difficult guest."

"I suppose so." I was still unconvinced. I could see, though, that Inspector Monroe was reluctant to consider Angus Mackay as a suspect. No doubt, as a respected local employer with established family history and ties in the community, Mackay was held in high regard and one of the last people that the detective would seriously consider for the murder.

"What about the staff?" I asked suddenly. "They were also in the castle last night and one of them could have been the murderer. In fact, isn't that more likely? Aileen sounded like a tough boss to work for—

a bit of a slave driver, to be honest. Maybe one of the staff members bore a grudge and wanted to get vengeance for some way she'd mistreated them?"

"Most of the staff do not sleep in the castle overnight," said Inspector Monroe. "In fact, Aileen Fergusson and Angus Mackay are—were—the only two people who lived on-site and provided a staff presence to the guests overnight. Mackay lives in a private wing on the upper floor; Fergusson had her own set of rooms on the ground floor at the rear of the castle. All the other staff members go home once their shifts are done."

"But last night—after I found Aileen's body and called for help—I'm sure I saw some members of staff in the library," I protested.

"Aye, there are some who work late, especially on the night of the Tasting Menu Dinner. Last night, there was Mairi and Rhona still finishing up in the kitchen and Jenny preparing the dining room for breakfast, but all the other staff members had already left."

"Can you verify that?"

He raised his eyebrows slightly at my audacity but answered readily enough: "Aye, it'll be easy enough to verify. There's a CCTV camera on the front gate of the estate and my men will be going through the footage in detail. I've had a quick look myself already and you can easily see several staff cars leaving the estate yesterday evening—a couple of the groundsmen, Bridget the head of Housekeeping, that young chap who's the ghillie, the other young lass who serves in the dining room—Izzy, I think her name is... The last one to leave was Hamish, who mans the reception and also acts as barman. He left around eleven. We'll be checking with their families, of course, and confirming the times they got home."

"And what about the staff who were still here—do they all have alibis?" I asked. Seeing his expression, I ducked my head apologetically. "Sorry, Inspector, I didn't mean to be rude or cheeky. I... you know... in a murder investigation, it's natural to wonder—"

"Actually, it would not be 'natural' for most people I interview. You seem to think much more like a detective," he said, looking at me curiously. "As for alibis, well, Rhona and Mairi were in the kitchen together, so they can vouch for each other. The girl Jenny was in the dining room alone so she has no alibi, as such, but she is only eighteen and I cannot imagine that she could be the killer."

No, neither could I. I had met Jenny the night before and the bubbly, rosy-cheeked girl was the last member of staff I would have picked as a murderer.

"In fact, Jenny was very upset when I spoke to her this morning," Inspector Monroe continued. "You see, she realised that she was probably the last person to see Aileen alive. They were in the dining room together and Aileen wasn't happy with the way Jenny had laid the tables for breakfast so she'd wanted them completely redone—that's why the girl was here so late. Then Aileen left the dining room, at around quarter past eleven, and then next thing Jenny remembers is hearing your voice calling for help."

"That was just after twelve," I said. "So that means Aileen was murdered sometime between eleven fifteen, when Jenny last saw her, and midnight, when I found her."

Inspector Monroe inclined his head. "Aye, that is the assumption we are working from." He looked at me with respect. "You do seem to be unusually familiar with the procedures of a murder investigation. In fact, I had been meaning to thank you, lassie, for doing such a good job securing the crime scene until my men arrived. If you had not made everyone leave the library and locked the door, it would have made things much harder for the Forensics team and caused more complications in the investigation. So I am most grateful."

"Oh, it's nothing," I said, blushing. "I... I've been at a few crime scenes before, so I know how important it is not to contaminate any potential evidence."

He gave me a quizzical look. "Do you work with the police, Miss Rose?"

"No, I run a tearoom," I said with an embarrassed laugh. "But I've... um... been involved in a couple of murder investigations. As a bystander, I mean," I added hastily. "And some of my observations and deductions helped to solve the case."

"Hmm... well, if you think of anything else

regarding this case, I'd be glad to hear it," said Inspector Monroe. He rose from his seat. "I think that's all for the time being, although I may need to speak to you again."

I rose as well and said hurriedly, "Inspector, may I ask: how was Aileen killed? I didn't see any blood..."

"She was garrotted."

"Garrotted?" I stared at him. "You mean, like, strangled with a rope?"

"Aye, although it could have been anything that's long and strong and can be wrapped around a person's neck and tightened."

"What about a fishing line?" I asked, thinking of the fishing rods I'd seen lined up against the wall in the library.

"Ah, you noticed the rods in the library," said Inspector Monroe, nodding approvingly. "No, fishing line would probably be too thin. It would just snap. Oh, you *can* garrotte someone with a length of wire, but it needs to be something thicker and stronger, like piano wire, maybe. That's what most people think of when they think of garrotting, because of movies like *The Godfather*. The Mafia certainly liked to use it. But in this case, the pathologist who inspected the body last night said that the bruising around Aileen's neck suggests the weapon was something like a rope or a cord. If it had been a wire, it would have cut into her flesh and there would have been a lot of blood. But there was no open wound."

"Does that mean the murderer brought some rope

with him, just to use to garrotte someone?" I asked sceptically. "That seems a bit convenient."

"No, no, lassie. Like I said, many things could have been used: a curtain cord, a tie, a scarf, a computer cable... that is partly what makes my job difficult," he said with a sigh. "The murderer could have used any number of things in the castle. We will be checking to see if any of those things are missing, of course, but with so many options, it will be impossible to cover everything." He gave me a grim smile. "So a better place to start may be 'motive' rather than 'means'. Who could have had a reason for wanting Aileen Fergusson dead?"

CHAPTER NINE

I was still pondering Inspector Monroe's question as I left the small parlour that he was using as an interview room. Who *did* have a motive to kill Aileen? The only person I'd observed in a conflict with her was Tariq Al-Mansouri, but surely you didn't murder someone just because they tried to discipline your child and answered you back! But if it wasn't him, who else could it have been?

I paused just outside the interview room, wondering what to do. The hallway led to the Great Hall and I could hear the hum of conversation from the guests gathered there; everyone was busy speculating about the murder and gossiping about Aileen's background. After the intense hour I'd just spent with Inspector Monroe, the last thing I felt like doing was spending more time discussing the dead woman. Turning decisively, I retreated down the hallway in the opposite direction until I came to the side door which let me out of the castle.

Stepping into the fresh air, I breathed deeply and felt some of the tension leave my shoulders. A dunnock sang nearby, its warbles and trills amazingly loud for such a small bird, and it was answered shrilly by a robin on the other side of the grounds. The mist from the night before had cleared, although the sky was still hazy with clouds and there was a sombre hue to the landscape. In the distance, the mountains looked dark and brooding, their peaks veiled with mist.

I turned away from the ominous view and began to walk along the terrace which bordered one side of the castle. *Maybe I'll go for a stroll around the castle grounds*, I thought. *It'll be good to get some fresh air and exercise. I wonder if Cassie—*

I paused as I rounded an enormous hydrangea bush and came across two men huddled together against the wall of the castle. One of them was Jerry Hudson and the other was Angus Mackay. The latter was talking earnestly to the American, his head bent in a conspiratorial manner:

"...same potential as that recent 1988 cask o' the Macallan which sold fer over a million poonds at auction... and it was bought fer jus' five thousand quid, can ye believe it? But this could match that or even beat it! Aye, and it's so easy: all held in bond fer ye, with nothing tae do but sit back and wait fer it tae mature... I couldnae believe it meself—" He broke off abruptly as he noticed me. "Ah... er... it's Miss Rose, isn't it?"

Quickly, he plastered a bright smile on his face, but not before I saw the look of annoyance that flashed across his features. Mackay was not pleased about being interrupted. Still, his manner was nothing but solicitous concern as he said: "I hope ye have recovered from yer ordeal last night? Mus' have been a nasty shock fer ye."

"I think it must have been a bigger shock for *you*," I said. "I mean, you knew Aileen personally. She was your manager."

"Aye, aye, it's a bloody guddle," said Angus Mackay. "I couldnae believe it when I went into the library and saw her body. And noo the polis in the castle everywhere..." He sighed and shook his head, then darted a look at me. "Ye been talkin' tae Inspector Monroe then?"

"Yes, I've just finished my interview with him." I paused, then added casually, "He was asking if I'd noticed any odd behaviour amongst the guests and whether I thought anyone at the castle might have wanted to harm Aileen."

"Aww, the man's haverin'!" said Mackay violently. "I told him it's obvious the killer's a hooligan from ootside! There's no call tae suspect any o' the guests or the staff!"

"I think he's just asking all the usual questions

that one has to in an investigation," I said.

"Och aye, well, ye have tae excuse me noo... I think I should speak tae Inspector Monroe agin," said Mackay. With an apologetic nod, he hurried away and disappeared around the side of the castle.

I turned back to Jerry Hudson who had been uncharacteristically silent during our exchange. Based on the Texan's behaviour yesterday, I would have expected him to barge into the conversation just now, loudly boasting about how murders back in America were "bigger and badder".

But Hudson looked a very different man from the braggart of the night before. His eyes were bloodshot and he looked like he hadn't slept much. He was wearing his trademark "cowboy" outfit but something about it didn't seem right. Maybe it was because the cowboy hat was slightly askew, his shirt collar was undone, and his belt was buckled in a slapdash manner, as if he had thrown the clothes on in a hurry.

What really caught my attention, though, were the nasty red swellings on one side of his face. "Are you okay?" I blurted. "Your face..." I gestured to the red lumps and blisters.

Hudson put a reflexive hand up to his temple, then cringed as his fingers brushed against one of the swellings, and he hastily jerked his hand away. "Oh... yeah... damned midges," he said, with a poor attempt at a dismissive shrug. "Stepped outside after dinner last night for a bit of fresh air and walked straight into a swarm."

I remembered my mother's warning about the famously fearsome Highland midges. *Maybe she was right after all,* I thought grudgingly. Hudson's injuries looked far worse than what you'd expect from tiny insects—he looked like he'd walked face-first into a wall of barbed wire!

"I didn't realise midge bites swell up so much," I said, eyeing him with concern. "The bites I've seen were always small red spots."

"Yeah, well... uh... I kinda got sensitive skin," mumbled Hudson. "I guess I must be having an allergic reaction or something."

"Maybe you should let one of the staff members have a look," I suggested. "Highlanders live with these midges and they'll know the best way to treat—"

"No!" said Hudson quickly. "No, no, I'll... I'll be fine. So you've been talking to the cops, huh?" he said, changing the subject. "What did you say to them? Who are you ratting on, huh?" he asked, trying to make a joke but not quite managing.

"No one. I'm not trying to point fingers at anyone. I simply told Inspector Monroe what I saw and heard last night, that's all," I said.

"Well, I didn't even go near that woman," said Hudson. "Didn't have nothing to do with her all day."

"Actually, that's not true. I heard the two of you speaking in the library earlier," I said. "Aileen was asking you for payment for something—"

"Hey, what's this? Were you spying on us?" he asked belligerently, taking an aggressive step towards me.

"No!" I said, taken aback. "I just happened to be sitting in that armchair by the window when the two of you came in. I wasn't hiding there on purpose."

"Well, what you heard was no big deal," said Hudson with exaggerated nonchalance. "And I didn't speak to Fergusson again after that. Anyway, I think Mackay is right: the murderer's gotta be some nutcase from outside the castle. I mean, the security here sucks, man! Anyone can come onto the estate and break into the castle—"

"I haven't heard about any signs of a break-in, though, have you?" I asked him. "The only damage seems to be a few things in the library last night, which probably happened during Aileen's struggle with her attacker."

The American shrugged. "So there wasn't a broken window, so what? Doesn't mean someone didn't get in from the outside. It's a damn sight more likely than one of us being the killer!"

"So you didn't notice anything unusual last night?" I prodded him.

"I told you, I didn't go near the woman!"

"Yes, but maybe you noticed something else, not necessarily directly related to Aileen but just anything odd—"

"I saw nothing, okay?" he snapped. "I had dinner and then I went to the bar. That's it. I was there the whole evening."

"Who were you with?" I asked.

He waved a hand in the direction that Angus Mackay had disappeared. "Mackay and that young English dude. Sinclair?"

"Tristan St Clair?"

"Yeah, that's him... and the Arab guy... Massoori or something. Anyway, Mackay brought out all these bottles of Scotch and we were doing shots and talking business, and then the next thing we knew, you were screaming the place down. So we all took off running to the library." He shrugged again, seeming to calm down a bit. "I thought you were kidding when you said she was dead. I mean, jeez, you just don't expect to walk into a freakin' murder scene, do you?"

Tell me about it, I thought. Still, if Jerry Hudson was telling the truth, then it meant that he had an alibi for the entire evening. He could hardly be murdering Aileen if he was drinking in a bar with three other men!

"Look, I gotta go," he said, glancing at his watch. "Gotta go make a call."

He started to turn away and, as he passed me, I realised what had been niggling me.

"What happened to your tie?" I asked.

Hudson froze. "M-my tie?" he stammered.

I pointed to his open shirt collar and the bare space in front of his chest. "Yes. Your... bolo tie, isn't it called? You were telling me about it yesterday."

"Oh yeah, right..." His eyes shifted away, not

meeting mine. "I... er... I was kinda in a hurry this morning and decided not to bother putting it on. Just too much trouble, you know."

I thought back to how proudly Hudson had showed me the accessory yesterday and his declaration that he never went out without his bolo tie—his "lucky piece". I wondered if he wasn't telling the truth. And as I watched Jerry Hudson walk away, I also couldn't help thinking that a bolo tie would make a very good garrotte weapon.

***

I returned to the castle to find that a self-service buffet featuring an ad hoc selection of cold meats, breads, pastries, and fruit had been laid out on a table at the side of the Great Hall. Obviously, in the shock of the murder, followed by the arrival of the police, the crime scene being processed, and the guests and staff being questioned, the usual breakfast service at Aberglinn Castle had been abandoned.

Still, it was an impressive spread, and the sight of the food reminded me that I hadn't eaten anything since the night before. As I paused to grab an oatcake with a slice of Bonnet cheese, I heard the sound of plates smashing in the kitchen and a babble of distressed voices. Wincing in sympathy, I wondered how the staff were coping with running the castle in the circumstances, especially without Aileen's eagle eye and tight management.

Still, it was unlikely that any of the guests would complain. *They all seem too busy gossiping about the murder to be paying much attention to the hotel service*, I reflected as I scanned the crowd in the Great Hall. It felt like everyone was gathered here, although when I looked closer I noticed that the Al-Mansouri family, Jerry Hudson, and Tristan St Clair and his girlfriend were missing.

Some people were attempting to present a semblance of normality: Connie and Bruce from Texas were bent over the vintage chess game, just like when I first saw them yesterday; the two elderly English ladies were perched on one of the sofas, sipping tea; and Shane and Luke, the gay couple from Sydney, were lounging on another sofa, flicking idly through magazines. But it was obvious that no one was really interested in anything other than discussing different theories on the murder.

"We think it was that Arab fellow," said one of the elderly ladies in a breathless voice. "Did you see how angry he was when he was arguing with Ms Fergusson about his children? Oh my goodness, I thought he was going to hit her!"

"People don't commit murder just because someone tells their littlies off," said Luke scornfully. "I reckon it's that Pom. The one with the fancy title." He made a dramatic gesture. "Omigod, he looks just like the type who would commit cold-blooded murder."

"Luke!" admonished Shane from beside him. "You don't know anything about Tristan St Clair to make a comment like that."

"I know enough just from watching him," retorted Luke. Then he paused and flexed his biceps (obviously the result of hours in the gym), and added, "Although now that I think about it, he seems a bit weedy. Don't know if he'd be strong enough to strangle anyone."

"Was she strangled?" gasped the other elderly lady, putting a hand to her own throat.

"Yes, I heard the staff talking," Connie spoke up. She gave a shudder. "They say that she was garrotted with a wire or something."

"*Garrotted!*" both elderly ladies squeaked.

"But... don't you need to be specially trained to use a weapon like that?" asked the svelte blonde who was standing by the fireplace once again. From her accent, she sounded Scandinavian—from Norway or Sweden, perhaps.

"Not necessarily," Bruce said, joining the discussion. He gave a diffident cough. "I served in the US Air Force as a pilot when I was younger. We didn't get serious combat skills training, but you pick up a few things here and there. One of the things I learned was that anyone can figure out how to use a garrotte pretty quickly. You sure as hell don't need to be Special Forces or something to do it. You just need a length of cord or something similar that will bear a good amount of weight and pressure, and the ability to sneak up on your victim undetected—or maybe just have them trust you enough to turn their back."

Everyone digested his words in silence.

"Well, I personally agree with Miss Wetherby and her sister," said Shane, nodding at the two elderly ladies who simpered back at him. "I still think it's more likely to be that Arab bloke, Al-Mansouri. I mean, we all saw him having a go at the victim. They have a 'history', as they say."

"If not him, then maybe it is one of other men in the bar," a soft voice spoke up.

I turned to see the young Chinese girl looking shyly around the room. She was sitting in an armchair, with her husband perched on one arm. They were listening soberly to the discussion and it was strange not to see them taking photos for once.

"I think must be one of them, because all other guests upstairs," she continued. "It is easy to go to library from the bar."

"Well, someone could have sneaked down from upstairs," argued Bruce. "I hate to say it cos that means it could have been one of *us*, but that's a possibility you can't ignore—"

"No." The blonde girl's companion spoke for the first time. He had an accent even thicker than hers, but his words still carried easily around the hall. "No, Anna and me—our room is right next to the landing at the top of the stairs. There is a creaking floorboard outside on the landing. Every time somebody is walking down the stairs, we hear it in our room. Last night, I was reading in the bed, and I did not hear any sound on the stairs after eleven... only around midnight, I hear somebody walk past and go downstairs."

"That would have been me," I said, stepping forwards at last to join them. "I went down just before midnight to look for my phone. I thought I'd left it in the library, which is why I went in there."

Everyone pounced on me and began peppering me with questions. How was I coping? Had I recovered from the shock? How did I feel when I first saw Aileen's body? Did I have any theories about who the murderer might be?

I parried their questions as best I could, then I turned to the blond Scandinavian and asked: "Are you *sure* you would have heard someone going downstairs before me?"

"Yes, I am sure," he said simply.

"So I am right!" cried the Chinese girl. "The murderer is somebody already downstairs."

"Yes, and I'm telling you, that Tristan St Clair was in the bar as well. So it *could* have been him," insisted Luke.

"So was Al-Mansouri!"

"What about our host, Mr Mackay? Do you think *he* could have done it?"

"You're not serious! Why would he want to murder his own manager?"

"Well, maybe they had something going on—"

An incredulous laugh. "You mean like an affair?"

"No, no..."

"What about the staff? One of *them* could be guilty..."

The voices rose once again to fill the Great Hall, and I sat down quietly at the side of the room to watch the others continue to debate their hunches and theories. It was fascinating to see how quickly everyone jumped at the chance to play detective.

At least the Old Biddies aren't here, I thought. It was bad enough to be mixed up in a murder mystery again, but at least I didn't have to worry about wrangling that meddling foursome. No one loved being amateur sleuths as much as Mabel, Glenda, Florence, and Ethel, and if they were here now, they would probably—

A familiar booming voice rang out behind me:

"Never fear, Gemma, we've arrived. Now, where did they find the body?"

CHAPTER TEN

I jerked up from my chair and stared in disbelief at the four little old ladies who were trotting into the Great Hall, their white woolly helmet-hair rigidly intact and their lavender handbags tucked securely under their elbows.

"What... what are you doing here?" I asked weakly as I stared at the Old Biddies.

"We've come about the murder, of course," said Mabel as they joined me.

I gaped at her. "The murder only happened last night! How on earth did you hear about it so quickly?"

"My cousin Graeme told me about it. He's one of the gardeners here at the castle, didn't I tell you?" said Mabel briskly. "Anyway, we were on our way up to Scotland, as it was. The recent calls with Graeme made me realise that I hadn't seen any of my family up here for quite a while—"

"And Scotland is such a marvellous place for a holiday..." Ethel piped up.

"...all those sexy Scottish men in their kilts..." said Glenda with a dreamy sigh.

"...and the Scottish cakes and sweets..." said Florence, just as dreamily.

"—yes, so we decided that it was high time we came for a visit," finished Mabel, trying to take back control of the conversation. "I rang Graeme up yesterday and, as luck would have it, he told me that he and his wife were just off on a last-minute holiday to Majorca—"

"It's the perfect arrangement!" Glenda cut in again, beaming.

"Yes, we can stay in their cottage and mind the place for them while they're gone," said Ethel.

"Of course, we didn't expect to find a murder waiting for us when we arrived at Inverness Airport this morning," said Mabel, rubbing her hands with relish. "Graeme was at the airport too, to catch his plane, and we'd arranged to meet in the terminal so that he could give us his house keys. Well, he told us all about the hoo-ha here at the castle last night. The news of the murder has gone all over Inverness-shire by now, you know."

"What, already?" I said, thinking that the local grapevine must be even more impressive than the village one back in Meadowford-on-Smythe. As far as I knew, Inspector Monroe hadn't even made an official statement to the media yet!

Mabel turned to regard the rest of the room, her arms akimbo. "Are those the other guests? Good. It'll be easier to question everyone if they're all gathered here."

"Now, hang on, hang on... this isn't like back home, you know," I said quickly. "You can't just barge into the murder investigation. The police here don't know you and they won't be as tolerant as Oxfordshire CID. Besides, I spoke to Inspector Monroe, the detective in charge of the case, this morning, and he seems like a very good investigator—"

"Pah!" said Mabel, waving a contemptuous hand. "These policemen never know what they're doing. Glenda, Florence, Ethel, and I have years of experience, with *hundreds* of murder cases—"

"Yes, murder cases in *mystery novels*!" I said in exasperation. "That's not quite the same thing—"

I broke off as a loud, petulant "*Meorrw!*" suddenly filled the air. Looking down in surprise, I realised for the first time that Florence had been carrying a cat carrier, which she had set down by her feet. I saw an inquisitive paw reach through the bars and grope around the flagstones, then a familiar little whiskered face peeked out of the carrier door.

"You brought Muesli as well?" I cried.

"Well, we couldn't very well leave her behind,

could we?" said Mabel. "I'm sure a bit of Scottish air will be good for her feline constitution."

"*Meorrw! Meorrw! Meorrwww!*" Muesli cried, butting her head against the carrier door.

"Aww, the poor little dear is so excited to see you," cooed Glenda, bending down to the cage. "She wants to say hello."

Before I could stop her, she had unlatched the cage door and lifted Muesli out.

"Wait, Glenda, I'm not sure that's such a good idea—" I broke off as a squirming bundle of fur was shoved into my arms. "*Oomph!* Er... hi, Muesli..."

I tried to hold the little cat more securely in my arms but Muesli was in no mood for cuddles. Her green eyes darted excitedly around as she took in the Great Hall. She was in a new place and she wanted to explore!

"Wait... Muesli... stop that," I said irritably as she began wriggling. I winced as her claws caught on my clothes and dug into my skin. "*Ow!* Muesli, stop that... no, wait. *Muesli!*" I gasped as my cat suddenly heaved herself out of my grasp.

She landed nimbly on the floor and trotted off without a backward glance.

"Muesli!" I cried. "Come back!"

She paid me no attention, darting between two armchairs and past the startled Chinese newlyweds before scampering across the Great Hall and disappearing in the direction of the dining room and kitchen.

"Muesli!" I hissed, chasing after her. "Come back here!"

I ran across the hall, my cheeks red with mortification as the other guests turned to stare. Then, as if things weren't bad enough, a blood-curdling mix of yowling and screeching filled the air.

I stopped in my tracks, looking wildly around, then I saw what was making the dreadful noise. Muesli had paused just outside the swinging baize door which led into the castle kitchen. And standing, facing her, was the black cat that had been skulking in the Great Hall yesterday. It now looked double its normal size, its fur standing on end, its yellow eyes narrowed to slits as it yelled feline insults at Muesli. And my little tabby wasn't taking it lying down. She had puffed herself up too, and her ears were flattened to her head, her tail whipping back and forth as she hissed a few choice words back. Between the two of them, the cats were making enough noise to wake an entire army of phantom pipers, and I could see the other guests grimacing and clamping hands to their ears.

"Hey... hey... stop it, you two!" I cried, hurrying towards them and waving my arms.

The black cat turned and spat at me. Then—with a last hiss at Muesli—it whirled and darted away down the hallway. I lunged to grab my little tabby, but she was too fast for me. Before I could reach her, Muesli had turned and streaked down the hallway after the black cat.

"Muesli!" I cried, furious.

I rushed down the hallway after them. We passed the doors leading to various offices and the one to the library—now sealed with crime-scene tape—and then the black cat darted into a room at the very end of the hallway. Without a pause, Muesli shot in after it.

There was a muffled scream inside the room, even more high and terrified than the cats' screeching, and my heart sank.

Oh no, I thought. *That's all I need: one of the guests being startled by the cats and tripping and falling or something.*

I hurried into the room and nearly collided with someone rushing out.

"Oh!" I caught the doorjamb to steady myself. Then I recognised the slim red-haired girl who was diving past me. It was the harpist, Lilian Monaghan.

"I'm... I'm sorry... *I need to get out!*" she gasped in a shrill voice as she shoved me aside and stumbled out into the hallway.

I glanced into the room and saw that it was a small, cramped bedroom with a single bed along one wall, a wardrobe in the other corner, and a table between them. There were various boxes, folding chairs, cushions, umbrellas, and other paraphernalia stacked around the room, as well as piles of hotel brochures and marketing material. A metal cot was folded up and squeezed against one wall, and next to it I could see a doorway which led into a tiny bathroom. This was obviously a spare bedroom, which had been co-opted into use as a storeroom and general overflow area.

The black cat had sprung up onto the bed and was now huddled among the blankets. It hissed and growled at Muesli, who was crouched beside the bed, eyeing her opponent and looking as if she was planning to pounce at any moment.

"Oh no you don't!" I cried, lunging and scooping her up.

Muesli gave an indignant wail and tried to wriggle out of my grasp, but I held firm. Keeping a strong hold on her, I hurried back out of the room and found Lilian standing outside in the hallway, several steps away from the bedroom door. She was rubbing her hands along her bare arms, as if she was cold, and her face paled when she saw me.

"I'm so sorry," I said. "I didn't mean to scare you. This is my cat, Muesli, and I wasn't expecting her to be here—she was brought in by some friends who arrived unexpectedly at the castle today. She escaped from her carrier and then met that—" I broke off as I realised that Lilian was backing away from me as I approached, her eyes wide with fear. "Lilian? Is everything all right?"

"Y-yes... I mean, no..." She took a shuddering breath as she shifted back another step. "I... er... I don't like cats. I mean, I'm... I'm scared of them," she said in a small voice.

"Oh!" I stopped in my tracks. Quickly, I reversed

my steps, putting more space between us. "I'm sorry. I didn't realise. You should have said."

Lilian flushed. "I was embarrassed. It's... it's such a stupid phobia, you know. I mean, who's scared of cats? But it's something I've had ever since I was a child and I can't seem to control myself—"

"Oh, don't feel bad," I said quickly. "People have phobias about all sorts of things, so why not cats? Listen, let me go and put Muesli away in her carrier and then I'll grab the other one as well."

"Th-thank you," she said, her eyes filling with relief. She backed away even further as I walked past her to return to the Great Hall. There, I found the Old Biddies already busily chatting to the other guests and I groaned inwardly as I wondered what nosy questions they were asking. But there was no time to worry about that now. Hurriedly, I put Muesli back in her cat carrier, ignoring her cries of indignation, and then went back for the other cat.

I found the black feline still huddled on the bed, although without Muesli on the scene, it seemed to have calmed down. It sniffed my fingers in a friendly way when I put out a tentative hand, and made no protest when I finally lifted it carefully off the bed. In fact, it even began purring as I tucked it into the crook of one arm and stroked its chin with my other hand.

I came out of the room to find Lilian still hugging the wall several feet away, and she watched fearfully as I carried the stray cat past her and out to the

Great Hall. Giving the area with Muesli and the cat carrier a wide berth, I made my way out to the front vestibule.

"My goodness, what have you got there?" exclaimed the bearded man sitting at the reception desk. I hadn't met him before, but I guessed that this was the "Hamish" that Inspector Monroe had mentioned, who manned the reception and also acted as barman. He gave me a friendly smile as he came forwards to look at the cat in my arms.

"I think it's a stray who hangs around the castle," I said.

"Oh yes, that's right. This one's always skulking around the back door of the kitchen," said Hamish, shaking his head. "Morag the head cook loves cats and so she's always feeding scraps to strays, even when she's not supposed to. She's got a soft spot for this wee one. Calls him Duff."

"Duff?"

He chuckled at my puzzled look. "It's from the Gaelic word 'dubh' which means 'dark'," he explained. He reached out. "Here, I'll take him off you and put him back outside."

"Thank you." I handed Duff over, gave his head a final pat, then returned to find Lilian.

CHAPTER ELEVEN

The harpist was hovering nervously in the doorway of her room and she gave me a grateful smile when I rejoined her.

"Thank you so much for doing that!" she said in a tremulous voice. "Um... there *were* just two, weren't there?"

"Yes, only those two," I assured her.

She flushed. "I'm sorry. It's just that it felt like a whole tornado of cats came in here."

I laughed. "They certainly sounded like a tornado of cats! It's amazing how much noise they can make without even laying a single claw on each other." I poked my head into the room. "They didn't damage anything, did they?"

"No, I don't think so," she said, looking critically

around. "To be honest, most of the stuff here isn't mine. I only brought that—" She indicated a small tote bag in the corner. "I wasn't planning to stay overnight."

I looked at her curiously. "Yeah, I remember you saying you were taking the last train home from Fort William?"

She nodded. "Ewan Campbell—you know, the castle ghillie—said he'd drop me at the station on his way home and it was all arranged, but then after dinner was over, I heard that there was some problem and the last train had been cancelled. That meant I would have had to take a taxi home, which would have been horribly expensive..." She made a face. "But then Bridget, the head of Housekeeping, was really lovely and she said that I could just stay the night here at the castle. Apparently Ms Fergusson had originally arranged for you and your friend to stay in here, but since Bridget put you in one of the guest rooms, this was free."

Thank God for Bridget, I thought, looking with distaste around the poky little room. If Bridget hadn't rescued us from Aileen's stinginess, Cassie and I would have had to stay in here—presumably with one of us sleeping on the camp bed. It was perfectly adequate, of course, but it would have been a much more uncomfortable stay.

She must have misread my expression because Lilian said hurriedly, "Oh, it might be a bit cramped, but the bed's very comfortable and I was just grateful to have somewhere to stay. Or at least, I *was* grateful until that thing happened with Ms Fergusson," she corrected herself with a grimace. "Now I wonder if I shouldn't have just stumped up the money for a taxi. Then I wouldn't be stuck here, caught up in a murder investigation." She gave a shudder. "It was so awful when I went into the library last night and saw her body..."

I tried to remember if I'd seen Lilian amongst the people in the library the night before but there had been so much confusion that everything was a blur.

"Have the police interviewed you yet?" I asked.

"No, not yet."

Something in the way she said that made me regard her curiously. "Have you got something you need to tell them?" I asked on an impulse.

She swallowed uncomfortably. "Well... it might be nothing, really..."

"But?" I prodded.

She hesitated, then said in a low voice: "This room is next to the library. Oh, I know it's not right next door," she amended, seeing my expression. "There's a small storeroom running most of the way between us. But the castle bends around here and the hallway forms a sort of L-shape, you see, with my room at the tip of the L. So that means that part of it backs onto the library—well, the bathroom does. It shares a section of wall with the library, right at the end, where the big windows are..." She gestured with her hands, trying to explain.

"And you heard something through the wall?" I guessed.

Her eyes opened wide. "How did you know? Yes, I was in the bathroom cleaning my teeth before bed last night and I heard muffled voices."

I felt my heartbeat quickening. "Did you recognise the voices?"

"One of them was Ms Fergusson. I'm sure of that. The other... the other was a man."

"What were they saying?"

"I only caught a few words and phrases. They sounded angry, like they were having an argument."

"Really?" I couldn't keep the excitement out of my voice. "What were the words you heard?"

"It was just snatches, really... nothing that made much sense."

"Try to remember," I begged her.

She frowned with effort. "I think the man said: '...what this castle means to my family...' And then, well, he said some swear words."

"And Aileen? Did she say anything to that?"

"I couldn't make out what she said, but it was in a really sarcastic tone, like... you know, like she was laughing at him." Lilian paused, as if remembering. "She's got the most horrible, jeering laugh."

"And that's it?" I asked, slightly disappointed.

"Well, they did speak a bit more after that. But the man seemed to calm down and they lowered their voices, so I couldn't really make out anything they were saying anymore. Anyway, by then, I'd finished cleaning my teeth, so I went to bed and shut the bathroom door."

"Do you know how much longer they were talking for?"

She shook her head. "Sorry, no. I was really tired so I just wanted to get to bed."

"What about outside? Did you maybe hear footsteps going past, like the man leaving the library?" I asked hopefully.

She shook her head again. "I fell asleep quite quickly," she said apologetically. "I suppose they could have come out of the library and walked past, but I wouldn't have heard because I'd already drifted off." She gave me a self-conscious smile. "In fact, I was in a deep sleep when your shouting woke me up. I thought maybe I was dreaming. Then I heard the commotion outside in the hallway so I forced myself to get up and go and see what was going on, but I was feeling awfully spaced out. You know that feeling when you've suddenly been dragged out of a deep sleep and you feel all confused and nauseous and weird?"

"Yeah, I know the feeling. It's horrible," I said, giving her a sympathetic look. "By the way, how can you be so certain that the woman you heard was Aileen?

"I... it just sounded like her. I'd heard her laugh earlier, in that same way. You know, when she was making fun of the little girl for being scared of cats," said Lilian tightly.

"What about the man? Did you recognise his voice at all?"

She hesitated. "I... I'm not sure..."

"It's okay. Just tell me who you *think* it was." I looked at her encouragingly.

"I..." She hesitated again and her eyes flickered. *She did recognise the voice*, I thought and waited with bated breath. But after a few moments, Lilian shook her head and said, "N-no... I... I couldn't tell who it was."

I heaved a sigh of frustration. "Okay, but you've still got to tell all this to the police. It's really important. You should go and insist on speaking to Inspector Monroe now."

She looked reluctant. "But it could be nothing, really—"

"It's not nothing! Lilian, don't you realise that you could have overheard Aileen talking with her murderer?"

She paled. "What... what d'you mean?"

"Well, think about it: one of the castle staff confirmed that Aileen was with her in the dining room last night until around a quarter past eleven. So she was last seen alive then. I found her just after midnight. So that means she was killed sometime in the forty-five minutes between eleven fifteen and midnight. When did you hear the voices?"

Lilian seemed to shrink into herself. "Around eleven thirty," she said in a small voice.

"There, you see?" I said triumphantly. "The man

you heard was probably Aileen's murderer! You've *got* to tell the police everything you told me!"

She looked uneasy. "But..."

"Lilian, it's your civic duty. This is a murder investigation and you've got to give the police any information you have which could help." I gave her a look. "Unless... you have some reason for wanting to protect the murderer?"

"No, of course not!" she cried, flushing. "I... all right, I'll tell the inspector."

I left her in the room, packing up her things, and returned to the Great Hall. As I passed the grandfather clock in the hall, I was surprised to see that it was already half past three. Where had the day gone? I was just wondering what to do with myself when I spotted the Old Biddies marching purposefully towards me.

"Time for tea, Gemma," said Mabel, catching hold of my elbow and propelling me ahead of her.

"Wait... what?"

I looked across to see an equally bewildered Cassie being dragged along by Florence, whilst Glenda and Ethel eagerly signalled one of the girls from the castle kitchen. A few minutes later, Cassie and I were unceremoniously plonked onto a sofa in the drawing room—a long gallery-style room which ran the length of one side of the castle, and which had windows that gave out onto another magnificent vista of the estate. We'd had a quick look in the drawing room during Bridget's tour of Aberglinn

Castle when we first arrived, and I gazed around in admiration again now. Seen up close, the surroundings were even more spectacular, with two ornate marble fireplaces, gold Rococo mirrors decorating the walls, and a host of beautiful antiques and delicate Chinoiserie-style ornaments displayed on side tables and shelves.

The Old Biddies had settled themselves on armchairs and sofas next to ours, with Muesli curled up in her cat carrier and tucked under a table next to us. Mabel watched with approval as one of the castle waiting staff carefully unloaded a "Highland Tea" from a silver tray onto the coffee table in front of us. Nestled between the teapot and cups made of fine bone china were plates of freshly baked scones alongside pots of homemade preserves and Scottish clotted cream. I had been about to protest that I didn't really want tea, but now I found my mouth watering as I inhaled the rich, buttery aroma rising from the warm scones.

The real star of the show, though, was the towering three-level cake stand which had been placed next to the tea and scones. This was filled with an assortment of gourmet bites inspired by traditional Scottish foods—from savoury snacks like Isle of Mull cheddar puff pastries, Perthshire ham rolls, and duck egg sandwiches with Arran mustard mayo to sweet treats like heather honey parfait, millionaire's shortbread oozing with caramel, and miniature Dundee cakes soaked in Dalwhinnie whisky.

That oatcake I had snatched from the buffet seemed ages ago and now, as I looked at all the delicious food in front of me, I realised that I was starving.

Florence heaped things onto our plates and watched with maternal satisfaction as Cassie and I tucked in. "You girls look even thinner than when you left Oxford," she said, clucking her tongue. "Have you not been eating properly since arriving in Scotland?"

"We have, but this is the best thing we've tasted so far, I think," said Cassie as she tackled a lemon macaroon with gusto.

"Yes, my cousin Graeme told me that Aberglinn Castle Hotel is famous for its afternoon tea," said Mabel. "So I made sure to book a sitting as soon as we arrived."

"It was a great idea!" I said, smiling gratefully.

As I sat back chewing a delicious mouthful of buttery shortbread, though, I couldn't help feeling slightly guilty. A woman had just been murdered and here we were, sitting in sumptuous surroundings, enjoying afternoon tea...

As if reading my thoughts, Mabel said: "One cannot think properly on an empty stomach, and we must have all our wits about us if we are to solve this murder."

"We're not supposed to be trying to solve the mur—" I started to say, then broke off as I remembered that I had been eagerly questioning Lilian myself earlier. Feeling slightly ashamed of my own hypocrisy, I said grudgingly, "Well, okay, I suppose we could *discuss* the potential suspects while we're eating. After all, all the other guests are doing it anyway. And as long as we don't interfere with Inspector Monroe's investigation—"

"We don't need to discuss potential suspects," announced Mabel. "We *know* who did it."

CHAPTER TWELVE

The Old Biddies looked smugly at each other and smiled as they saw Cassie's and my reaction.

"You know who the murderer is?" I said disbelievingly.

"Oh yes. It's that loud, rude man—the one from Texas."

"Jerry Hudson?" Cassie said in surprise. "Why do you think it's him?"

"Because he has the perfect motive, dear! We've been chatting to the kitchen staff and to the lady who is head of Housekeeping—Bridget, that's her name—and they've been telling us all about the guests," said Florence.

"Yes, there's a pair of sisters—the Miss Wetherbys—from Bath, who recently received a windfall after an elderly relative died and left them a small fortune," said Ethel. "So they've decided to do all the things they've always wanted to—"

"Oh, are they ticking off their bucket list?" said Cassie, smiling. "How sweet. I suppose one of the things is staying in a castle?"

Ethel nodded. "Yes, just like the couple from Sweden—Anna and Mikael. Well, except that it's not just one castle for them. They love castles and are trying to stay in as many as they can—"

"A very odd hobby," said Mabel with a disapproving sniff. "They told us that they've visited most of the castles in Germany and also in France, and now they're starting on the castles in Scotland. Still, I suppose it's better than that young chap from Sydney who seems to talk about nothing but hair and clothes."

"Oh, I think he's rather a dear," protested Glenda. She fluffed her white hair. "Luke told me that I had wonderful skin for my age and gave me some make-up tips for 'mature' ladies."

If he can get you to stop putting fuchsia rouge on your cheeks, that will be a big achievement already, I thought, eyeing the usual twin spots of bright pink colour on Glenda's face. Still, I had to admit that the overall effect was quite pretty and charming and suited Glenda's perpetually girlish personality.

"There's also a lovely young Chinese couple who have just got married and are on their honeymoon," continued Florence. "And a retired couple from Texas who are doing a tour of the UK... and an Arabic family from Dubai who are very wealthy—"

"Yes, yes, but the one we're interested in is Mr Hudson," Mabel cut in impatiently.

"Yes, especially as Mr Hudson comes from America too. It's very fitting, don't you think?" said Ethel brightly.

I looked at her blankly. "What?"

"Don't say 'what', say 'pardon', Gemma," said Mabel, tutting. "You know your mother would be horrified to hear you."

I swallowed an irritable sigh. "It's just... I didn't understand what Ethel meant—"

"Oh, the saying 'to have a chip on your shoulder' originated in the United States too. In the nineteenth century, dear," Ethel explained eagerly. "When the young men there were spoiling for a fight, they would place a chip of wood on their shoulder and dare someone to knock it off. So that's why we use it now to mean someone who's sensitive about a grievance and always challenging other—"

"Yes, but what does that have to do with Jerry Hudson?" I asked in exasperation.

"Well, he has a chip on his shoulder," said Ethel.

"About what?"

"About his money."

"What do you mean? The guy never stops rabbiting on about how rich he is," said Cassie, rolling her eyes. "You should have heard him at dinner last night, boasting about his big house and cigars and luxury cars to anyone who would listen. Why would he be sensitive about his wealth?"

"Because the money isn't really his," said Mabel succinctly. "Jerry Hudson didn't make his money—he married it. He was lucky enough to meet the daughter of a Texas oil baron when he first moved to Dallas and he persuaded her to elope to Las Vegas with him. And since then, he has been living off his wife's money and enjoying a very nice life, pretending that he's a billionaire oil tycoon himself."

"He's obviously pretending to be single too," I said dryly, thinking of his heavy-handed flirting. "I didn't even realise that he was married. He never mentioned his wife. Why hasn't she come to Aberglinn Castle with him?"

"She doesn't like the countryside so she has stayed in London," Glenda explained. She gave a wistful sigh. "I must say, the shopping *is* wonderful in London."

"The shopping in Oxford is just as good," said Mabel staunchly.

"Oh no, the farmers' market is the best place," protested Florence.

"Well, *I* think the post office shop in Meadowford-on-Smythe has everything you could want," said Ethel loyally.

"Anyway, so you're saying that Jerry Hudson is coming up here and pretending to be a rich bachelor, just so he can play out his 'lord of the castle' fantasies on a Scottish estate?" said Cassie, trying to steer the conversation back on track.

Glenda nodded. "Apparently, some of the staff have overheard him on the telephone to his wife and he sounds completely under her thumb." She put on a very bad American accent: "'*Yes, honey*' and '*no, honey*' and '*of course, honey*'... and they could hear her through the speaker as well. She was talking to him like a pet dog."

"That must get up his nose," said Cassie, grinning.

"Ooh yes. They say he's awfully grumpy after each call, but he would never dare talk back to his wife. He barely dares to sneeze without her permission, because if she got angry and decided to leave him, he would lose everything. His in-laws never liked him, you see, and they've signed all sorts of legal documents to make sure that he would be left without a penny if their daughter divorced him."

I shook my head in mingled disbelief and admiration. In the half day since they'd arrived, the Old Biddies had already managed to befriend half the castle staff and extract more information than the police!

"But surely you're not suggesting that just because Hudson is henpecked, that makes him a murderer?" I said.

"Well, it might do if you're terrified of your wife finding something out," said Mabel with a meaningful look. "You see, we also heard that Mr Hudson has 'roving hands'."

"Oh God, tell me about it," Cassie groaned. "He tried to cop a feel of my bum during the pre-dinner drinks last night."

"Ah!" said Mabel. "That ties in perfectly with what we were thinking. It's the perfect motive!"

I looked at her disbelievingly. "Are you saying Jerry Hudson tried to grope *Aileen*?" I thought back to the steely-eyed castle manager with her high turtleneck, prim wool skirt, and frosty manner. I couldn't imagine any man being tempted, never mind daring, to make a pass at Aileen Fergusson!

"No, no, not Aileen—but he has definitely tried to paw several of the female members of staff," said Mabel. "Izzy and that young girl Jenny who works in the dining room both told us that he kept 'accidentally' brushing against them whilst they were serving him."

"What a tosser," said Cassie with an expression of disgust. "If he tries anything on me again, I'm going to give him a bloody good walloping."

"I still don't see why this gives Jerry Hudson the 'perfect motive'," I protested.

Glenda sat forwards. "Well, what if Aileen found out about Mr Hudson's disgusting habits?"

"And what if she decided to use it as leverage for blackmail?" added Florence.

"Yes, what if she told him that unless he paid her money, she would tell his wife?" said Ethel excitedly. "He couldn't afford that, because otherwise he might lose the high life that he's become used to, so he had to do something to silence Aileen."

"That's a lot of 'what ifs'," I said doubtfully.

"It could make sense, though, Gemma," said Cassie, looking thoughtful. "I mean, Hudson's one of those 'big game hunter' types who loves to brag about the dead animals they've killed, isn't he? So he's already comfortable with taking a life. And he's so full of himself, he probably thinks that he's above the law. I mean, look at the way he swaggers around in that stupid cowboy hat and outfit—"

"Oh!" I sat up straight. "His outfit! I've just remembered: when I saw Jerry Hudson this morning, he wasn't wearing his bolo tie."

"His what?" said Cassie.

Quickly, I explained about the American's prized accessory and how he had claimed that it was his lucky piece and that he never went anywhere without it.

"Except that he was definitely 'without it' this morning," I said. "And when I asked him about it, he got quite evasive." I paused, then added excitedly, "Inspector Monroe told me that Aileen had been garrotted, and to do that, you need a length of something that's flexible and strong, like a cord or a belt... or a bolo tie!"

"Aha!" said Mabel triumphantly. "I told you we were right. Jerry Hudson is our man."

"Oh, but wait... Hudson has an alibi," I said, remembering. "He was in the hotel bar the whole evening, drinking with some of the other male guests."

"Perhaps he sneaked out while the others weren't looking," suggested Cassie.

"That bar is tiny. Surely the others would have noticed if Hudson suddenly wasn't there?"

"The alibi is a minor detail," said Mabel, making a dismissive gesture with her hands.

"How can you say that?" I spluttered. "The alibi is the most common way to prove someone's innocence, because you can't be committing murder in one place when you're definitely somewhere else."

"Well, if it's not Hudson, who do you think it could be then?" asked Cassie.

I shrugged. "I don't know... what about the castle owner himself? You know, Angus Mackay was acting very oddly last night when Tariq Al-Mansouri complained about Aileen."

Cassie looked at me. "What do you mean, 'oddly'?"

I repeated what I had told Inspector Monroe about Mackay's weak attempts to mollify the Dubai businessman while shying away from disciplining his castle manager for her insolence.

"It was almost as if Mackay was intimidated by Aileen in some way," I said as I finished. "Most bosses would have at least disciplined her for speaking to a guest like that, if not actually fired her—especially given that this is a luxury hotel. You know, 'the customer is always right' and all that. Wealthy people pay a lot of money in places like this just to be pandered to. Not providing that kind of obsequious service is practically asking to lose business. But Mackay seemed willing to jeopardise all that."

Cassie shrugged. "Maybe it's like the inspector said: Mackay would rather lose one difficult guest than lose an excellent manager who runs his hotel really well—especially if he secretly agreed with Aileen. I mean, you have to admit, those children were absolute brats, and somebody needed to tell those parents some hard truths. Anyway, wouldn't Angus Mackay have the same alibi as Jerry Hudson?" she pointed out. "He was in the bar drinking with the other men as well, wasn't he?"

"Oh yeah... you're right," I said, sitting back, crestfallen. "I'd forgotten about that. Inspector Monroe said all the men in the bar last night vouched for each other."

"I'm telling you, dear, Jerry Hudson is our man and we shall find evidence to prove it," said Mabel as the other Old Biddies nodded in agreement. "In fact, if we can get into his room, I'm sure we could—"

"Ohhh no!" I said, frowning at them. "Don't even think about it! You're not breaking into Jerry Hudson's room to snoop in his things."

"Oh, it wouldn't be difficult," Ethel said. "The rooms here all have old-fashioned keys, so it would be very easy to pick the lock. I once read a book all about burglars and how they pick locks, when I was working as a librarian, and I can still remember the instructions very well. We can practise on the lock in your room, dear, and—"

"No," I said in exasperation. "No, you're not practising on our lock or any other lock in the castle!" Before the Old Biddies could argue, I quickly waved to the plate of scones on the table in front of us and said brightly, "Um... has anyone tried the scones yet? I'd love to know how you think they compare with the Little Stables'..."

To my relief, the distraction worked. The Old Biddies turned their attention to the plate of still-warm scones, and soon everyone was engrossed in tasting and rating them.

"Wow, these are *good*," said Cassie with her mouth full.

I picked one up myself and carefully cut it in half lengthwise, then slathered clotted cream, followed by a dollop of home-made strawberry jam, onto one of the halves. Taking a bite, I chewed appreciatively. It was rich and buttery, with a soft, crumbly exterior that contrasted beautifully with the light and fluffy insides of the scone—and all melding with the lovely flavours of the strawberry jam and Scottish clotted cream. I didn't think I had tasted such amazing scones in a long time. In fact, it seemed sacrilegious to think it, but these might have been even better than the ones we served in my own tearoom.

"They really are amazing," I agreed, swallowing the last crumb. "I wonder if Morag the head cook will let me have a peek at her recipe. I did ask Aileen about spending some time in the kitchen, but she rejected it immediately. She said that she didn't want me wasting staff time. Now that she's gone, though, maybe I can—" I broke off and made a face. "Sorry, that sounded a bit heartless, like I'm revelling in her death or something."

"Oh, don't be silly. It's perfectly reasonable to make the most of the situation," said Cassie. "Besides, do you think anyone at the castle is really going to miss her? I mean, they might have respected her managerial skills—you know, keeping everything running efficiently—but I get the impression that nobody really liked her."

As I poured myself a fresh cup of tea, I thought: *the real question is—did anyone at the castle dislike Aileen enough to want to murder her?*

CHAPTER THIRTEEN

By the time we finished afternoon tea and rejoined the other guests in the Great Hall, I noticed that the mood had changed. Everyone's excited speculation about the murder had been replaced by boredom and impatience with the rigmarole of the investigation. Inspector Monroe had given instructions that no guest or member of staff would be allowed to leave the castle until everyone had been questioned and all alibis established, and so people were forced to loiter around, awaiting their turn to be interviewed.

In a desperate bid to provide entertainment for his guests, Angus Mackay had persuaded the inspector to allow them to take part in some of the activities which had originally been planned for the weekend. And luckily, British Summer Time meant that the sun didn't set until nearly ten in the evening, so there was still ample light for the workshops to take place, even this late in the day.

Looking as relieved as the guests to be doing something at last, Cassie rounded up her motley crew of aspiring artists and took them out onto the terrace to set up their easels. I followed at the rear of the group and was just about to settle down to watch them when I noticed another coterie of guests gathered around a familiar figure. It was Ewan Campbell and he was handing out fishing rods and protective eyeglasses to the group. As he turned to lead the way out to the wide front lawn beyond the terrace, he saw me and waved enthusiastically, beckoning me over to join him. I hesitated for a moment, then—ignoring Cassie's glower—turned and went over.

"Hi! I didn't expect to see you today," I said as I fell into step beside him.

"Well, no one told me not to come so I arrived for work as usual this morning. I must say, I was gobsmacked when I heard what had happened," Ewan said, shaking his head. "Bloody hell, murder! Who would have believed it? Anyway, the police said they need to speak to me as well, eventually, so I decided I might as well stay. There's been so much confusion and disruption that the staff really need an extra hand around the place. Plus, Mr Mackay told me he wanted me to stick to the original plan for the ghillie experience... so here I am."

He looked at me with gentle concern. "But how about you? Are you okay? I heard that you discovered the body."

"Oh, I'm fine. In fact, I feel a bit bad that I'm not more upset," I confessed, thinking back to my guilt during the afternoon tea. "It seems a bit wrong to be doing anything 'normal' when Aileen has just been murdered, you know?"

He glanced back at the row of people following us. "Yes, I know what you mean. It feels weird for me to be here doing the ghillie experience as if nothing has happened. But I suppose there's no point sitting around moping. It's not going to help with the investigation. And this will at least keep the guests occupied and distracted. Not that this is completely 'normal', anyway. Inspector Monroe wants to keep everyone under his eye, so we're not allowed to go too far out into the estate; we have to stay here by the castle—which is a bit of a pain when typical ghillie activities include foraging in the forest and fishing in the rivers," he said with a rueful laugh. He indicated the lawn in front of us. "Still, most of this lot seem to be complete novices at fly fishing so I should be able to keep them busy enough just practising their casting on the lawn."

"Did you see Aileen last night?" I asked.

"I had a quick chat with her just before I left... around ten thirty, I think? I'd collected a good batch of chanterelles during my foraging first thing yesterday and I wanted to ask if I could take some home. The castle has first dibs on anything I find growing on the estate, you see," he explained. "And, of course, chanterelles are top of everyone's wish list."

"Oh, are those the golden-coloured mushrooms we had at dinner last night? They *were* delicious—so silky and chewy, with this lovely flavour," I said, remembering.

Ewan nodded. "Chanterelles are famous for their special flavour and texture. Smells sort of like apricot, doesn't it?"

"Yes, that's exactly it!" I cried, laughing. "I thought I was imagining it."

"Aye, chefs go absolutely mad for chanterelles. They're beautiful even just fried with a knob of butter and some fresh herbs, in a copper pan over an open fire. It's why they're so valued—you know they're one of most expensive mushrooms in the world?"

"Wow, really?" I wondered at the cost of the degustation dinner that Cassie and I had enjoyed. No wonder Aileen had been grudging in her welcome!

"Yes, it's cos you can't farm chanterelles. They're a mycorrhizal fungus, so they only grow around certain species of living trees and their mycelium has to interact with the tree roots in a certain way for them to thrive. We haven't figured out a way to replicate that yet, so the only way to get chanterelles is to find them in the wild.

"And even then, it's not that easy because they only appear at certain times of the year for a few days at a time. You need to know exactly where and when to find them." Ewan winked at me. "That's where the ghillie expertise comes in. I found a great patch in a birch grove yesterday morning and there were loads of mature caps, so I brought a big bundle back. More than enough for the dinner menu, with some to spare, so I thought it should be okay for me to take a few back—I live with my uncle and he adores chanterelles. It would have been a real treat for him."

"Well, especially if you found them, it's only fair that you get to keep a few for yourself," I agreed.

"You'd think that," said Ewan, his mouth tightening. "But Aileen was a right mean tightwad and—" He broke off with an apologetic smile. "Sorry. Probably shouldn't speak ill of the dead. Anyway, she wouldn't let me have any. Said that Morag needed extra for a new recipe. To be fair, that was probably true. I know Mr Mackay was talking about adding some new items to the menu." He shrugged. "Anyway, so I left and that's the last time I saw her."

He glanced back at the group behind us, then lowered his voice and asked: "Have the police got any suspects?"

"They seem to think that it could have been a random intruder from outside, who broke in looking to steal valuables. But it's odd that nothing's been reported missing."

"Maybe Aileen disturbed the thief before he had a chance to steal anything. You know, he got scared and scarpered."

"After he went to the trouble of murdering her?" I said sceptically. "If he was bold enough and ruthless enough to kill her, wouldn't he have at least grabbed some things on his way out? Conversely, if he was the type to get scared off, wouldn't he have run away as soon as she saw him instead of hanging around to kill her?"

"Well, maybe he didn't mean to kill her. Maybe they got into a tussle and he killed her by mistake—"

"She was garrotted, Ewan," I said, giving him a look. "If she'd been hit on the head, I might have believed that, but you don't garrotte someone by mistake. That's a deliberate act of violence."

He raised his eyebrows. "You sound very familiar with all this stuff."

I coloured. "I... um... I've been involved with a few murder investigations before. Just as a civilian," I added quickly. "But... you know... you pick a few things up."

"So who do *you* think might have done it?"

I threw a glance back at the group myself. "I don't know. But I think it's most likely to have been someone who was on the ground floor last night."

"Were there some people still downstairs?"

"Yes, several of the male guests were still drinking in the bar, plus Mr Mackay himself. And then there were the staff in the kitchen, of course."

"Aww, you're not thinking that Mairi or Rhona or Jenny could have done it?" said Ewan, looking scandalised.

"Well, no one on the staff really liked Aileen, did they?" I said bluntly.

He hesitated. "No. But there's a big difference between not liking your boss and murdering her!"

I sighed. "Yeah, you're right. And no, I don't really think any of the women could have done it. But the men in the bar..."

I trailed off as we had reached the centre of the lawn by now, and Ewan reluctantly ended our conversation in order to turn to his group. I scanned the people gathered around him, then glanced over at Cassie's group in the distance. *So much for all modern efforts to avoid gender stereotyping*, I thought with a wry smile. The participants for the two activities seemed to have neatly divided themselves along gender lines. Cassie's art workshop was mostly made up of women whilst Ewan's "ghillie experience" was filled with male guests. I ran my eye over the group: there was the young Chinese husband, the gay couple from Sydney, Bruce from Texas, the model-handsome Mikael from Sweden, and Tariq Al-Mansouri, the businessman from Dubai.

Jerry Hudson wasn't in the group, which was hardly surprising given that he was an experienced hunter and would probably have turned his nose up at such a "beginners" activity. In any case, I'd glimpsed him as we were coming out and he'd looked happily ensconced in one of the armchairs in the Great Hall, flirting with Tristan St Clair's voluptuous companion. St Clair himself had been nowhere in sight and I wondered where the arrogant Englishman was. Perhaps being questioned by the police?

The one female in Ewan's group was the Swedish girl, Anna, looking as svelte and chic as ever despite wearing a dull army-green mackintosh and matching gumboots. She pushed her blonde hair back as she took her place beside her partner Mikael, and everyone listened keenly to Ewan's instructions.

"...depending on the type of fish and the kind of place you're planning to cast your fly. Here in Scotland, that's usually lochs and streams, but you can also fly-fish for large trout in stocked reservoirs and for big game fish in the open sea. Of course, the size of your fish will determine the size of the rod and the weight of the fly line." Ewan held up several spools of gleaming fishing line in various sizes. "Lines of #4 to #8 weight would be fine for tackling grayling and trout on small and medium rivers... and you'd go up to something a bit heavier like this #10 for trout in larger waters or pike and salmon. Of course, for big fish like marlin and tuna, you'd need a line with real weight and strength, like a #14—not that you'd be meeting any of those here in the Highlands," he said with a chuckle. "So we don't bother carrying those types of lines."

Then he picked up his own rod and began demonstrating how to attach the fly and cast a line whilst the guests attempted to copy him. I backed away to a safe distance as people began casting their flies haphazardly across the lawn, metal guides flashing, reels spinning, and fishing lines tangling everywhere. Ewan darted between them, trying to help, and I admired his patience with their ineptitude.

"...no, no... don't hold the line too tightly between your fingers, otherwise the friction will prevent the line from running out as you cast... yes, that's it! Well done..."—

he smiled at the young Chinese husband, then walked over to the couple from Sydney—"...yes, that's good... careful not to move your wrist too much... keep the rod straight, so that the line can travel straight out in front of you..."—he turned to the Swedish girl, Anna—"... don't stop your rod during the back cast, otherwise the line will drop downwards and—eeughh! Yes, like that..." He winced as Anna's fly flew backwards and got caught in her hair. She twisted and yanked at it frantically, trying to free herself. Ewan rushed to her side. "No, no... wait! Let me do it for you, otherwise you might hook the fly into your skin..."

I noticed that Tariq Al-Mansouri seemed to be having less trouble than the others and, as I watched him, I realised that this could be the perfect opportunity to speak to the Dubai businessman. *Maybe he can tell me if Jerry Hudson did sneak out of the bar after all?*

CHAPTER FOURTEEN

I wandered casually over to Al-Mansouri and stood watching as he carefully cast his fly out in a straight line along the lawn.

"You seem to be a natural," I complimented him.

He gave me a perfunctory smile. "I do it before," he admitted. "They build man-made river in Dubai, with pump and different levels and artificial rapids, you know? So you go and it is like you are fishing in a river in Europe."

"Really?"

He laughed at my expression. "It is nothing if you know Dubai," he said smugly. "We can build anything there. We even have skiing. Yes, there is a big indoor mountain slope with a black diamond run, with artificial snow and even penguins. They import them into the desert."

"Wow..." I murmured. "I guess it's true that money can buy you everything."

"Not everything," Al-Mansouri admitted, looking up at the spectacular Highland scenery around us. "You cannot compare to the real thing."

"Yes, but to come and experience the 'real thing', you need money too," I said with a dry smile.

He grinned at me, this time with genuine friendliness. "Yes, you are right. I see you are clever, like my Safa."

"Er... last night must have been a bit of a shock for you?" I said, hoping to draw him out so that I could ask him about the murder.

It was the wrong move. His face closed and he said in a guarded tone: "It was shock for everyone."

"Yes... well, I remember that you were one of the first people who ran into the library when I was calling for help," I said ingenuously. "So you must have been somewhere nearby?"

"I was drinking in the bar with the other men. Mr McKay invite us to taste some more whisky. We go after dinner and we stay in the bar the whole evening. Only when we hear you shouting, then we come out together," he said quickly, reeling the sentences off like it was something he had practised many times.

"Ah, right... so you didn't see Aileen earlier in the evening?"

"I see her at dinner, but after that, no. Which good because I don't want to see her face," he said with loathing. "That woman is a *kalba*—a female dog! I am still angry how she disrespect me. And Mackay is like a camel: he let his manager ride on his back!" He raised a fist. "If I am her boss, I know how to teach her lesson, to punish her." Then, perhaps remembering that he was talking about a murdered woman, he hastily unclenched his fist and added, "But I don't really hurt her, of course. It is very sad that she is killed."

He started to turn away and I could see from his expression that he wasn't inclined to talk to me anymore. I bit my lip in frustration; I hadn't even managed to ask him about the alibis of the men in the bar. Then, as I glanced across at Cassie's group, I spied his daughter Safa standing in front of an easel, busily dabbing paint on the canvas. I had a brainwave: *the way to this man's heart is through his children...*

"How are your kids coping?" I asked in an exaggeratedly solicitous tone. "Safa is such a sensitive and perceptive girl. I hope she hasn't been too upset by what's happened."

Al-Mansouri turned back to me, his face brightening. "Ahh... thank you for asking. My wife want us to leave immediately—as soon as the police allow us to go—but I think it is better for the children if we stay. I show them murder is not serious; nothing to be scared. Anyway, Hamid is too young to understand, but, like you say, Safa knows everything. But she is not scared," he added proudly.

"You know, she is reading a lot, especially the books called *Nancy Drew*. I buy the whole set for her."

"Oh yes, I know *Nancy Drew*," I said, smiling in reminiscence. "I read those books too when I was about Safa's age, and I was desperate to be a 'girl detective'!"

"Yes, yes, Safa is the same. She told me she will catch the murderer before the police," said Al-Mansouri, chuckling indulgently. "*Wallah*, maybe she will do it. She is very, very clever. I think her brain level is like a genius, you know?"

"Mmm, she seems incredibly bright," I gushed. "I could tell as soon as I met her. I'm sure she's top of her class?"

Al-Mansouri beamed. "Always number one. And her teacher said she will go to top university like MIT or maybe Harvard or Oxford..."

"I'm sure she inherited her brains from her father," I said, giving Al-Mansouri a look of wide-eyed admiration. "I mean, you're one of the most successful businessmen in Dubai, aren't you? Anyone can see that you're the kind of man who is always top of his field."

Al-Mansouri made an expression of false modesty but I could tell that he was flattered. I continued slyly, "Actually, it's a shame *you're* not in charge of the investigation, Mr Al-Mansouri. You're so brilliant—I'm sure you'd get results faster. Especially as the police seem to be completely stumped, you know. Because the most likely suspects are those who were on the ground floor, but everyone there has an alibi. The staff in the kitchen can vouch for each other, and of course you said all the men in the bar were together the whole time. It's a shame because I think the police might suspect Mr Hudson," I added, lying shamelessly. "But since he has a solid alibi..."

Al-Mansouri hesitated, then he glanced around and said in a low voice, "Not all the time. We are not together all the time."

I caught my breath. Keeping my voice offhand, I asked, "What do you mean?"

Al-Mansouri hesitated again, then said: "Mackay and Hudson and St Clair—they talk to me and we decide it is better to tell police that we are all together in the bar. Because even we know we did not do the murder, but sometimes, police ask too many questions and then it becomes big problem, you know? So this way it is easier. We all say the same thing—we are together in the bar—and we keep everything simple."

"So are you saying that you *weren't* in the bar the whole evening?"

"No, *I* stay there but Hudson—he went out. Also the Englishman, Tristan St Clair. They go to toilet."

"Oh... what time was that?"

Al-Mansouri frowned. "I don't remember. After eleven o'clock. I know this because I promise my wife that I go up at eleven, but when I get up, Mackay said he has very special whisky to show us. He said it is the best and most expensive. I want to see this, so I stay. Then Hudson said he must go to toilet first. And after he went, St Clair said also he needs to go."

"So they didn't go together?"

He gave me an odd look. "It is not like you are going for coffee."

"I mean, did they leave the bar at the same time?"

"No, Hudson went first. Then after... maybe five minutes? St Clair said he also must go."

"And what about Angus Mackay? Did he stay in the bar with you?"

"Yes... ah, except just before they come back, he also went outside."

"Outside? You mean out of the castle?"

Al-Mansouri nodded. "He go out to smoke pipe. I asked him why don't smoke in the bar, but he said Aileen will be angry. She is not allowing smoking in the castle. But Mackay is the owner!" he said in disgust. "He is so scared of that woman, like he is small boy and she is his mother."

"So after they all came back, did you—"

I broke off suddenly as my eyes caught sight of something in the distance. Just visible through a gap between the tall shrubs planted along the side of the castle was an external metal staircase which had been fixed to the wall, no doubt to provide an escape route in the event of a fire. And creeping furtively up the steel gratings were four familiar figures with white helmet-hair and Marks & Spencer cardigans. As I watched incredulously, the first figure pointed jubilantly at a window beside the stair platform and the others scampered after her as she began to make her way towards it.

I gave a strangled groan. It was the Old Biddies, and they looked like they were trying to break into one of the castle rooms using the fire escape!

CHAPTER FIFTEEN

Hastily making excuses to Tariq Al-Mansouri, I raced across the lawn, past the terrace, and around the side of the castle. I reached the bottom of the metal staircase just in time to see the Old Biddies disappearing around the bend at the top of the first flight of stairs.

"Mabel!" I called. "Glenda! Florence! Ethel! What are you *doing*?"

Four wrinkled old faces appeared over the railing and peered down at me.

"Ah, Gemma, perfect timing. You can come and help us," said Mabel briskly.

"Help you do what? What on earth are you doing up there?" I demanded.

"We're conducting a search of a suspect's room, of

course. What does it look like?" said Mabel.

"You see, dear, we went to see Inspector Monroe after tea and tried to explain how we could help him with the investigation, but he just wouldn't listen to us," said Glenda indignantly.

"Yes, so we've decided that since the police aren't investigating Jerry Hudson properly, we'll just do it ourselves," Florence said.

Ethel beamed at me. "And isn't it lucky that this fire escape happens to go past the bathroom in his suite? Since you said we can't pick the lock to his door, we thought this was a marvellous alternative. We can just climb in the bathroom window and—"

"What? No, you're not climbing in anyone's bathroom window!" I spluttered. "You need to come back down. Wait, where are you going...? Mabel? Glenda? Ethel? Florence?" I called as the four heads disappeared from view.

Aaarrgghh! I stared up in frustration at the empty railing for a moment, then sighed and started climbing up the metal staircase myself. Above me, I could hear excited whispering and muttering, although the bend of the staircase meant that I couldn't see the Old Biddies. By the time I finally reached the first platform, I was horrified to find that the only sign of the geriatric foursome was a pair of stout legs, clad in beige knee-high stockings and sensible orthotic shoes, disappearing through a large window.

"Unbelievable," I muttered as I rushed over to the

window myself.

It was an enormous double-sash affair, with the lower section raised to reveal a large gap—just wide enough for four little old ladies to crawl through. I ducked my head through the opening to see the Old Biddies standing inside, dusting themselves off.

"Ah, Gemma, about time," said Mabel. "I would have thought you young people could move a bit faster."

"You shouldn't be in here!" I hissed. "Do you realise you're breaking into a guest's private room? You need to get out now before somebody finds you—"

"Somebody is much more likely to find us with you hanging out of the window like that," Mabel pointed out. "Now, either come in or go back down. You are jeopardising our mission, young lady."

"I..."

Furious, I threw a look over my shoulder. Mabel was right: the window was in full view of everyone on the terrace and out on the lawn. I could see Cassie, bent over an easel, pointing something out to one of the women guests and Ewan busily demonstrating something to Bruce using the latter's rod. They were both too engrossed to look this way, and all the other guests were too, but that was just luck. Any minute now, one of them could look up and spot me, or a member of staff could come around the side of the castle and see me as well...

I deliberated for a second more and then, with an

infuriated sigh, I ducked even further and climbed in through the open window. As I straightened up inside, I stared around the vast bathroom suite. *My God... and Cassie and I thought our ensuite was fancy. This place is practically the size of our entire room!*

There was a marble vanity unit with a double sink and matching mirror spanning one wall, accompanied by a white leather ottoman big enough to take a nap on. Opposite the vanity unit was a beautiful ornate fireplace—no doubt where water used to be heated for baths in the olden days—and beyond that stood an enormous claw-foot bathtub, dominated by a heritage mixer tap in gleaming polished brass, complete with vintage spout, crosshead handles, telephone-style shower and cradle, and ceramic details. Turning, I realised that the bathroom even extended around the corner, leading into two alcoves—one housing a high-tech bidet toilet and the other expanding into a spacious shower cubicle with modern chrome fittings and an overhead rain shower.

The sound of giggling made me jerk my head around, and I was aghast to find the Old Biddies clustered around the vanity unit, poking through Jerry Hudson's toiletries.

"...it's quite nice, don't you think?" said Glenda as she spritzed a bottle of aftershave on her wrist, then held it out for the other Old Biddies to sniff.

"Mmm, yes, lovely... I wonder if they do a similar

fragrance for ladies?"

"Or bath salts. That would be handy—"

"What are you *doing*?" I exclaimed in exasperation as I hurried over to them. "I thought you were here to search the room, not sample toiletries like you're in a department store!"

"Observing a man's personal grooming habits can lead to important clues about his character," said Mabel loftily. "Really, Gemma! If you want to be useful, you can begin searching the bedroom while we complete our examination in here."

Grrrr. I started to retort, then realised that the quickest way to get the Old Biddies out of the room was to convince them that the search was done. I sighed. *If you can't beat 'em, join 'em...*

Just outside the bathroom, I found a walk-in wardrobe and I paused in the doorway, glancing curiously inside. There were a couple of Western-style jackets hanging on the rails and piles of jeans, trousers, shirts, and other clothing on the shelves. On a hunch, I stepped inside and quickly rummaged through the clothes, paying particular attention to any accessories. There were various belts and buckles, shoes and laces, a watch, and even a pair of cufflinks, but no bolo tie. I stepped out of the walk-in wardrobe and peered into the main bedroom. There were a few things tossed over the chairs, but unless Jerry Hudson had stashed his bolo tie in one of the drawers in the antique writing desk or side tables—highly unlikely—it looked like his bolo tie wasn't anywhere in the suite.

So he was lying when he said that he couldn't be bothered to put it on, I thought. I distinctly remembered him telling me that he'd left it back in his room that morning, but it was obviously not here. So where was it? Had Hudson lost it? If so, why hadn't he just said so? Or had he deliberately got rid of it... perhaps because it could be used as evidence to incriminate him?

The sound of footsteps in the hallway outside interrupted my thoughts and I froze as I heard them approaching the suite door. The next moment, I heard someone fumbling with the door handle.

Whirling, I ran back into the bathroom, where the Old Biddies were still hovering around the vanity unit.

"There's someone at the door!" I gasped. "It must be Jerry Hudson coming back to his room. We need to get out!"

I grabbed Ethel's elbow and started trying to drag her to the bathroom window, but Mabel put out a hand to stop me.

"There's no time. We'll never get through the window fast enough," she said decisively. "Quick, in here!"

Before I realised what was happening, I found myself being bundled around the corner and thrust into the huge shower cubicle, with the Old Biddies crowding in around me. Mabel pulled the glass door silently closed and the five of us stood there holding our breaths. In the room outside, I heard the creak of the door opening and the soft *click* as it closed and latched again. There was a long pause, as if the person was standing still, listening.

Did he hear us? I wondered wildly. *What if Hudson decides to come in here and take a shower? How are we going to explain what we were doing in his bathroom?* I tried frantically to think of a good reason why he would find four little old ladies and me huddled under his rain shower. The image was so absurd that I felt a sudden hysterical urge to laugh.

"*Shush!*" whispered Mabel, digging me in the ribs with her elbow as I gave a muffled snort.

I took a deep breath, getting control of myself, then strained my ears to hear what was going on in the main bedroom. There were footsteps moving around but, as I listened, something struck me as odd. These didn't sound like the footsteps of someone moving confidently around his room. In fact, they sounded hesitant, almost furtive. *Why is Jerry Hudson creeping around his own suite?* I wondered.

Then, beyond the room, I heard a commotion in the hallway outside and voices and footsteps approaching the suite door once more. There was a sudden rustle of movement in the bedroom and the sound of someone hurrying into the bathroom. The next moment, someone came barrelling around the side of the alcove wall, yanked open the shower door, and thrust himself into the cubicle with us.

I sprang back in surprise as I found myself staring

not at Jerry Hudson but at Tristan St Clair.

"You!" I cried. "What are you doing here?"

"I..." St Clair paused and cocked his head to listen. Outside, the footsteps and voices passed the suite door and then faded away down the hallway. He turned back to me, his shoulders relaxing and his face settling into his trademark arrogant smirk. "I could ask you ladies the same question," he said coolly.

"I asked you first," I retorted.

He gave a nonchalant shrug. "My girlfriend Jemima was feeling chilly so I came up to fetch her a wrap."

"From Jerry Hudson's room?"

"Yes... er... well, we popped in here to chat to Jerry earlier and Jemima thought she might have left her cardie in his room," said St Clair smoothly.

There was no way I could disprove his story and since I, myself, had seen Hudson flirting with Tristan's girlfriend downstairs, it might even have been true. Tristan St Clair *could* have been on friendly enough terms with the American to come up to Hudson's room by himself... but somehow I doubted it. The man was lying through his perfect white teeth.

"So why did you rush in *here*? Was Jemima wearing her cardigan in the shower?" I asked sarcastically.

St Clair flushed and said quickly: "*You* still haven't answered the same question. I'm sure Jerry would be interested to know what *you* are doing in his bathroom?"

"I... er..." My mind went blank and I cursed myself for not being able to match his quick tongue.

"That's really none of your business, young man," said Mabel, stepping forwards and elbowing me out of the way. "But since you ask, I was chatting to Mr Hudson about shower fixtures—I'm redoing the bathroom in my house, you see... it's twelve years old now and getting a bit creaky, if I do say so myself... the Carron bath is still marvellous, of course—you wouldn't expect anything less from a British company that's been making baths for over 250 years—but the shower could do with new fittings... and I've been hearing everyone talk about 'rain showers' but I'd never seen one myself. Well, Mr Hudson told me that he had one in his room and he invited me to pop up here to try it out if I like..."

Tristan St Clair blinked, looking slightly stunned as Mabel paused at last for a breath. Then—before he could move—she reached out and twisted one of the taps, sending cold water shooting out from the rain shower overhead. The other Old Biddies and I jumped hastily out of the way and scurried out of the shower cubicle just in time, but St Clair wasn't fast enough. He gave a yelp as he was suddenly drenched.

"Hmm... yes... very impressive," said Mabel, stepping back and eyeing the stream of water critically. She turned the tap off, then dusted her hands. "Well, I think I've seen enough. Now, I think it's time for a cup of tea. Come along, girls!" she said.

And before St Clair or I could react, she marched out of the bathroom with the other Old Biddies trotting behind her. A minute later, I heard the door of the suite shut behind them and their footsteps receding down the corridor.

Grrrrr! I don't believe it—they've just abandoned me here with Tristan St Clair! I fumed as I turned back to look at the young aristocrat. He was stepping gingerly out of the cubicle, shaking water from his hair, his expression a mixture of angry disbelief and grudging admiration.

"Don't tell me you're installing a rain shower in your house too?" he said with a sneer. "That old biddy might have a quick tongue but we both know they didn't really come in here to check the shower."

I looked at him levelly. "Just like we both know you didn't really come in here to get your girlfriend's cardigan."

He inclined his head, acknowledging the hit. "*Touché.* In that case, how about we agree that the hotel management don't need to know that your little old lady friends are breaking into guest bedrooms... if Jerry Hudson doesn't need to know that I was here in his room."

I gritted my teeth. It galled me to have to make a bargain with St Clair, but unless I wanted to get the Old Biddies in trouble—and myself too—I had no choice.

I gave a curt nod, then said: "So what are you really doing in here? Is it something to do with the murder?"

He laughed. "The murder? What makes you think I have anything to do with that?"

"Well, you lied to the police about your alibi, for one thing," I said.

His expression sobered and his eyes shifted uneasily. "What are you talking about?"

"You told the police that you were in the hotel bar with Jerry Hudson, Angus Mackay, and Tariq Al-Mansouri the whole evening, but I know that's not true. In fact, you left the bar during the window of time when Aileen Fergusson was murdered."

"I went to the loo, okay? I just forgot to mention it to the police," he snarled. "I mean, it's such a mundane thing, it's not as if I went somewhere important. To all intents and purposes, I *was* in the bar all evening. I just happened to pop out for a few minutes to relieve my bladder. That's hardly a crime." His face took on a crafty look. "And if we're talking about people with fake alibis, then the person you should really be looking at is Jerry Hudson."

"What do you mean?"

"Well, he said he was going to the toilet first, and I followed a few minutes later. But when I got to the downstairs Gents, there was nobody there. So where was Hudson?"

"Maybe he came upstairs to use his own toilet," I said, indicating the alcove next to us. Then I recalled the Swedish couple with their room next to the landing. If Hudson had come upstairs, he would surely have triggered the squeaking floorboard at the top of the staircase... and yet Mikael had been adamant that he had heard no one walking past on that landing.

As if confirming my thoughts, St Clair said: "No, Hudson left his room key in the bar. I saw it on the bar counter, next to his wallet, after he went out. Without it, he couldn't have got into his room. So if he wasn't in the toilet downstairs and he wasn't up here, then where was he, eh?" He turned away from me and sauntered towards the bathroom doorway. "Now, if you'll excuse me, I need to go and find a cardigan for my girlfriend."

He disappeared out into the bedroom, and a minute later I heard the door of the suite close. I stared after him. Were the Old Biddies right? Was Jerry Hudson the murderer after all?

174

CHAPTER SIXTEEN

It was with a sense of relief that I saw the Old Biddies off that evening as they left the castle—with Muesli in tow—to return to Mabel's cousin's cottage. Hopefully, there would be no mischief they could get up to overnight, at least. I did feel slightly guilty as I bade my little cat goodbye for I had barely spent any time with her. But I couldn't keep Muesli at the castle—not unless she was to remain cooped up in her carrier all the time. I just didn't dare risk letting her out, even in our own room, in case she escaped and caused another scene. *At least at Graeme's place, she'll be able to run around and stretch her legs,* I thought. And I was sure the Old Biddies would spoil her rotten and feed her all sorts of treats for dinner!

Thoughts of dinner made me wonder about Cassie's plans for *our* evening, and I hurried back to our room to find my best friend. She was busily rummaging through my case and looked up with relief as I stepped into the room.

"Oh good, you're here. Quick, get changed and dolled up. You can wear this top with these jeans—it always looks good on you."

I took the clothes she thrust at me in bewilderment. "Does it really matter what I wear? We're just having something simple downstairs, aren't we? It's not like we're going to another degustation dinner."

"We're not eating at the castle tonight—we're going out to Fort William for dinner."

"To Fort William? But why? I thought you said room and board was included in your contract?"

"Not for you," she pointed out. "You have to pay a supplement."

"Well, okay, but *your* meal is still complimentary. Cass, if you're getting free food here anyway, it seems silly to—"

"We're going to Fort William," insisted Cassie. "I've booked a taxi already to come and pick us up. There's... um... a pub I want to try. I've heard that the food there is really good. Come on, Gemma! You don't want to come all the way up to Scotland to stay cooped up here in the castle all the time, do you? Don't you want to experience a bit of the local culture, try out some of the local places?"

"I suppose so..." Cassie was right. After all, we *were* supposed to be on holiday, and it would be a shame not to explore the area a bit. Then I remembered the murder investigation. "But what about the police? I thought Inspector Monroe didn't want anyone leaving Aberglinn?"

She waved a hand. "I've checked with him and he said it's okay. They've interviewed most of the guests today and people can leave, as long as they remain in the vicinity and are easily contactable by the police. Fort William is only about fifteen minutes' drive away."

"Most of the guests seem to be opting to remain in the castle, though," I said. "As I was coming up, I saw the staff preparing the dining room and laying out all the places."

I didn't add that I'd been hoping we could have dinner in there too, so that I would have more of a chance to observe the other guests—in particular, Jerry Hudson. For once, I would have been happy to sit with the loud American and listen to him talk!

Cassie read my thoughts. "Look, Gemma, I know you want to hang around here because you're thinking of the murder investigation, but you know, having a break away from the castle might be good for you. It'll give you a chance to see things from a distance, get a better perspective."

"Right now, I don't need a better perspective, I need more information," I said in frustration. "If I could spend some more time observing the guests, I might notice something I hadn't even thought of."

"Yeah, well, there's definitely one suspect you haven't thought of," muttered Cassie. "Ewan Campbell."

I looked at her in disbelief. "Ewan? You're not serious?"

"Why not? I mean, you heard him on the drive from Inverness Airport; it was obvious he didn't like Aileen."

"Cassie, *nobody* on the staff liked her," I said. "And Ewan hardly spoke about her, unlike some of the other staff, like Bridget, who really complained about her during our tour. Anyway, Ewan has an alibi. He left the castle at ten thirty, well before the time Aileen was murdered, and Inspector Monroe said it was confirmed on the CCTV camera footage."

"So? He could have come back."

"I'm sure the police would have checked all the alibis of the staff who left the estate. Inspector Monroe told me they were going to speak to the families to confirm the times they got home."

"Alibis can be faked," said Cassie stubbornly. "Besides, didn't you say that Aileen was garrotted? Well, I was watching Ewan on the lawn today and listening to him talk to his group. He certainly knows his way around a fishing line. He's got access to the perfect murder weapon right there."

I shook my head. "I already asked Inspector Monroe about that. He says the fishing line used in those rods is too thin and light to garrotte anyone—

it would just snap. You might be able to do it with the heavier lines used for catching big game fish like tuna, but they don't keep those spool sizes at Aberglinn because you don't meet those kinds of fish here in Scotland," I said, recalling Ewan's talk to his group. "Anyway, Inspector Monroe said the murder weapon is more likely to have been a rope or cord or something thicker like that—not a wire because that would have cut into Aileen's neck and there wasn't broken skin, only bruising."

"Well, fine, he could have used something else," said Cassie impatiently. "The point is, he could have done it."

"But so could anyone else!" I said, exasperated. "Honestly, Cassie, I don't know what you have against Ewan. He's not a murderer—he's a decent guy."

"You just don't want to suspect him because you've got a crush on him."

"I do *not* have a crush on him!" I cried indignantly.

"Aww, come on—he's just your type, Gemma. All dark and handsome, with those incredibly blue eyes... remind you of anyone?"

I flushed. "Rubbish! I... I don't have a 'type'! I mean, okay, yes, I admit that Ewan is very good-looking. Any woman with eyes in their head can see that. But that doesn't mean that I'd be blind to his potential as a murder suspect—*if* there was actually some decent reason to suspect him! You seem to be accusing him simply because he didn't like Aileen...

which pretty much describes every other person at Aberglinn."

Cassie didn't answer, but her expression was mutinous as she went into the bathroom to get ready. I sighed and started to get changed myself, wishing I could understand my best friend's strange hostility towards the handsome ghillie. By the time we were ready, I was glad we were leaving the castle for a night. Perhaps the break would help to give Cassie some perspective too, and it would certainly distract us from our disagreement.

The town of Fort William was nestled right at the foot of Ben Nevis, the highest mountain in the British Isles, and therein lay most of its claim to fame. In fact, Fort William was one of the three forts which cut across the Highlands from coast to coast, and which were built just after the unification of Scotland and England by a nervous government who wanted to control the Highland clans that still supported an independent Scottish monarchy.

Sadly though, unlike Fort Augustus on the banks of Loch Ness and Fort George with its commanding view across the Moray Firth, Fort William wasn't an especially scenic place. In fact, for a town known as the "capital of the Highlands" and surrounded by such spectacular scenery, it was surprisingly underwhelming. I blamed this on the faded Sixties-style buildings, incongruously plonked on street corners, and the ugly dual carriageway cutting the town off from the nearby sea loch—all of which managed to cancel out the charms of the pedestrianised High Street, with its cobblestones and elegant stone buildings housing quaint shops and pubs.

Still, the bustle on the High Street more than made up for the slightly disappointing aesthetics. It was full of tourists and visitors making the most of the long summer days. Crowds spilled out of pub doorways and formed queues outside restaurants, and Cassie and I had to navigate around them as we walked past the souvenir shops and eateries. We stopped at last in front of a pub doorway, from which raucous laughter and the enticing smell of hot cooking wafted out into the night air.

"This is the place," said Cassie enthusiastically, tugging my arm. "I heard they even do haggis on baked potatoes here!"

I made a wry face as I followed my friend in. Oh, I wasn't repulsed by haggis like many people were. Yes, I knew that the crumbly mixture was traditionally made up of the minced liver, heart, and lungs of sheep, together with beef or mutton suet and oats and onions. But once cooked and seasoned with a lovely mixture of pepper and spices, haggis really looked just like a delicious savoury mince, and I quite enjoyed the unique earthy, peppery flavour. Still, I didn't share Cassie's passion for this traditional Scottish dish. She absolutely adored haggis and pounced with excitement on anything that was haggis-flavoured. It was probably one of the highlights of a holiday in Scotland for her: being able to have haggis at every meal!

Inside the pub, it was warm and cosy, with exposed stone walls and dark wood furniture. We pushed our way through the crowd and managed at last to secure a spot at the bar counter. A harassed-looking barman turned towards us and gestured to the row of draught beer taps in front of him.

"What'll ye have, luv?" he asked.

"A pint of Tennent's Lager, please," said Cassie. She sent me a teasing look. "I suppose you'll be having your usual shandy?"

My best friend never lost an opportunity to tease me for being a lightweight when it came to alcohol and for my usual choice of drink: shandy—a weak mix of beer and lemonade that was usually the preserve of young adolescents and "ladies" who couldn't hold their liquor. Tonight, though, I surprised her by turning to the barman and saying:

"Actually, I'd like to try a Scotch whisky, please. Can you recommend something for me?"

He eyed me speculatively. "Ye wantin' the stuff that all the tourists ask for? The Glenfiddich and Macallan and the like? Or ye wantin' a single malt from a local Highland distillery?" he said in tones which suggested that the latter choice was the only proper one.

"Um... I'll try one of the local ones," I said bravely.

"And ye be wantin' a nip or a dram?"

I looked blankly at him. "What are they?"

He grinned. "A nip's a small shot o' whisky; a dram's a larger pour."

"Oh. Right. Well... a dram, then," I said, thinking: *In for a penny, in for a pound.*

A few minutes later, a tulip-shaped snifter glass filled with a rich amber liquid was placed in front of me. Conscious of the barman's expectant gaze, I lifted the glass to my lips and took a big gulp.

Oh my God! It was as if someone had poured liquid fire into my mouth. I coughed and choked, my eyes watering as I grabbed the bar counter for support.

"Ye all right, lassie?" asked the barman in concern.

"Er... yes, yes... fine," I spluttered, feeling the amused gazes of people nearby. "It... um... just went down the wrong way," I lied, whilst wondering despairingly if there could be a "right" way for whisky to go down.

Lifting the glass, I took another—more cautious—sip. It still burned just as badly as the first time and I had to make an effort not to screw my face up at the bitter, fiery taste.

"Um... do you think you could add some Coke to this?" I asked the barman.

You would have thought that I'd asked him to add some arsenic. He gave me a look of abject horror. "Ye wantin' to add Coke to a fourteen-year-old Clynelish?"

"Er... never mind then," I said hastily.

"I can add some water or ice to the glass if ye like,"

said the barman grudgingly. "But a quality single malt like that should be drunk neat."

"Oh... er... okay, I'll stick with it as it is," I said and hurriedly retreated to where Cassie had bagged two seats at a nearby table.

"Well done for finding seats," I said as I slid into the chair next to her. "This place is packed!" I glanced around. "I don't see anyone eating though."

"There's a proper restaurant upstairs," said Cassie. "But I thought it would be nice to have a drink down here first—you know, soak up the atmosphere." Her eyes kept straying over my shoulder and she seemed to be scanning the room as she sipped from her pint glass.

"What?" I asked, turning around to look over my shoulder. "What are you looking for?"

"Nothing," said Cassie quickly. "Just looking around... you know, it's interesting to check out the locals."

I looked at her in puzzlement. She made it sound like they were animals to be viewed on safari or something. In any case, I wasn't sure how many people in the pub *were* "locals". I turned in my seat to scan the room myself. Most of the patrons looked like overseas tourists, backpackers, and out-of-town visitors, with one large group of young men, in particular, looking like they might be military types, given their short haircuts and toned, muscular bodies.

Then the group of young men shifted as one of

them made a joke and several began clapping each other on the backs, roaring with laughter. As the bodies parted, I caught sight of a dark-haired man standing in their midst.

I gasped. This time, there was no mistaking those strong, handsome features, the firm, sensual mouth, and those piercing blue eyes.

It was Devlin O'Connor.

CHAPTER SEVENTEEN

At the same moment that I spotted him, Devlin glanced across the room and our eyes met. Everything and everyone around me seemed to recede and it was just us, staring at each other across the room. Then Devlin said something to his companions and began threading his way through the crowd towards me and Cassie. I had often seen Devlin in full CID detective mode, handling crowds at crime scenes with a calm authority, but even off duty and dressed in a casual T-shirt and jeans, he was a commanding presence. Men instinctively shifted aside to make way for him and women eyed his tall figure with open admiration as he passed.

I was annoyed to find that my heart was beating uncomfortably hard in my chest as he approached.

True, I hadn't seen Devlin for several weeks now—not since that fateful night when he'd suggested that we "take a break"—but it was ridiculous to be getting so worked up over meeting him again. This was the man I'd known since my student days at Oxford, for heaven's sake! *And the man you most trusted and felt closest to, who turned your world upside down by suddenly wanting time apart*, a voice in my head reminded me. Feeling the sense of grievance and betrayal fill me once more, I raised my chin and kept my expression aloof as Devlin came to a stop next to us.

"Devlin! What a surprise to see you here!" cried Cassie with such exaggerated disbelief that I wanted to roll my eyes.

I shot a dagger look at my best friend, suddenly understanding why she had been so insistent that I accompany her to Scotland and even out to Fort William and this pub this evening. Ever since our tiff, Cassie had been itching to personally instigate a reconciliation between Devlin and me. With her direct, fiery temperament, she'd had no patience with concepts like "taking a break" or the idea of having time and space apart to resolve issues. As far as she was concerned, if a relationship had problems, they should be hammered out there and then—with a screaming match that lasted until 4 a.m. if necessary!

It had been a struggle to restrain her from trying any romantic meddling, but I'd thought that my heartfelt pleas (mixed with threats to never speak to her again) had worked. Now, I could see that I'd been fooled. Cassie had simply redirected her efforts into more sly scheming, and tonight was obviously the culmination of a convoluted attempt to stage an "accidental" meeting between Devlin and me.

It also explained, I realised, Cassie's strange hostility towards Ewan Campbell. Suddenly having a handsome, charming young man claiming my attention was the last thing she needed and an unexpected threat to her carefully laid plans. No wonder she'd reacted with peevish belligerence and animosity towards him!

Cassie must have known what I was thinking but she pretended to ignore my thunderous expression, turning instead to Devlin and saying blithely: "Isn't this an amazing coincidence?"

To his credit, Devlin looked as taken aback and surprised as I did, and I felt slightly better that he'd obviously not been party to Cassie's scheming.

"I hadn't realised that you girls were coming to Scotland," he said.

"What are you doing here?" I blurted, then blushed at my tone. As the first thing to say after not seeing him for weeks, it was blunt to the point of rudeness.

Devlin didn't react, although his voice was cool as he said: "I'm here for my LSO—Licensed Search Officer—training. It's a specialist course I have to do once a year to keep me practised and up to date with security coordination and missing person search techniques." He gestured to the group of young men on the other side of the room. "It's run by the Police National Search Centre; that's a joint police and military unit, so you get trainers combining the best expertise from the Royal Engineers and the UK police service."

"Oh... er... how interesting!" said Cassie in an unnaturally high voice, darting nervous looks between me and Devlin. "I remember you mentioning this course when I ran into you in Oxford a couple of weeks ago, Devlin, but I didn't realise that it was being held in this part of Scotland."

Liar, I thought. Cassie must have looked up exactly where the course was being held and then realised that Aberglinn Castle was just "down the road" in the same area of the Highlands. She must have been secretly ecstatic when the plumbing problems at my tearoom had given her the perfect excuse to drag me up here. No wonder she had kept going on about how it was "meant to be"!

"They run it in different parts of the country, but yeah, choosing the Highlands is a great call, I think," said Devlin. "You can't find a better place than the Scottish wilderness to test search-and-rescue and forensic recovery skills. You've got some of the harshest terrain and most challenging weather conditions in the world out here."

"What, in the summer?" I said sarcastically.

This time, Devlin couldn't hide the flicker of

irritation in his blue eyes, and I felt a stab of satisfaction. It was childish, I know, but a part of me wanted to lash out at him, to provoke some kind of reaction and see him feeling as angry and upset as I was.

Cassie hastily drained her pint and said in the strained silence: "Er... how about I get us some more drinks? Back in a mo!" And she disappeared through the crowd, leaving us alone.

Silently cursing my best friend, I looked up at Devlin and said, "I had *no idea* you were coming to Scotland."

It came out more aggressively than I intended, probably because I didn't want Devlin to think that I'd been trying to engineer some way to throw myself into his path. I knew it was just silly pride, but I desperately wanted to show Devlin O'Connor that I didn't care about our "break" and that I was managing fine without him in my life, thank you very much.

His brows drew together and he said curtly, "I'm sorry I didn't warn you beforehand so that you wouldn't have your holiday spoiled by running into me, but I didn't know you were coming up here either."

I flushed. "That's... that's not what I meant," I said quickly. "I just..." I broke off miserably. I couldn't believe that having not seen each other for weeks, the first time we were in the same room again, we were fighting already.

Taking a deep breath, I said in a more conciliatory tone: "I'm sorry, that came out wrong—"

Devlin sighed and ran a hand through his dark hair. "No, *I'm* sorry, Gemma. I didn't mean to... Look, let's start again, shall we?" He gave me the ghost of a smile. "So how come you're here in the Highlands?"

I told him about the plumbing repairs at the Little Stables and how I'd ended up on this impromptu holiday with Cassie.

"I'm sorry about your tearoom," said Devlin, frowning. "That must be costing a fortune and be a lot of extra stress."

I was touched by the genuine sympathy and understanding in his voice. Whatever else might come between us, Devlin had always understood what the tearoom meant to me.

"Thanks," I said. "Hopefully it won't be too bad. The cost is partly covered by insurance, and actually it'll be nice to have a modern system at last. Besides, Cassie said it was high time that I took some time off from work and she's probably right," I added with a wry look. "I haven't had a real break since opening the tearoom over a year ago... and who would turn down the chance to stay in an ancient Scottish castle?"

Devlin's gaze fell to the snifter of whisky on the table next to me and he raised an eyebrow. "I didn't realise you were starting to drink the hard stuff."

I laughed a bit self-consciously. "I'm not. It's only because I felt like I ought to try a Scottish whisky while I'm here and I asked the barman to recommend one." I looked at the glass and gave a shudder. "I wish I hadn't bothered though. It's really horrible. And now I'm left with this glass of whisky that I've paid for so I don't want to waste it, but I can't drink it without retching!"

Devlin looked amused. "Surely it's not that bad?"

I picked up the glass and thrust it at his lips. "You try it! Go on—taste it and tell me that it isn't horrid."

As Devlin hesitated, I realised belatedly how intimate my gesture was. It was the kind of thing romantic partners did, like offering a spoonful of food across the table for the other to taste, and I felt my cheeks warming. Hastily, I began to withdraw my hand, but Devlin reached out and caught it, gently extricating the snifter glass from my grasp. Pretending not to notice my embarrassment—for which I was grateful—he raised the whisky to his lips and took a measured swallow.

"It's a bit on the peaty side," he said, lowering the glass and looking at me thoughtfully. "Probably not what I'd recommend to a beginner, but it's very smooth... very nice." He took another swallow. "What is it? A traditionally peated Glendronach or an Old Pulteney? Or maybe an aged Clynelish? It's definitely a peated malt from the Highlands."

I looked at him in surprise. "How on earth did you know that? Yes, the barman said it's a 'fourteen-year-old Clynelish'—whatever that is."

Devlin smiled at my dismissive tone. "Clynelish is

an iconic distillery up on the northern coast of Scotland. It's famous as producing one of the whiskies that are blended together to make Johnnie Walker." He raised the glass. "This is actually considered by connoisseurs to be a classic 'low peat' malt, with very good flavours of sea and salt that's balanced by honey and vanilla—"

"Honey? Vanilla?" I said incredulously. "You've got to be joking!"

Devlin chuckled. "You have to develop the palate. I agree it's probably a bit strong for a beginner—and especially someone like you who doesn't really drink at all—but trust me, this is a very good whisky. It's just unfortunate that it's the one you started with; it's smokier than most Highland whiskies. Usually it's the Islay distilleries, and some from the islands like Skye that produce the famous peaty single malts. Highland whiskies tend to be less smoky and have more spicy, dried fruit flavours and aromas like oak and heather—"

"I never realised you knew so much about whisky," I said, staring at him.

His blue eyes twinkled. "Well, there are still some things you don't know about me, Gemma Rose."

I felt a warm glow deep in my chest. It had been a long time since Devlin had taken that playful tone with me. In the past few months, we'd always seemed to either be arguing or intently discussing a murder investigation. In fact, now that I thought about it, this was the most relaxed I'd ever seen Devlin in recent times. He didn't have that tense jaw and the strained, tired look about the eyes that I'd grown used to seeing back in Oxford. Maybe having a break and getting away from it all was good for him too...

I realised that he was watching me and I wondered if he could read my thoughts. Feeling suddenly embarrassed, I looked around for Cassie, keen to have someone break the tension. I spied my best friend on the other side of the room, glass in hand, talking and laughing with the group of young military men, obviously with no intention of coming back. *Traitor*, I thought. Still, I had to admit that, in a way, I was glad Cassie wasn't there. Things were awkward enough between Devlin and me without an audience watching.

Turning back, I saw that Devlin was still watching me. "It's good to see you, Gemma," he said at last, his blue eyes soft.

I gave him a shy smile. "It's good to see you too."

There was another pregnant silence. Then Devlin cleared his throat and said: "So... you're staying in a Scottish castle, eh? What's that like?"

"Very posh," I said, gratefully seizing the opening he offered. "Full of rich, egotistical businessmen and snooty aristocratic types. Actually, that's not totally true," I amended. "There are some very nice people there. There's a sweet Chinese couple on their honeymoon and a lovely couple from Texas who are doing the retirement travel thing, and also a pair of elderly ladies—sisters—who inherited a lot of money and are now finally able to do all the things on their bucket list, one of which is to stay in a castle. Oh, and there's a gay couple from Sydney and a young Swedish couple who seem quite nice too. But it's definitely the kind of place that Cassie and I would never normally be able to afford—you know, all swanky suites and luxury four-poster beds and enormous fireplaces—so it's a real treat to be able to stay there." I paused, then added, "Although I have to say, right now, it feels more like a police incident room than a luxury hotel."

"What do you mean?" asked Devlin in surprise.

"Oh, hadn't you heard? You're obviously not on the Inverness-shire grapevine," I said with mock disdain. "The castle manager was murdered last night. She was found strangled in the library."

CHAPTER EIGHTEEN

Devlin shook his head and gave an exasperated laugh. "I don't believe it, Gemma. You come all the way here to Scotland and you still manage to get involved in a murder!"

"Well, I didn't do it on purpose," I retorted. "It's not like I go around trying to stumble over dead bodies!"

"You discovered the body? That must have been unpleasant," said Devlin, his expression softening.

I sighed. "Yeah, it was pretty horrible." Quickly, I told him the events of the previous night, from the dramas during the pre-dinner drinks to the details of the murder and a summary of the possible suspects.

"You know what's the worst thing? I didn't even realise that she was there at first. It was so dark in that corner and the armchair was so deep, with such a tall back... and even after I saw her, I thought that she'd just fallen asleep..." I trailed off, shuddering as I saw the slumped, lifeless body in my mind's eye once more.

"You said she was strangled?" said Devlin, frowning.

"Garrotted, actually. That's what Inspector Monroe said. But it's basically the same thing, isn't it? She was choked to death."

"Well, it depends on what you mean by 'choke'. When people say 'choke', they usually think of preventing someone from breathing, but garrottes more often kill by a 'blood choke'. That means the ligature cuts off the carotid artery and blood is prevented from going to the brain, starving it of oxygen," Devlin explained. "Essentially, you lose consciousness and become brain-dead even before the ligature cuts off your windpipe."

I shivered. "The whole thing sounds barbaric."

"Yeah, it's not a particularly nice way to die," said Devlin grimly. "Garrottes were actually invented by the Spanish Inquisition as a method of execution, and the original version used an iron collar that was tightened around your neck. Of course, nowadays it's usually done using a flexible length of cord... or anything, really. That's one of its benefits as a weapon: it's very simple and very effective. You don't need any specialist equipment and you don't even need that much training to use it."

"Yeah, there's a guest at the castle who used to be a pilot in the US Air Force who said something similar. He said you don't need to be Special Forces or anything to learn how to use a garrotte."

Devlin nodded. "Basically, if you can get the length of cord or whatever around the victim's throat, cross the ties and pull in opposite directions, the natural tightening action will do the deed for you."

"Do you have to be strong, though?" I asked. "Like... would the killer have to be a man?"

"How big and tall was Aileen Fergusson?"

I thought back and said in surprise, "You know, it's funny, I have it in my mind that Aileen was a formidable woman, but now that I think about it, she wasn't actually that big or tall. No more than five foot two, at the most, and very thin, almost scrawny. It was her manner and presence that made her seem so much bigger than she was."

"Well then, if she wasn't a very big person, a woman *could* have garrotted her—especially if the woman was bigger than her—but it's probably still more likely to have been a man."

"The top suspects are all men anyway," I said thoughtfully. "I mean, the police seem to be favouring the theory that it was an outside intruder who was trying to steal valuables from the castle, and most burglars are men, aren't they? But I think they're wrong, anyway. I don't think it's someone from the outside."

"Mm... yes, the logistics don't make sense," agreed

Devlin. "You said she was found in the library, wasn't she? Now, I assume there might be valuable first editions and things like that in the library, but an average thief wouldn't necessarily know that. In any case, it would be more efficient for him to target the drawing room or Great Hall where there are obvious antique pieces and other valuable ornaments out on display."

"That's exactly what I said to Inspector Monroe!" I exclaimed. "The library has mostly books and hunting trophies, and some equipment like fishing rods and binoculars and that sort of paraphernalia. It's just not the sort of place a random thief would go to look for loot! Besides, as far as I know, nothing's been stolen—although apparently Mackay is still checking the inventory to be sure," I conceded.

"Who suggested the 'outside intruder' theory?" asked Devlin. "Was it Angus Mackay, by any chance?"

I looked at him, impressed. "How did you know?"

Devlin gave a cynical smile. "It's not hard to see why the owner of Aberglinn Castle would want to push that version of events. The last thing he needs is for the killer to be one of his guests—or a member of staff. If it's a random criminal from the 'outside', there's no direct link with the castle."

"Yes, and especially if the killer might have been Angus Mackay himself," I added.

Devlin raised his eyebrows. "Ah... you're thinking of Mackay's strange behaviour when Tariq Al-

Mansouri complained about Aileen?"

"Yes!" I said, delighted at the way he effortlessly followed my thought process. "There was just something really 'off' about his manner. It wasn't just that he didn't want to lose a good manager, like everyone keeps saying—it was more than that." I thought back to what I had said to Inspector Monroe. It had seemed a bit far-fetched, but now I was more convinced than ever that it was true. "It was like he was *scared* of her..."

"You think Aileen had some kind of hold over her boss," said Devlin. It was more a statement than a question, and I nodded eagerly.

"Yes, not just from his behaviour but *hers* too," I said, recalling Aileen's smirk as she stood watching Mackay from the other side of the room. There had been a sense of power and satisfaction in her smile. "She wasn't remotely worried about being fired, you know. It was as if Aileen knew that she could behave however she liked and Mackay would never dare to challenge her."

I paused for a moment, then added excitedly, "And do you know what else? I had a long talk with Lilian— you know, the girl I told you about who was playing the harp during the pre-dinner drinks. She ended up staying at the castle last night because her train was cancelled. She was put in a room on the ground floor, down the hallway from the library, and her bathroom happened to back onto a section of the library wall. Anyway, she told me that she heard voices through the wall at around eleven thirty—which would be right within the window of time the murder was committed—and it sounded like a man and a woman arguing. Lilian is positive that the woman was Aileen... and I think the man could have been Angus Mackay!"

I leaned forwards, warming to the idea. "Maybe Mackay was angry about the way he had been emasculated in front of his guests and he went to Aileen to complain, but she just mocked and taunted him. In fact, Lilian told me that she heard Aileen laughing in a jeering way. So maybe Mackay lost it and decided that he'd had enough of being controlled by his own manager, and he decided to get rid of her once and for all."

"Hmmm... that's a pretty weak motive," said Devlin critically. "People don't just murder their employees because they're angry that their complaints are ignored. If that was the case, managers would be murdered all over the world, every day!" said Devlin half jokingly. "It would be different if you knew for certain that Aileen *did* have some kind of hold over Mackay, because wanting to break the control she had over him would be a viable motive. But without that... you need to be careful of jumping to a conclusion and trying to make the facts fit your hypothesis," he warned. "Remember, also, that while it's possible that the man overheard *was* Mackay, it could just as easily have been any one of the male guests in the castle—"

"No, it had to be one of the men who were downstairs," I insisted. "The Swedish couple have their room right by the landing at the top of the staircase and they can hear anyone going past because of a creaky floorboard. They're sure that nobody went downstairs after eleven last night— except me, when I went down to the library and found Aileen's body. So the murderer had to be someone who was already downstairs." I paused, then sighed. "But you're right, I suppose it could have been one of the male guests who were still downstairs."

I gave him a brief rundown on each of the men in the bar. "What I want to know is where Jerry Hudson really went when he left the bar... and what happened to his bolo tie? And Tristan St Clair—why was he sneaking around Hudson's room today?"

"To my mind, the most important question is whether Tariq Al-Mansouri was telling the truth when he said he was the only one who remained in the bar," said Devlin. "Because if that's the case, then that means none of them really has an alibi." He leaned forwards, his blue eyes intent. "Alibis are the key to everything. They're the best way to narrow down the list of suspects. Where was everyone at the time of the murder and what were they doing? Do you have corroborating witness statements of their movements?"

I hid a smile. Devlin was in full investigator mode now and there was something thrilling to see the way his mind focused. It also hit me sharply how much I missed being able to discuss a murder like this. There was no one else who could debate hunches and theories like this with me, no one else who had such an intuitive understanding of what I was thinking. And for all the conflict that it often caused in our relationship, working on a case with Devlin had been one of the things I most enjoyed doing together. My smile turned sad. *Why does the thing that brings us closer together also have to be the thing which drives us apart?*

"Gemma?"

I blinked and came out of my thoughts to see Devlin looking at me expectantly. "Sorry, I didn't catch that," I mumbled.

"I was asking if any of the men in the bar—"

"Gemma!"

I turned in surprise at the new voice and saw Ewan Campbell striding across the room towards us.

"I didn't realise you were coming to my favourite pub!" he said in delight as he reached out and gave my shoulder a friendly squeeze.

"Oh... um... I didn't know this was your favourite pub," I stammered, conscious that Devlin had stiffened next to me and was now giving the handsome ghillie a narrow-eyed look.

Almost unconsciously, I found myself looking Ewan over as well. I remembered the day Cassie and I had arrived at Inverness Airport and how I'd almost mistaken Ewan for Devlin when I'd glimpsed him across the crowded terminal. Now, though, seen together at close quarters, there was no question of confusing the two men. Although superficially similar with their tall, athletic figures, dark Celtic colouring, and handsome looks, there was a hardness to Devlin, a brooding intensity, that Ewan didn't possess.

Out of the corner of my eye, I saw that Devlin was noting Ewan's hand, which was still on my shoulder, and I hurriedly took a step back, breaking the contact.

I cleared my throat. "Er... this is Ewan. He works at Aberglinn Castle as the ghillie and—"

"And general dogsbody," said Ewan with a self-effacing laugh as he extended a hand to Devlin. "Nice to meet you, mate."

Devlin shook his hand. "Likewise," he said, although his tone was cool.

Ewan looked at me expectantly, obviously waiting for me to introduce Devlin, and I suddenly found myself tongue-tied. What should I say? "This is my boyfriend"? "My ex-boyfriend"? "My possible-ex-boyfriend-if-we-don't-work-out-our-issues"?

"Um... this... this is Devlin. He's... he's a detective inspector with the Oxfordshire CID," I mumbled at last, opting for the safe-professional-title option.

I saw Devlin glance sharply at me and knew that he had noticed my omission of our relationship and hadn't liked it. I felt a prickle of irritation. *Well, we wouldn't be in this situation if you hadn't wanted a break,* I thought, my old feelings of betrayal and resentment returning.

"A detective?" Ewan looked at Devlin with new eyes. "You're not involved in the murder investigation at Aberglinn, are you?"

Devlin shook his head. "No, I'm up here on a training course, actually, and just happened to run into Gemma. But she was telling me all about the case and I suppose you could say that I have a professional interest." He gave Ewan a speculative look. "I understand that you weren't at the castle when the murder occurred?"

"No, I was off the premises," said Ewan. "I finished my shift and left at around ten thirty."

"And you live nearby?"

Ewan shrugged. "Depends on what you mean by 'nearby', but yes, I live in a village about twenty minutes' drive from the castle."

"Do you live alone?"

"No, I live with my Uncle Mac, actually," said Ewan, looking slightly taken aback by the barrage of questions. "He's retired and alone now, so it's good to be able to keep him company."

"So he would have been home last night and can confirm the time you got home—"

"Hey," I interrupted, frowning at Devlin. "What are you doing? You're interrogating Ewan like he's a suspect or something!"

"It's okay," Ewan said to me with a good-natured smile. "I don't really mind, and I suppose it's natural to ask." Turning back to Devlin, he added, "Aye, the police came round to speak to my uncle this evening and he confirmed that I got home before eleven and didn't go out again after that. So I've got a solid alibi," he said with a grin.

"You don't need a solid alibi because you're not a suspect," I said, scowling. I turned on Devlin. "I can't believe you're suggesting that Ewan might be the murderer!"

"I'm not suggesting anything," said Devlin evenly. "But anyone who is innocent would have no problems being questioned about their movements at the time of the crime."

I bristled. "You have no business questioning anyone since you're not officially leading this investigation."

"Neither are you," he snapped. "But that never stopped *you* sticking your nose in where it didn't belong, did it?"

I drew in a sharp breath, shocked and hurt. My hands shook. I was so angry I almost wanted to slap him, and I could see my fury mirrored in Devlin's eyes.

Ewan shifted his weight, looking uncomfortably at us. "Er... maybe I should leave you two—"

"No, I'll leave," said Devlin, his voice curt. "I'm sure Gemma would infinitely prefer your company to mine."

With that, he turned and stalked away.

CHAPTER NINETEEN

I groaned as I rose from bed the next morning, struggling to shake off that groggy, heavy-headed feeling so often associated with a bad hangover. But it wasn't a night of alcoholic excess that had caused my suffering—no, my throbbing head was more due to the emotional strain and tension of my meeting with Devlin the night before, followed by hours of lying awake in bed, furious and fuming as I replayed our encounter in my mind over and over again.

Still, in the cold light of morning, I found some of my anger and resentment fading. I was still mad at Devlin, but I had to concede that I hadn't behaved particularly well myself either. And perhaps Cassie was right—perhaps I did get defensive about Ewan too quickly...

Sighing, I got out of bed and walked over to the window. There was a mist this morning, blanketing the mountains and stretching like a soft, fleecy blanket across the castle grounds. As I tilted my head and looked up at the sky, I caught sight of a light drizzle falling steadily from the clouds overhead. This was what the Scots called "smirr"—that awful, irritating drizzle of moisture which somehow didn't seem substantial enough to merit the label "rain" (and therefore give you an excuse to stay indoors), and yet was still enough to lend a humid dampness to everything and make you feel wet through.

So much for summer in Scotland, I thought as I turned towards the ensuite bathroom to wash and dress. Cassie had obviously risen already and gone downstairs, leaving me to sleep in. I had a feeling that the move had been less an altruistic one and more because my best friend was keen to avoid me for a while, after her role in my confrontation with Devlin.

When I finally arrived in the Great Hall downstairs, I found that most of the guests seemed to share my view of the "smirr" and had opted to stay in the dry comfort of indoors. People were either lazing on the various sofas and armchairs in the Great Hall or standing by the windows, gazing out at the misty landscape, or lingering over breakfast in the dining room. Cassie was nowhere in sight— probably looking for an alternative place to continue her workshop indoors—but the Old Biddies had already arrived and made themselves at home on one of the sofa suites in the hall. They had also, I saw with a sinking heart, brought Muesli with them again in the cat carrier.

"Well, we couldn't very well leave her alone in Graeme's cottage," declared Mabel when I went across to join them and expressed my dismay. "She would have been lonely, all by herself in a strange place. I'm sure Muesli would much rather be here with us. She can still enjoy everything just by watching through the bars of her cage."

Glancing down at my little tabby cat, I was doubtful. Muesli was vigorously pawing and butting her head against the door of her carrier, trying to push it open, whilst giving us indignant looks and letting out a petulant "*Meorrw!*" every so often.

"Aww, poor thing—it does seem cruel to keep her cooped up," said Glenda, watching in sympathy. "Are you sure we can't let her out, just for a little bit?"

I hesitated. I did feel mean for keeping Muesli confined to her carrier, but I just didn't dare let her loose in the castle again.

"How about if I take her outside?" I suggested. "I could let her have a little sniff and walk around on the terrace, out at the front of the castle, or maybe in the flowerbeds around the lawn..."

"Excellent idea," said Mabel approvingly. "And while you are there, you can check to see if there are any suspicious footprints."

I rolled my eyes. "I'm sure the police will have done all that—"

"Never trust anyone to do as good a job as yourself," admonished Mabel, wagging a finger at me. "Especially the *police!*"

A few minutes later, I stepped out of the castle, lugging Muesli's carrier in one hand. I was pleasantly surprised to find that the drizzle had subsided and that my raincoat was unnecessary. I set Muesli's carrier down on the terrace overlooking the front lawn and gingerly unlatched the door of the cage. The little tabby stepped out and gave herself a good shake, then looked around, her green eyes wide with curiosity. I had half wondered if the open space of the castle grounds would faze my cat, but I should have known better. Muesli was definitely not a shy, nervous feline and she trotted confidently across the terrace, pausing to sniff at the various stone urns holding potted plants before weaving between the legs of the wrought iron tables and chairs provided for guests to sit and enjoy the view.

I began to relax and my own gaze drifted to the vista stretching out beyond the terrace. The mist was lifting and a hint of blue was streaking across the grey skies. *Maybe Cassie will be able to continue her workshop outdoors after all,* I thought, turning back. *Maybe she can—*

I stopped and stared at the empty terrace.

"Muesli?" I called.

Silence. With a sense of foreboding, I began bending and peering under the chairs and tables arranged on the terrace, but there was no sign of a little tabby cat. *Where has the bloody minx gone?*

"Muesli!" I called again. "Muuuuuuuesli!"

"*Meeowrr?*"

I jerked my head up and found a cheeky little whiskered face peering down at me from a ledge above my head. Somehow, Muesli had managed to climb up the side of the castle wall and was now perched precariously on a carved stone ledge which ran the length of the building. *Great,* I groaned inwardly. I had forgotten that cats didn't just operate in two dimensions. To any feline, gaining height was second nature, and you didn't just explore sideways—you went *up* as well.

"Muesli, what are you doing up there?" I called, annoyed. "Come down!"

"*Meorrw!*" she said, twitching her tail defiantly.

Then, as if to illustrate her point, she turned and began walking along the narrow ledge away from me.

"Ohh... careful!" I cried, watching anxiously as she placed one paw daintily in front of the other. But I needn't have worried. Muesli balanced with expert skill and soon reached the end of the ledge as it met a turret on the corner of the castle wall. But if I had hoped that the architectural barrier would deter my little cat and send her obediently back down to me, I was disappointed. Muesli simply sat back on her haunches, looked up at the crenellated battlement encircling the top of the turret with a measured eye, then launched herself upwards like a rocket exploding from a launchpad.

I gasped and held my breath as I watched Muesli grab on to the parapet, half hanging off the side of the battlement as she scrambled to get a foothold, her back claws digging into the pitted stone surface. Then she hauled herself up over the edge and sat upright on one of the merlons.

"*Meorrw!*" she said triumphantly, shooting another cheeky look down at me. Then she turned and trotted along the top of the parapet circling around the turret and disappearing over to the other side of the castle.

"Muesli!" I called, infuriated as I rushed around the corner myself to try and keep her in sight.

I found her happily traipsing along the duplicate stone ledge of the wall on the other side of the castle. This time, however, when she reached the end of the wall, Muesli didn't attempt to skirt the next turret. Instead, she climbed up to a window ledge and— ignoring my threats and pleas—settled down to give her face a leisurely wash.

"Arrrrggghh!" I growled, standing underneath and watching in exasperation. I sighed. It looked like I had no choice but to go up and get her. I eyed the window speculatively, wondering if I could reach out and catch Muesli. It looked like it was on the upper floor, and I hoped that it was accessible from a corridor rather than being a window in one of the private guest rooms.

I was in luck. When I finally made my way back into the castle and upstairs, I found the window to be at the end of a hallway. I crept up to the opening, approaching from the side so that Muesli wouldn't see me, and peered around the edge of the window frame. *Aha.* Sitting enticingly close was the back view of a rounded feline bum, accompanied by a little furry head with two perky ears on top.

Eyeing the window latch, I considered my options. Although Muesli was currently facing away from me, it wouldn't take her two seconds to turn around and see me as soon as she heard me trying to open the window. Could I be quick enough to open it and grab her before she could dart away?

Well, there's only one way to find out, I thought grimly as I took a deep breath and unlatched the window. It swung open with an ear-splitting creak of the hinges and Muesli sprang to her feet, her fur on end and her green eyes startled. She relaxed slightly as she saw me, but, to my dismay, she gathered herself to jump off the window ledge.

"No... Muesli, come here!" I cried, lunging out of the window to try and grab her.

For a moment, I thought I had her, as my fingers met a furry, wriggling body. Then the next moment, there was an indignant yowl as Muesli squirmed out of my grasp and tumbled off the ledge.

"*Oh my God—!*" I screamed, lurching forwards and nearly falling out of the window myself as I tried to save my cat.

I was too slow. Muesli plummeted downwards.

But my cry of horror trailed off as I saw that my

little tabby was somehow flipping herself in mid-air. As I watched in awe, she twisted around and landed gracefully on her feet on the ground a moment later, next to a tall, spiky grey plant growing at the base of the castle wall.

"*Meorrw!*" said Muesli, sending a reproachful look back up at me. Then she turned and trotted off, disappearing into the shrubbery at the side of the castle.

"Hey, wait... Muesli!" I called futilely after her.

Sighing, I was about to withdraw my head and close the window when I paused and squinted down at the ground again. Something was glinting up at me from the depths of the grey, spiky plant. *What's that?*

I shifted my position to try and get a better look. No, I wasn't imagining it. Something shiny was catching the light and gleaming between the prickly stems of the plant. Overcome by curiosity now, and with Muesli temporarily forgotten, I shut the window, then ran back downstairs and out to the spot beneath the window.

My steps slowed, though, as I approached the large grey-green plant. It was a Scottish thistle: well over six feet tall, angular and arresting, and bristling with vicious thorns. I recalled the story Ewan had told me about how the Norse army had failed in their invasion of the Highlands. Looking at the plant now, I couldn't help feeling sorry for the hapless Viking warrior who had stepped barefoot on this prickly weed and inadvertently alerted the Highland clans to the ambush. *Ouch!*

Taking a careful step closer, I simultaneously raised on tiptoes and leaned forwards to peer into the mass of spiny stems. *Yes, there...* I caught the gleam of silver once more and, as I squinted harder, I realised suddenly what I was looking at: an ornamental silver clasp, studded with turquoise stones and carved with an eagle feather pattern. The very same clasp I had seen on Jerry Hudson's bolo tie.

CHAPTER TWENTY

So this is where the bolo tie is! I thought. As I peered closer, I saw that two long lengths of leather trailed out from either side of the clasp. *Did Hudson know it was here? Had he hidden it here himself?*

I raised my head and looked around, noting my surroundings for the first time. This side of the castle looked out on a view I recognised: it was the same beautiful vista I had seen from the big bay windows in the library. In fact, I saw now that the large windows protruding from the castle wall, several feet away, *were* the ones that looked out of the library. Which meant that these other windows must have belonged to the offices situated along the same hallway. I raised myself on tiptoe again, and this time peered into the window right beside where the thistle was growing. Yes, it looked like a personal office: I could see a desk piled high with papers and folders, a large annual planner mounted on the wall, filled with scribbled entries, a lush spider plant gracing a macramé hanger, and several filing cabinets in the corner. As I strained my eyes, I noticed a few photographs pinned to a bulletin board on the wall, all sharing a common figure: Aileen Fergusson. This must have been the castle manager's office.

What had Jerry Hudson been doing here? I wondered. *Had he been skulking around Aileen's office? Or...* My gaze drifted down to the library window a few feet away. *Was it the library that he had been aiming for?*

If Hudson had murdered Aileen that night and wanted to get rid of the murder weapon, this vicious, thorny plant would have been the perfect hiding place. He could depend on no one coming close without good reason—in fact, I myself would never have seen the bolo tie hidden in the depths of the plant if I hadn't been looking down from that window right above it. And no doubt that was why the police had missed this vital clue as well. Mabel had been right about not always trusting the police to do a thorough job, I conceded grudgingly as I crouched down next to the thistle and peered into its depths. I could just imagine a junior officer, ordered to search the grounds, taking one look at this prickly weed and deciding that it wasn't worth bothering to come closer.

Now, though, I could let Inspector Monroe know, and once the police retrieved the bolo tie they could send it for forensic analysis. If traces of Aileen's skin and DNA were found on the leather straps—

My thoughts were interrupted suddenly by the sound of rapid footsteps approaching. The next moment, a large figure came around the side of the castle, moving with furtive speed. It was Jerry Hudson, and he was so busy throwing nervous looks over his shoulder that he didn't see me crouched next to the thistle until he was practically stepping on me.

"*Unggh!*" He stopped short, his eyes widening in dismay as he saw me.

He was breathing fast, obviously agitated, and there were beads of sweat on his forehead. His eyes darted nervously to the thistle and then back to me.

I rose slowly to standing. "Hello, Mr Hudson. You seem to be in an awful hurry."

"Uh... call me Jerry, please," he said, making a weak attempt at casual camaraderie. "Yeah, well, looks like it's gonna be a nice day. Thought I'd go for a walk, you know, get a bit of fresh air..."

"Oh? This seems like an odd place for a walk," I said, gesturing to the section along the castle wall. Then I looked pointedly at his shirt collar and said, "You're not wearing your bolo tie again, Mr Hudson. I remember you told me that it's your 'lucky piece' and you never go out without it."

He flushed. "Oh, yeah... well... uh... I kinda decided to lay off the tie while I'm here in Scotland.

You know, try to fit in more with the locals."

"So you haven't lost the tie?"

"Lost it? Oh, hell no," he said quickly. "It's... uh... safe up in my room."

"Really? That's odd, because I've just found it in the middle of that thistle, there," I said, gesturing to the spiky plant next to us.

Hudson gulped. "Uh..."

I gave him a hard look. "You lied to me about the tie. Just like you lied to the police about your alibi."

He stared at me. "My alibi?"

"Yes, you told the police that you went to the toilet when you left the hotel bar, but Tristan St Clair told me that he never saw you in the Gents. You couldn't have gone upstairs to your room either, because you'd left your room key behind in the bar... so where *did* you go, Mr Hudson? Was it the library?"

I paused as I recalled the Old Biddies' theory about Aileen blackmailing Hudson, and suddenly it clicked with another memory: that first day when I'd overheard Aileen and Jerry Hudson in the library.

I looked him in the eye. "Was Aileen blackmailing you? That was it, wasn't it? That first day in the library, I heard the two of you arguing and Aileen saying she needed payment by the end of the day. She cleverly made it sound like a 'quote' for some hotel service but, in fact, she was talking about payment for her silence. And if you didn't pay, she threatened to 'approach the other interested party'— who was probably your wife, right? Was that when you decided to murder her? So that she wouldn't be able to keep threatening you?"

"What? No! I never murdered no one!" cried Hudson, looking aghast.

"Then why did you hide your bolo tie in the thistle?" I asked. "You knew it would incriminate you as the murder weapon used to garrotte Aileen, so you decided—"

"NO!" shouted Hudson. "I didn't hide it in there, okay? It fell in and I couldn't get the damned thing out!"

I faltered. "What...?"

Hudson scowled. "Look, okay, you're right: that greedy bitch *was* trying to blackmail me. Sometimes, I get a bit... uh... 'friendly' with the maids. You know, it's just a bit of fun, no big deal, but my wife's real uptight about stuff like that. Anyway, Aileen told me that she got evidence—secret photos and videos and stuff like that—which she would show my wife unless I paid her money. So yeah, I was pissed about it... but I didn't murder her! In fact, I wired money to her account that night, before dinner. You can check my bank statement if you like."

"Just because you paid her doesn't mean you *didn't* murder her," I said doggedly. "You could have decided that you didn't want to be stuck paying her any *more* money, so you got rid of her once and for all—"

"No! I tell you, I didn't murder her!"

"Then why is your bolo tie in there, if you didn't

hide it on purpose?" I demanded, pointing at the thistle plant.

Hudson sighed. "That was an accident, okay? Aileen told me that she kept the 'evidence' in her office, and after a couple of drinks in the bar that night, I got it into my head that I could break into her office and maybe find the evidence and destroy it or something. Then she wouldn't have a hold over me anymore, right? So I pretended to go to the restroom and I went to her office instead. But the door was locked, so I came out here to try my luck through the window. I thought maybe there was some way I could force it open and get into the office... Anyway, so I climbed up on the window ledge to get a better look at the latch and then somehow—I don't know what happened—I kinda lost my balance. My foot slipped or something. Anyway, I fell off, right into that damned plant over there!"

He shot a dirty look at the thistle next to us. "Man, it hurt! That thing has got fangs! And it's like, the more you struggle to get free, the more the barbs dig into your skin—"

"Oh, the swellings on your face," I said, suddenly remembering the angry red marks I'd seen the next morning. "Those weren't midge bites at all!"

"Yeah, I lied about that," Hudson admitted, putting a hand gingerly up to one cheek. "That thistle got me good. I was thrashing around, trying not to make too much noise, and then when I finally got myself free, I realised that my bolo tie had got loose and was still inside the plant." He shook his head in frustration. "I tried to get it out, but it was so dark I couldn't see properly and, jeez, those freakin' thorns! They're everywhere! Couldn't put your hand in without getting stabbed. So in the end I gave up. Besides, the other guys in the bar were probably wondering where I'd gone. I was just thankful that it was pretty dark in the bar, so they didn't get a good look at my face when I got back. Otherwise, I would have had a hard time explaining why I looked so messed up."

He glanced at the thistle again. "When you found Fergusson's body and the police came and I heard that she'd been garrotted... well, I realised that my tie could get me in trouble. So I tried to come out and get it back. But there were so many damned police officers crawling around out here yesterday, it was impossible to get close enough! So I thought I'd lie low and try again today. Inspector Monroe never saw me before yesterday, so he never knew I had a tie. You're the only one who noticed."

He looked at me pleadingly. "You're not gonna rat on me, are ya? I mean, okay, I lied about a coupla things, but you could say that I'm the real victim here, you know, cos that woman was squeezing me for money."

"If anyone is a victim, it's the poor girls you sexually assaulted," I said, looking at him with disgust. "I'm not going to hold information back from the police. It will help them to eliminate suspects from the investigation—*if* they *can* eliminate you," I added with heavy emphasis.

"Hey, I didn't murder anyone, okay?" said Hudson angrily. "If you're looking for a suspect, you should check out the person Fergusson was talking to in the library."

I looked at him sharply. "What do you mean?"

"I heard voices talking when I was out here that night," said Hudson. "Someone was with Fergusson in the library."

I recalled what Lilian Monaghan the harpist had told me about hearing voices through her bathroom wall. "What time was this?"

Hudson shrugged. "I don't know. Sometime around eleven thirty maybe? I left the bar around eleven twenty and I was back again by eleven forty."

"Did you see who it was?" I asked eagerly.

"Nah. I didn't go up close enough to the library window to look in."

"Okay, what about the voices you heard? Did you hear what they said?"

"Sorry. Couldn't really make out words. It was just like a rumble coming through the glass. I think I heard someone laughing at one point—sounded like a woman."

That tallies with what Lilian overheard, I thought, remembering the girl's description of Aileen's jeering laugh.

"And the other person? Was it male or female?" I asked.

Hudson shrugged again. "Like I said, I wasn't close enough to look through the window. The only thing I saw was their shadows on the wall. There was one smaller figure—that was probably Fergusson cos she was kinda short, wasn't she? The other shadow was tall and skinny. But it could have been a guy, could have been a girl. The silhouette was kinda fuzzy, you know?"

CHAPTER TWENTY-ONE

I walked slowly back into the castle, musing over what Jerry Hudson had told me. If the American was telling the truth—and it certainly seemed like he was, this time—then it meant that he was off the hook as a suspect. It also meant what whoever had been talking to Aileen in the library that night was very likely to have been the murderer after all. But who could it have been? I wondered in frustration. It had to have been someone on the ground floor of the castle that night... which meant that it was most likely to have been one of the other men at the bar. Tristan St Clair? Tariq Al-Mansouri? The castle owner, Angus Mackay?

My money was on Mackay. I couldn't shake off the memory of that odd scene I'd witnessed and the strong feeling I'd had that Aileen Fergusson had had some kind of hold over the castle owner. Well, if she had been willing to blackmail Jerry Hudson, why not her own boss too? It would certainly explain why he had seemed to be so "under her thumb" and unwilling to antagonise her, even at the expense of offending one of his guests.

And it would certainly fit the sequence of events that had occurred that night. As I'd suggested to Devlin, the scene with Al-Mansouri could have been the trigger, with Mackay deciding that he'd been humiliated enough and that the situation was untenable. It might have even been a matter of honour. I thought of the Scottish national motto that Ewan had told me about: *nemo me impune lacessit,* and I recalled the impressive sight of Mackay in full Highland regalia, with his black Prince Charlie jacket, tartan kilt, and sporran... It was not hard to imagine the Scotsman living up to that motto and deciding that those who had provoked him would have no impunity. So he had marched to the library to have it out with his manager, and that was the conversation that both Lilian and Jerry Hudson had overheard. In fact...

I thought back to my conversation with Lilian. I'd always had the nagging feeling that the harpist was holding something back—I was *sure* she'd had some idea of who the "second voice" was but had just been unwilling to tell me. Now, I wondered if it was because she *had* recognised the second voice as belonging to "Uncle Angus"—an avuncular figure she'd known since childhood and who she'd probably looked on with some affection. It was no surprise, then, that she would have been reluctant to name him and make him a prime suspect in the murder investigation.

Still, this was all conjecture, I realised with a sigh, remembering Devlin's warning. The whole thing hinged on my hunch that Aileen had been blackmailing Angus Mackay too, but there was no proof. *It would help if I had some idea of what Aileen could have been blackmailing her boss about,* I thought as I made my way to the castle reception desk.

I was hoping to ask if Hamish or one of the other members of staff might have seen Muesli. I had searched around the exterior of the castle after parting from Hudson but all I had found was the empty cat carrier still sitting on the terrace. There hadn't been any sign of my little tabby cat and now I was beginning to imagine all sorts of horrors.

What if she was stuck somewhere? What if she was hurt? I should have just left her in the carrier instead of letting her out, I berated myself. *I'll never forgive myself if something has happened to her...*

As I was entering the outer vestibule, I ran into Safa coming in the other direction. The little girl was clutching an enormous vintage magnifying glass in both hands and she looked up at me eagerly.

"See what the reception man give me?" she

beamed, brandishing the magnifying glass at me. "Now I can look for mystery footprints like Nancy Drew!"

I smiled at the girl's enthusiasm. "I don't suppose you might have seen a little grey cat during your sleuthing?" I asked her.

The little girl drew back slightly. "Grey cat?"

"Yes, she won't hurt you," I assured her. "It's my cat. Her name is Muesli. She's a grey tabby cat—that means she has dark stripes on her coat—and she also has a white chest and paws. Have you seen her? I really need to find her."

Safa frowned, then said: "I think I see a grey cat like that in the kitchen. I want to go in to look for clues but then I see the cat." She shuddered. "I hate cats! I am going to tell Baba, then he will make trouble and kick them out," she said with malicious glee.

Vicious little spoilt brat, I thought, watching her skip away. Still, she had assuaged my worries about Muesli. It sounded like my little cat had made herself at home with the kitchen staff. Turning, I headed towards the dining room and the corridor which led to the castle kitchen. Breakfast seemed to be over, and I could see the staff rushing around, clearing the tables, relaying them for lunch, serving drinks, and responding to other requests from the guests. I felt a tug of sympathy as I caught sight of the strained, harassed expressions on their faces—it reminded me of the days when I was run off my feet at the tearoom.

On an impulse, I turned to Bridget, who was walking briskly past with a pile of folded sheets in her arms, and asked:

"Bridget, do you need an extra hand around the castle? I'm free and I'm happy to help. I run a tearoom, you see, so I have some experience with catering and hospitality."

"Oh, bless ye, dear, but yer a guest!" she said, looking scandalised. "Yer here tae relax and enjoy yerself—"

"Well, I'm not really a paying guest," I said, slightly embarrassed. "You know I just tagged along with my friend and I don't want to take advantage of—"

"*Wheesht!*" said Bridget, waving a dismissive hand. "Yer not takin' advantage o' anyone. Yer a sweet, polite girl—not like some others." She cast a dark look across the hall. "There are some not payin' a penny either but actin' like Lord and Lady Muck, wantin' this and wantin' that, and complainin' all the time..."

I followed her gaze to where Tristan St Clair and his girlfriend were sprawled across one of the sofas next to the window. "They're not paying guests?" I said in surprise.

"Aye, Hamish handles the check-ins and he told me. Staying fer free, it seems. Mr Mackay's invitation."

"Oh, perhaps they're his friends," I said.

Bridget made a sceptical face. "Never heard Mr Mackay mention 'em nor seen them at any o' the castle events." She gave Tristan St Clair another look and added with a contemptuous sniff: "Ye wouldnae think anyone as posh and rich as *he* is would need tae scrounge a free bed, would ye?" She shook her head. "But I've seen big billionaires actin' like the meanest bastards ye'd ever meet—and I've known homeless folk give ye their last penny."

She went off, still shaking her head, and I continued to the baize door that led into the kitchen. Pushing it open hesitantly, I peeked inside. I was surprised to see a large modern kitchen, all gleaming stainless steel and modern appliances, which was completely at odds with the vintage interior of the rest of the castle.

A wonderful, rich aroma of cooking and baking permeated the air, and as I stepped into the room and peered through the steam wafting up from various pots and pans, I saw two women in white chef's tunics hovering over the workbenches. *These must be the sous chefs, Rhona and Mairi*, I guessed, and beyond them was an older woman also dressed in white—Morag the head cook, no doubt—standing by a door which opened onto the rear of the castle grounds. I caught a glimpse of a potager garden through the open doorway, with vegetables and herbs arranged in neat, geometric lines.

I was just about to step forwards to introduce myself when I realised that Morag was bending down to place a heaped bowl in front of a grey tabby who was reclining luxuriously on a folded plaid blanket just inside the door. Morag cooed and stroked the little cat, whilst simultaneously handfeeding her tasty morsels from the bowl.

"Muesli!" I cried accusingly. *Unbelievable.* Here I was, worrying about her being hurt or in trouble, and all along the little minx was here in the lap of Scottish luxury!

Morag straightened and looked at me in surprise. "Hullo... can I help ye, miss?"

I hurried over. "Hi... it's Morag, isn't it? I'm Gemma. I'm staying at the castle... and this is my cat, Muesli," I said, indicating the little tabby who was looking up at me with a smug expression on her whiskered face.

Morag's face brightened. "Ah, I was wonderin' who the mite belonged to. She didnae look like a stray tae me." She reached down and began scratching Muesli under her chin. "Will ye look at that gorgeous wee face? I was just thinkin' o' takin' her home, since she cannae stay here."

"I'm sorry if she's been causing you trouble—"

"Trouble?" One of the sous chefs spoke up with a laugh. "You fair made Morag's day. No one is as crazy about cats as our Morag. You should have seen her face when your kitty turned up at the back door." She smiled at me. "I'm Rhona, by the way. And this is Mairi. And you must be one of the girls who's come to teach the painting workshop? Bridget's told us all about you. A nicer pair of girls you couldn't meet, she said."

"Oh... thanks," I said, blushing slightly. "It's lovely to meet you all. Yes, my friend Cassie is teaching the painting workshop. I'm just tagging along, really."

"Ahh, so you don't do the painting too?"

"Bloody hell, no," I said with a laugh. "I can barely draw stick figures! No, I run a tearoom in England. Near Oxford. In fact..." I turned and looked at Morag shyly. "I was hoping that I could watch you do some baking. We sampled the afternoon tea yesterday and it was absolutely delicious, especially the scones! I don't think I've ever tasted such amazing scones. I would love to see how you bake them... if you don't mind?"

Morag smiled warmly at me. "Och, of course you can watch. Why would you think I would mind?"

"Well, it's just that... I asked Aileen when I first arrived and she refused. She said that she didn't want me wasting your time—"

"Ah, pay no mind tae that crabbit coo," said Morag with a scowl. "Aye, I know yer not supposed tae speak ill o' the dead, but that woman was a menace. Always countin' money, always rabbitin' on aboot 'efficiency' and 'productivity'... treated us all like slaves! Ye should have seen hoo she pushed the poor girls ootside—"

"Yeah, she had Jenny in tears the other day and Izzy threatenin' to hand in her notice," Mairi chimed in.

"She was a witch," Rhona agreed. She turned to me. "You know, Jenny suffers terribly during her monthly periods. The poor girl gets these terrible cramps, and I told her to come in the kitchen for a minute so I could make her a hot water bottle to put on her tummy—but then Aileen came in and saw her and started yelling at her for skiving off... For God's sake! The poor girl was suffering! Anyone could see that! What difference would five minutes have made?"

"S'no surprise that Aileen lived alone and had no family," said Morag with a sniff. "Not even a cat would have her."

Mairi sighed. "Things were so different when Lesley was still here. The castle was a real happy place then and we were all like one big family."

"Is Mr Mackay widowed? Was Lesley his wife?" I asked.

"Oh heavens, no. Angus Mackay is a confirmed bachelor," said Rhona, rolling her eyes. "No, Lesley was the previous castle manager. She was the loveliest woman you could ever meet. She was a local girl, grew up in this area, so she knew everyone and was like everyone's favourite aunt. That girl, Lilian, who came in to play the harp the other day, for example—she used to live on the same street as Lesley, you know. She was telling us how she used to go round to Lesley's place after school and have bannocks with home-made jam, and it was the best she ever tasted."

"Aye, there's no way Lesley would've let the poor child come here withoot givin' her some supper that night," said Morag, compressing her lips with disapproval. "I tried tae tell Aileen tae at least let me make the girl a sandwich, but that woman was heartless!"

"Yeah, everythin' would be so different if Lesley was here," said Mairi sadly. "It was a tragedy when she passed away."

"Well, I still think she died o' a broken heart," said Morag, pursing her lips. "I know what they said aboot her but I never believed it. There must've been some mistake, somewhere."

Seeing my confused expression, Rhona explained: "Lesley was fired, you see. Apparently, Mr Mackay found out that she had been fiddling the castle accounts. He didn't bring any charges against her, out of respect for the fact that she'd been working at the castle for over twenty years, but he let her go and cancelled the retirement package she would have received. She left under a cloud and everyone was talking about it for ages afterwards. We were all so shocked. Lesley was the last person on earth you'd think would do something like that..."

"Is that how Aileen ended up as the manager?" I asked.

Rhona nodded. "She had been hired to help out in the office part-time and so she sort of stepped into Lesley's place. Nobody liked her much, but Mr Mackay thought she did a good job running the hotel. He's desperate to keep that side of things going smoothly because he really needs the money, you see."

"Yeah, Aberglinn is beautiful but it's a nightmare to maintain," said Mairi, glancing up at the high-domed ceiling of the kitchen. "And the estate is huge; it costs a fortune to run. Since he lost the income he used to get from the big shootin' parties, Mr Mackay's been desperate to find other ways to make money."

"Just as long as he disnae start dockin' our pay," said Morag grimly. "Or he'll be findin' himself a new cook!"

CHAPTER TWENTY-TWO

I emerged from the kitchen ten minutes later, Muesli firmly clutched in my arms, and started to make my way to the terrace, where I'd left the cat carrier. The Great Hall seemed to have emptied out, with many of the guests obviously deciding to take advantage of the improved weather to venture outside. The only ones who had remained were Tariq Al-Mansouri's wife, who was sitting flicking through a fashion magazine while her son played with toy cars on the sofa next to her, and the two elderly English sisters, who were standing by the grandfather clock next to the staircase, talking to Tristan St Clair.

I was surprised to see the young aristocrat with them; the Miss Wetherbys seemed to be the last choice of company he would want to keep. But he was talking enthusiastically to them, smiling and gesticulating and making them laugh.

"...couldn't believe my luck, you know. I mean, this could have the same potential as that 1988 cask of Macallan single malt. Did you hear about that?" St Clair looked at the two elderly women and, when they shook their heads blankly, he said: "Aww, you must have read about it in the papers, surely? It was the most expensive whisky ever sold. Over a million pounds at auction, can you believe it?" He whistled and shook his head. "And the lucky bugger bought the cask for just five thousand pounds! Now *that's* good investment returns!" He laughed. "Anyway, this looks like it could be just as good—or even better! That's why when the chance was offered to me, I jumped on it right away." He paused, then snapped his fingers and pointed at them. "You know what? *You* should invest in this too! You two ladies recently inherited a large sum of money, didn't you? Well, this is a wonderful opportunity you shouldn't miss."

"Oh, I don't know..." said one Miss Wetherby with a nervous twitter. "We're not clever young men like you, Mr St Clair. We really don't know anything about stocks and shares and investing money. Our solicitor says it's best to leave things to a financial advisor—"

"Sod financial advisors!" said St Clair. "I've got one too and the man's a bloodsucker. I just decided to do this myself. That's the beauty of this, you see—you don't need any specialist knowledge. You don't need to know about stocks and shares and hedge funds and all that nonsense—you just buy a cask, it's held in bond for you at the distillery, and you've got nothing to do but sit back and wait for it to mature." He grinned and rubbed his hands appreciatively.

"Well, perhaps we might—" the other Miss Wetherby started to say, then broke off as she noticed me standing behind St Clair. "Oh, hello, dear. Is that your cat? She is just adorable." She hurried over to me and began stroking Muesli, with her sister following close behind.

Tristan St Clair swung around, and paused for a moment before saying with a supercilious smile. "Ah... Miss Rose, isn't it? And where are your inquisitive elderly friends? I hope they haven't... er... got lost in any more rain showers?"

I kept my expression neutral, determined not to let him get to me. "I was looking for them, in fact. Have you seen them, by any chance?"

"Oh yes, we got chatting to them earlier," said one of the Miss Wetherbys warmly. "They're ever so friendly. Mrs Cooke gave us her contact details and said that we must look them up if we should ever be visiting Meadowford-on-Smythe."

"They asked us to tell you that they've gone outside to sit on the terrace," her sister added. "We were just about to follow suit when we bumped into Mr St Clair."

"Yes, well, I'd better run," said Tristan St Clair,

flashing a look at his Rolex. He swept the Miss Wetherbys an exaggerated bow which had them giggling and blushing. "Lovely chatting to you, ladies. I'll catch you later!"

"*Such* a nice young man," said one Miss Wetherby with a dreamy sigh as we watched St Clair hurry up the main staircase.

"Yes, so handsome... and so well mannered!" her sister tittered. "You would think that he would have no time for two old spinsters like us, but he was so kind and interested in us..."

"Can I hold your gorgeous puss, please?" The other sister turned to me and held her arms out. "I'd love to give her a cuddle."

"Oh, of course," I said, handing Muesli over. "Just be careful not to let her go! I was actually on my way out to the terrace myself to put her in her cat carrier."

"Oh, we'll take her out for you," said Miss Wetherby, cuddling Muesli close as she began leading the way through the door out to the terrace.

Her sister accompanied her and they soon disappeared outside. I followed more slowly, my mind thoughtful. Maybe it was cynical of me, but somehow I just didn't believe that Tristan St Clair would genuinely want to spend his time chatting to little old ladies. Was he up to something? And did it have to do with his snooping in Jerry Hudson's room yesterday?

My musings were interrupted by the sight of a familiar tall figure coming from the front vestibule of the castle. I stopped in my tracks.

"Devlin!" I cried, feeling a twinge of delight before I remembered that I was supposed to be angry with him. "What are you doing here?"

"I came to see you actually," said Devlin as he came over to join me.

He was looking ruggedly handsome in a casual zip-neck jumper paired with dark denim jeans, and his dark hair was slightly windswept, lying in tousled waves across his forehead. I had a sudden urge to reach up and smooth them down. Hastily I tucked my hands into my pockets and tried to keep my expression cool and detached as I waited for him to speak.

Devlin took his time scanning the area around us. I followed his gaze and noted that, to all intents and purposes, we were alone. The Wetherby sisters had gone out onto the terrace, and the only other people in the vicinity were Mrs Al-Mansouri and her son, who were on the far side of the hall and not paying us any attention. In the distance, I could hear the clink of crockery and the murmur of voices coming from the dining room and kitchen area, but there were no staff nearby.

Seemingly satisfied, Devlin lowered his voice and said: "I can't stay long but I just wanted to come and give you some information. I've been doing some checking up for you."

I looked at him, puzzled. "Checking up?"

He nodded. "About the murder case here at

Aberglinn. I've got a few contacts at Inverness CID so I rang them up this morning to see if I could get any background on the case and any updates. The police here don't know you, unlike back in Oxford, so they're unlikely to share any progress in the investigation with you."

"Oh!" I stared at him. After the way he had stormed off the previous night, the last thing I'd expected was for Devlin to make this kind of effort for me. The gesture touched me more than anything else he could have done and I felt the last of my anger melt away.

"Thank you!" I said. "That was really sweet of you."

Devlin looked embarrassed. "It's nothing really. Just a quick phone call," he said gruffly. "Anyway, I thought it might interest you to know that none of the main suspects have a record, except Tristan St Clair."

"St Clair? What's he done?"

"He's got himself into trouble multiple times over various businesses he's set up. In fact, he has several failed businesses to his name—which is not a crime in itself, of course, but when you dig a bit deeper, you start to notice that all the businesses had similar issues with compliance and murky accounting..."

"So has he been arrested for anything?"

"No. He's a slippery sod. Knows all the loopholes in the law and how to use them to his advantage. The police have never managed to get enough proof of wrongdoing, so he's always managed to wriggle free each time. Actually, the last time he came onto the police radar he was listed as officially bankrupt, so I'd like to know what he's doing in a place like this," said Devlin dryly, glancing at the lavish décor.

"Well, I suppose people from his kind of aristocratic background always have privileged help. I mean, St Clair is a member of the landed gentry and his father owns estates across half of England—"

Devlin gave a bark of laughter. "Are you taking the mickey? Aristocratic background? The man is as working class as I am. His real name is Terrence Starkey and he comes from Liverpool. His father was a mechanic, and the only thing Starkey Senior owned was a council flat in one of the city's rougher neighbourhoods."

I stared at him. "I knew it! I knew he was up to something. So he's using a fake identity?"

"Yes, Tristan St Clair is nothing but a small-time conman."

"And he's not really rich? He's been showing off all this wealth since he arrived here, you know," I said. "Vintage Rolls-Royce, bragging about investing in whisky, swaggering around in Savile Row suits and Rolex watches... is that all fake too?"

Devlin shrugged. "He could have genuinely come into some money, maybe via another scam he's run, or it could be borrowed money that he's using to create a front. It's not that hard to project a false image. People are very suggestible. All you need is to provide some well-known 'markers' of perceived wealth: an expensive watch, champagne, caviar, designer labels, a flash car... and the next thing you know, everyone is impressed and in awe of you. It's why conmen are so successful. They know how to manipulate people's expectations."

"So you think St Clair is running a con again?"

"I wouldn't be surprised. As the saying goes, a leopard doesn't change its spots." Devlin glanced around again at our opulent surroundings. "And this would be his perfect hunting ground. A hotel like this would be full of rich—and probably gullible—victims."

"Hey! Do you think Aileen found out and was going to expose him, and that's why he murdered her?" I said, excited.

Devlin frowned. "I don't know. It's possible... but in my experience, professional scammers are not killers; they're liars and cowards. Oh, they're ruthless and heartless in their own way, of course, but when trouble strikes, their default is to cut their losses and run. Being exposed is part of the game for them, so it's something they're used to dealing with. Their priority is to escape and live again to scam another day. The last thing they're likely to do is get involved with a cold-blooded murder."

He paused for a moment, thinking, then said: "Did you say that St Clair was bragging about investing in whisky, just now?"

"Yes, I overheard him telling a couple of the other guests. Why?"

"What did he say exactly?"

"Well, I only heard the tail end of the conversation, but it was something about buying a cask and waiting for it to mature. He'd just invested in some himself, I think, and he was telling the Wetherby sisters—they're those two elderly ladies who've just inherited a large amount of money—that they should invest in it too. He seemed really enthusiastic, even saying that he'd done it without consulting his financial advisor."

"Hmm..." Devlin looked thoughtful. "That could be a classic whisky investment scam. They've become very common in recent years, especially because there have been some high-profile sales of whisky casks or bottles that have appreciated hugely in value—"

"Oh! I remember my father talking about that," I cried, suddenly recalling the tea with my parents at Mabel Cooke's house just before Cassie and I left for Scotland. "Dad was telling us about one of his colleagues who was interested in a whisky investment scheme. He said that some had shown amazing returns, far more than traditional investments or even things like antiques and art."

"Yes, that's the hook," said Devlin cynically. "The idea is that you get the chance to buy a cask of premium new-make spirits at discounted wholesale rates from the best distilleries, or maybe a new distillery that shows great promise. And these are often limited-run casks, which means there is a rarity factor increasing their value. Then the casks are stored for you by the distillery in a secure bonded warehouse while you wait for the whisky to mature. By law, spirits must mature in oak casks in Scotland for at least three years to be called 'Scotch whisky', but that's still a fairly short period of investment time, compared with other assets. And in that short time, the whisky could increase dramatically in value. You can then sell your cask back to the distillery at a profit or have it bottled privately and then sell the bottles yourself, or even auction off your cask to other investors and collectors. It's what makes these schemes so inviting: the promise of a quick and possibly very high return."

"Wow. It sounds too good to be true," I said.

"It often is," said Devlin with an ironic look. "There was a recent whisky scam in which a hundred and fifty elderly pensioners in the US were conned out of ten million pounds."

"Ten million pounds?" I gasped.

He nodded grimly. "Yeah. They were approached by scammers using fake names and talking in British accents, pretending to be from a specialist whisky broker in the UK. And they were convinced to wire large sums of money to this company to invest in a portfolio of premium Scotch whiskies which were supposedly held in a warehouse in the UK, waiting to mature and be sold for profit. Well, it turns out that the whole thing was a fraud and they never got their money back."

"God, those poor people," I said, horrified. Then I looked up urgently. "Devlin, St Clair was talking to the Wetherby sisters—they'd be the classic victims, wouldn't they? They're elderly and trusting and they've suddenly come into a lot of money..." I paused and frowned. "The only thing is, St Clair wasn't trying to sell them the scam. He actually said that he'd invested in the scheme himself—"

"That could have been a clever lie," said Devlin. "It's a well-known tactic of conmen and it's part of St Clair's front of presenting himself as a wealthy aristocrat. By telling them that he had invested in the scheme himself, he would lull them into a false sense of security. I'm willing to bet anything that St Clair is behind the whole scam. He's probably got a partner who's representing the 'official broker' side of things and they're working together behind the scenes. St Clair softens the victims up by pretending to be nice and helping them by sharing a good investment opportunity, and then sends them to his partner."

"Oh my God, I think I know who his partner might be!" I said suddenly. "I think it's Angus Mackay!"

CHAPTER TWENTY-THREE

I looked at Devlin eagerly. "I remember now—the first morning, after the murder, I bumped into Mackay talking to Jerry Hudson outside the castle. I thought he looked a bit furtive, and he definitely wasn't pleased when I interrupted them. And now that I think about it, he was using almost identical words to what I heard Tristan St Clair telling the Wetherby sisters just now. He mentioned the 1988 cask of Macallan single malt which was bought for just five thousand pounds but then sold at auction for over a million pounds. And he talked about how easy it was, with everything *'held in bond, with nothing to do but sit back and wait for it to mature'*... I'll bet Mackay was trying to convince Jerry Hudson to invest in the scheme too!"

"Mmm, you could be right," said Devlin. "If the owner of Aberglinn Castle is in on the scam, it would certainly help St Clair since he would have *carte blanche* to target the hotel guests."

"I'm sure of it! It also explains why St Clair is staying here for free." I told Devlin about my earlier conversation with Bridget. "Mackay is probably giving St Clair free lodgings in return for the latter's help in perpetuating this scam. Having a luxury suite here also contributes to St Clair's front of a wealthy aristocrat, and it allows him easy access to the guests." I paused, then continued excitedly, "And you know what? I'm sure it was Mackay who was with Aileen in the library that night, right around the time that she was murdered. The only sticking point was motive: I couldn't figure out *why* he would have wanted to murder his own manager. Well, here's the perfect reason! If she found out about his scam and was blackmailing him about it—as well as intimidating him so that he was completely under her thumb—he would have wanted to get rid of her."

Devlin still looked slightly sceptical. "Mackay is a strong possibility. But you have to be careful of jumping to conclusions, Gemma. You don't know for sure that Mackay was in the library with Aileen Fergusson that night—it's only a hunch."

"I have witnesses!" I insisted. "Jerry Hudson confirms that he saw someone with Aileen in the library. I talked to him this morning; he was skulking around outside the window because he was trying to break into Aileen's office to destroy some blackmail evidence—it's a long story," I said, waving a dismissive hand as I saw Devlin's confused expression. "It's not important, anyway. Jerry Hudson isn't the murderer. But he did see and hear the murderer talking with Aileen in the library just before she was killed."

"Did he actually see their faces?"

"No, he only saw silhouettes," I admitted. "But one was definitely Aileen and the other must have been her killer. And it all fits with what Lilian the harpist told me!" I continued jubilantly. "Remember I told you that she overheard voices in the library? I'm certain that the second voice she overhead belonged to Angus Mackay—she just wasn't willing to admit it. I think because he's family or something; she calls him 'Uncle Angus'."

"Well, Aileen Fergusson certainly seemed to be blackmailing *some*body," Devlin conceded. "That was the other piece of information I wanted to tell you. The police have checked her bank account, and the statements show that she'd been receiving regular large deposits of cash in her account over the past few months. It's not solid proof of blackmail, of course, but it's highly suggestive."

"I'm telling you, it all fits!" I said. "I can't wait to tell Inspector Monroe all of this. I know he wasn't keen to accept Angus Mackay as a murder suspect, but with all these things, surely he has to take the possibility seriously? We now know that Mackay has the perfect motive, plus he doesn't have an alibi for the time of the murder. In fact, there's a witness who may be able to identify him—or his voice, at least. So what else do you need?"

"There's still the issue of the murder weapon," Devlin reminded me. "Oh, that reminds me—there was one other thing I thought you ought to know: the full autopsy report came back, and it seems that the forensic pathologist has revised his opinion of how the victim was murdered."

"What do you mean? Are you saying she wasn't garrotted after all?"

"No, no, the cause of death was definitely asphyxiation by a ligature-type weapon. Aileen was garrotted. But the pathologist hadn't taken her clothes into account. She was wearing a thick, high-neck sweater, which would have protected her neck from any skin wounds. In other words, they originally thought that she could only have been garrotted with something like a rope or a cable—but in fact, the murderer *could* have also used something thinner, like a piano wire. It wouldn't have cut into her skin because the thick high neck of her sweater would have protected her from the abrasion, but it would still have been enough to kill her with the choking action."

"Oh," I said, thinking that it was just as well that I had already eliminated Jerry Hudson and his bolo tie. "Well, I suppose that just means that the murderer—Mackay—could have used anything. He had an entire castle to choose from anyway, didn't he?"

"Mm..." Devlin glanced distractedly at his watch.

"Do you need to go?" I said quickly, suddenly feeling awkward. Talking to Devlin had felt so comfortable, so easy and familiar, that I'd completely forgotten myself. "Sorry. I didn't mean to keep you—"

"No, it's fine." He hesitated. "I've actually got the afternoon off, but I was planning to meet the lads for a late lunch in Fort William and then head out to the hills with them for some more evacuation practice on rough moorland..."

He trailed off. I thought suddenly, with a leap of the heart: *Does he not want to go? Is he looking for an excuse to stay with me a bit longer?*

Before I could think of what to say, Devlin cleared his throat and said, "Anyway, I hope some of this info is helpful. Not that I really want you getting involved in the investigation, but..." He sighed. "Nothing I say seems to stop you anyhow." His blue eyes met mine. "Just... take care, Gemma, okay?"

He turned away. I reached out on an impulse and grabbed his arm.

"Wait, Devlin!"

He turned around. "Yes?"

I gave him a hesitant smile. "Do you... would you like to stay and have something to eat here at the castle? They do an amazing afternoon tea here. I'm sure the staff would be happy to serve it a bit earlier, if I ask them. In fact, I'd love you to taste their scones and tell me how you think they compare with those at the Little Stables..."

Devlin's face softened. "You know I always think your scones are the best, Gemma," he said with a smile that made me warm all over. "But sure, I'd be happy to—"

"Gemma! Here you are! I've been searching all over for you."

My heart sank as I turned and saw Ewan come in through the door from the terrace.

The handsome ghillie nodded a greeting to Devlin, then turned to me and said brightly: "You know you were telling me that you'd love to visit a whisky distillery? Well, I've got some time off this afternoon so I can take you on a personalised tour." He gave me a boyish grin. "And we could even go for a spot of fly fishing afterwards. It doesn't get dark at the moment 'til around ten o'clock. I know this great little spot down in the glen, which is totally private. I can ask Morag to make us a picnic dinner and we can take it down and enjoy it by the river..."

I cringed at the romantic image that Ewan's words conjured up and stole a glance at Devlin. His face was like stone, his blue eyes frosty.

Cursing the bad timing, I stammered "Er... that sounds lovely, Ewan... um... but I'm not sure... I mean..." I glanced at Devlin again. "Well, I might be busy this afternoon—"

"Don't worry on my account," said Devlin curtly.

"I was just leaving."

Turning, he stalked out of the Great Hall. For a moment I was tempted to rush after him, then I stopped myself as irritation flashed through me. Why should I chase after him? *It's Devlin's own stupid fault if he wants to get jealous!* After all, he was the one who wanted to "go on a break"! Still, as I followed Ewan out to the terrace, I couldn't help feeling a wave of chagrin washing over me, or a sense that I was spending the afternoon with the wrong man.

I saw Cassie look at me sharply as Ewan and I joined her on the terrace.

"Was that Devlin I saw through the window?" she asked, her face eager.

"Yes. He... um... he came to give me some information about the investigation," I said.

"Oh." Cassie looked deflated for a moment, then she said in an indignant tone, "Didn't you ask him to stay for tea or something?"

"I did," I said defensively. "But he... um... he said he had to go."

"Did I barge in on something?" asked Ewan, looking contrite. "Sorry... I didn't realise that you guys—"

"We're not... I mean, it's... it's complicated," I mumbled, flushing and cringing at the clichéd expression. I could see Cassie sending Ewan a murderous look, obviously blaming him for ruining a potential rapprochement between Devlin and me. Hastily, I changed the subject:

"Um… Devlin told me something really interesting: apparently, Tristan St Clair is a fraud. He's not a wealthy aristocrat at all but a small-time conman. In fact, we think he might be here working a scam and that—"

I broke off, suddenly conscious of Ewan standing next to me, listening. Angus Mackay was his employer and I had no idea what kind of relationship the ghillie had with his boss, nor what sort of loyalty he felt towards the castle owner. The last thing I needed was for Ewan to warn Mackay of my suspicions before I could report everything to the police.

"Um… yes, well, so St Clair has a record of criminal behaviour," I finished lamely.

Cassie looked sceptical. "So you think he might have killed Aileen? Because she found out that he was really a con artist? Seems like a weak motive to me. Besides, didn't you say that he had an alibi?"

"Well, if you believe what Tariq Al-Mansouri told me, none of the men in the bar that night actually had a solid alibi. Jerry Hudson and Tristan St Clair both left the bar to go to the toilet, although Hudson really went to try and break into Aileen's office. I'll tell you about it later," I added to Cassie as she started to frown in puzzlement. "And Angus Mackay supposedly went outside to smoke his pipe, which left Al-Mansouri alone in the bar. But there's no one to verify that either."

"So they all lied to the police?" said Cassie.

I shrugged. "It's hardly surprising. You know most people lie to the police about *some*thing when they're questioned in a murder investigation."

"Aye, I certainly lied about the speed at which I drove home," Ewan said with a laugh. "I mean, I told them that I got back at around ten to eleven, which would be about right if I was driving below the speed limit. But you know, at that time of the night, the roads are empty and... well..." He grinned. "It's hard to resist the temptation to push that speedometer a bit. Especially after a long day at work, you really want to let your hair down, you know? Turn the music up loud, floor the pedal, feel the rush..."

"So it didn't take you twenty minutes to get home?" said Cassie.

Ewan gave her a sheepish look. "No, I did it in about ten. But don't tell the police. The last thing I need is a speeding ticket!"

"Yeah, I'm sure there are loads of similar white lies from the other people questioned," I said. "For example, I don't think Lilian was telling the whole truth either—"

"Lilian?" Ewan looked at me in surprise.

"Yes, Lilian Monaghan, the girl who was hired to play the harp—"

"Aye, I know Lilian. I've known her since we were wee kiddies, actually. We went to the same school and practically grew up together. She used to live just down the road from me."

"Oh. Do you know her well?" I asked with interest.

255

Ewan shrugged. "I suppose so. She's always been very shy and quiet, never spoke to me much. I used to feel a bit sorry for her, actually. Her parents were really ambitious and they had very high expectations. They were fairly well off, you see, and they were always sending Lilian off to music lessons and private French classes and God knows what else. I heard that they even hired a professional nanny to teach her 'proper manners' and etiquette and all that shi—" Ewan broke off and hastily amended his words: "—er, all that kind of stuff. The nanny sounded like a real dragon, though. I remember Lilian coming to school with her eyes all red from crying."

"Did the nanny abuse her?" asked Cassie, aghast.

"Well, I don't think she hit Lilian or anything like that. She was just a heartless cow. Like, she knew about Lilian's cat phobia—you know, Lilian's always been terrified of cats, for some reason. All the kids in school knew about it but even the bullies never teased her, because we knew she really couldn't take it. But this nanny... well, Lilian once told me that the woman forced her to pat cats and hold them on her lap, and she'd laugh and make fun of Lilian if she cried. Said it was 'tough love'." Ewan shook his head.

"Oh yeah! I remember now. Lilian got really worked up over that cat in the Great Hall," Cassie said.

"Yes, on our first night here—the night of the murder," I told Ewan. "We were all having drinks before dinner and one of the castle strays got into the hall. Al-Mansouri's little girl saw it and freaked out—mainly because of the ghost story that Angus Mackay had been telling us earlier, I think—but anyway, she made such a fuss that Aileen came to quieten her down. But Aileen was quite brusque about it; she even started mocking the child's fear of the cat, and Lilian went rushing over. She seemed almost a bit hysterical."

"Really?" said Ewan, his face sympathetic. "I thought Lilian would have got over her cat phobia by now. Don't they say you grow out of these things?"

"She was probably traumatised by her experience with that terrible nanny," said Cassie darkly. "Really! It's disgusting what the woman did to her. Forcing people to confront their phobias that way doesn't help at all! If I were Lilian, I would have—"

"Shh!" I elbowed Cassie suddenly as I glanced across the terrace and saw a group coming towards us. It was the Old Biddies, and with them was the very girl we had been discussing: Lilian Monaghan.

CHAPTER TWENTY-FOUR

"Ah, there you are, Gemma," said Mabel in her usual bossy tones as they joined us. "We were just looking for you. This poor child was wandering around the castle gardens all by herself. We told her we'd take her to find the company of some other young people."

"I'm... I'm fine, honestly," protested Lilian weakly, looking embarrassed. "I quite enjoy being on my own. I was just having a look around the flowerbeds before I left. I love the hydrangeas at this time of year..." She trailed off as her eyes darted shyly from Ewan to me and Cassie. "Um... I hope we haven't interrupted anything—?"

"Oh no. We were just standing around chatting. I didn't realise you were still at Aberglinn," I said.

"Well, Inspector Monroe didn't get a chance to see me until late yesterday evening. And by the time we finished, Ewan had left, so there was no one to take me to the train station," Lilian explained. "So Uncle Angus said I might as well stay another night."

"Shame we didn't know, otherwise we could have taken you in our taxi," said Cassie. "We went out to Fort William last night and we could have dropped you off at the station."

"That's okay. I think you'd gone by the time the inspector finished his questions. I didn't mind, anyway. Morag gave me a lovely supper and I went to bed early."

"Are you off now?" asked Ewan. "I can run you down to the train station, if you like."

"Oh, but... but I don't want to bother you if you're..." Lilian gestured vaguely towards me and Cassie.

"It's no bother, Lil," said Ewan, giving her a lazy grin. "It'll take me fifteen minutes in the car. Save you having to trek to the nearest bus stop."

"Th-thank you," said Lilian, her cheeks pink. "That would be great."

Ewan held out a hand. "Where are your bags? I'll give you a hand."

"I've only got this," said Lilian, indicating the tote bag slung over one shoulder. "I didn't come with any luggage because I wasn't expecting to stay."

"Have you been stuck here without a toothbrush or any toiletries for two days, dear?" asked Glenda in dismay.

"Yes, and clean underwear?" added Florence, looking horrified.

"No, no, I've been fine," Lilian assured them. "I always carry a little pouch with a toothbrush and change of underwear and some toiletries in my handbag."

"Ah. Very sensible," said Mabel, nodding approvingly.

"It's something my mother always insisted on," Lilian confessed. "I used to think that Mum was being pedantic, but I'm really glad I followed her advice now."

She turned expectantly towards Ewan, obviously waiting to follow him to his car, but he held up a hand.

"Actually, you know what? I've just remembered that I've parked my Land Rover down by the outbuildings. Why don't you wait here and I'll bring it round to the front?"

He turned and loped off. Lilian watched him for a moment, then seemed to rouse herself and turned back to us.

"The staff have been so lovely to me," she confided with a smile. "Bridget even gave me some of the hotel toiletries to use, and one of the gorgeous guest bathrobes as a nightie." She giggled. "I think it's the poshest thing I've ever worn to bed!"

"Oh, that reminds me..." said Cassie, turning to the table next to her. "One of the girls asked me to give you this to take with you when you go." She indicated a large foil tray—the kind usually used to roast a ham or turkey in the oven—which was covered with a snowy white napkin.

"For me?" asked Lilian, looking surprised. "What is it?" She lifted the napkin and gasped at the mountain of food that was revealed. There were several scones and bannocks, three generous slices of Dundee cake, a couple of Scotch eggs, a few wedges of hard cheese, some smoked salmon wrapped in baking parchment an enormous pork pie in a glossy pastry shell, and, tucked in the side, a cluster of rich, buttery shortbread fingers.

"Apparently, Morag thought you looked a bit skinny and wanted to make sure that you went home with good supplies," said Cassie, chuckling.

"My God, I'm going to be eating this for a month!" said Lilian, staring at the tray. She glanced at the door leading back into the castle, then looked worriedly down the driveway. "I should really go into the kitchen to thank her—"

"Oh, don't worry, I'll let her know," Cassie offered. "Anyway, I'm sure you'll be back."

"I hope so," said Lilian wistfully. "I'd love to have a regular gig to come and play the harp at Aberglinn. It's such a gorgeous place."

"Yes, and you must have lots of happy memories of coming here as a child?" I said, trying to sound casual.

She turned surprised eyes on me. "No, I never

came to Aberglinn that much. Why would you think I did?"

"Oh, because you said Mr Mackay knew your parents and you call him 'Uncle Angus'. I thought maybe you were related or something—"

"Oh, no, not really," said Lilian with an embarrassed laugh. "Mr Mackay isn't really my uncle—I mean, not a blood relative. But he *is* an old friend of my parents. Mum and Dad always told me to call him 'Uncle Angus' and I suppose it's stuck. And I *have* known him since I was a little girl, so I suppose he does feel a bit like family."

"That's why you didn't want to name him, isn't it?" I asked suddenly.

She drew back from me. "I... I beg your pardon?"

"When you were telling me about the voices you overheard in the library, you said that you didn't recognise the second voice—but I think you were lying."

Lilian took another step back, her face paling. "L-lying?"

"Yes, you recognised the voice; you knew who it was—you just didn't want to admit it because you didn't want to incriminate him and get him in trouble with the police."

Lilian licked her lips. Her face was ashen now, her green eyes wide and scared. She looked desperately from me to Cassie to the Old Biddies. "I... I..."

Next to me, Cassie stirred uneasily and put a hand on my arm. "Gemma—"

I hesitated for a second, the girl's anguished face tugging at my sympathy. Then I hardened my heart. *If Lilian is covering up for a murderer, then she has to be exposed,* I thought grimly. Her testimony was absolutely crucial to proving Mackay's guilt. I couldn't let a bit of mawkish pity stand in the way of finding the truth.

Looking Lilian straight in the eye, I said: "It was Angus Mackay that you overheard, wasn't it?"

The girl shook her head weakly.

"Wasn't it?" I pressed.

"I... okay, yes! Yes, it was!" she said at last in a trembling voice.

I felt a flicker of satisfaction and turned to look triumphantly at Cassie but, to my surprise, she was scowling at me. Even the Old Biddies were looking at me with reserve. Cassie started to say something, then broke off as we heard the sound of a powerful engine. The next moment, a mud-splattered Land Rover pulled up in the driveway in front of the castle.

Lilian turned towards it, her face slack with relief. "Oh, the car's here! I... I have to go," she said, throwing us a wan smile. "Er... bye."

She began trying to lift the enormous tray of food from the table but her tote bag kept swinging from her shoulder and knocking against the tray as she bent over.

"Here, let me get that," said Cassie, reaching over and picking up the tray. She nodded to Lilian. "I'll help you carry it to the car."

"Oh, no... I don't want to give you any trouble. I can manage..." Lilian started to say. Then—as Cassie simply turned and began walking towards the Land Rover, the tray of food in her arms—she hurried after my friend, babbling, "That's really kind of you... thank you!"

The Old Biddies and I watched as Ewan got out and helped Lilian into the Land Rover while Cassie opened one of the rear doors and leaned in to lay the tray on the back seat. She fumbled for a few minutes, obviously trying to find a way to secure the tray so that it wouldn't go flying if Ewan had to swerve or brake suddenly, then stepped away from the car and shut the door.

Ewan gave us a wave, then got back into the driver's seat, and a few minutes later the Land Rover roared away down the driveway. Cassie walked slowly back to the terrace, her hands in her jeans pockets and her expression thoughtful. When she rejoined us, she gave me a disgusted look.

"What got into you, Gemma?"

"What do you mean?" I said, surprised.

"You were so hard on that poor girl! The way you kept badgering her about the voices in the library—you were practically bullying the poor thing."

"I wasn't bullying Lilian!" I cried, stung. "I was just trying to get her to admit that she recognised the voice. Sometimes you need to put a bit of pressure on people to get them to tell the truth—"

"Yes, but how did you know that she was lying?"

argued Cassie. "She could have really not known who the voice was."

"Oh, that young lady *was* lying," Mabel spoke up. She glanced at the other Old Biddies and they nodded in agreement with her. "But we're not sure if she *did* tell you the truth either," she added to me.

"What do you mean?" I asked, even more confused now. "Are you saying that Lilian didn't hear voices at all? Why would she lie about that? No, there were definitely voices." I told them about my confrontation with Jerry Hudson earlier. "He confirmed that he heard someone talking with Aileen in the library at around eleven thirty, as well."

"Did he think it sounded like Angus Mackay?" asked Mabel.

"No, he was standing outside and only heard the voices faintly through the glass of the library window, so he couldn't really make out enough to tell," I admitted. "But he did see their silhouettes and he said the other person was tall, so it's likely that they were a man."

"Hmm," was all Mabel said.

I glanced at Cassie. "What do you think?"

My best friend looked up distractedly. She had been staring at her phone screen, scrolling up and down. "Um... I don't know... I think you're too focused on Lilian. The poor girl is terrified of her own shadow! How do you know you can believe anything she says? She might be really neurotic and imagining things or making stuff up just to appease you. I mean, children are known for doing that, aren't they? That's why they're unreliable witnesses. They'll make up things or agree with things you suggest, just to please you."

"Yes, but Lilian is hardly a child," I protested. "I'd agree with you if you were talking about that seven-year-old, Safa, but this is a young woman in her twenties—"

"I don't know. Lilian seems very young and vulnerable to me," said Cassie. "If I were a detective, I would consider her an 'unreliable witness'."

I turned to the Old Biddies, waiting for their comments, but to my surprise they weren't paying Cassie and me much attention. Instead, they had their heads together, murmuring amongst themselves.

What mischief are they cooking up now? I wondered. "Er... I hope you're not planning to break into another guest room," I said, only half joking.

They looked up at me. "Certainly not," said Mabel with great dignity. "We are discussing what we'd like for tea." She glanced up at the sky, which had clouded over ominously again. "It looks like it might start raining again. We're going to return to Graeme's cottage for a bit of a rest."

"Yes, I'm sure poor Muesli would like to have a snooze on Graeme's sofa instead of being crammed in that cat carrier," added Glenda, looking at the cage on one of the tables nearby.

The Wetherby sisters had deposited my cat in her

carrier as promised, and I could see Muesli inside, curled up, dozing. The morning of climbing around the castle walls had obviously exhausted the little tabby. Still, Glenda was right—it would be much nicer for Muesli to be stretched out on soft cushions in a warm, cosy sitting room, rather than hunched in the cramped confines of her cage.

"Would you like a hand carrying her back?" I offered.

"We can manage," said Mabel briskly. "Graeme's place is not that far. They converted some of the castle outbuildings into cottages and he snapped one up as soon as they offered the tenancies. Very shrewd, my cousin Graeme." She nodded at the other Old Biddies. "Come along!"

I watched them trundle away, Muesli in tow, then turned back to Cassie. "Do you think they're up to something?" I asked.

"Hmm...?" Cassie had been back on her phone, reading something intently on the screen, but now she hastily put it down.

"What are you looking at?" I asked.

She hesitated for a moment, then said, "Nothing... just checking something..."

I gave her a suspicious look, wondering if she was devising another ploy to throw me and Devlin together. "Cassie, please don't—"

I broke off as the sound of a car engine alerted us to Ewan's return. He parked the Land Rover at the side of the main castle door, then came over to join us.

"Bad news, Gemma. I passed that whisky distillery on the way back and it looks like it might be shut to public visitors today. It seems that they're doing some maintenance," he said regretfully.

"Oh, that's okay," I said quickly, trying to ignore the sense of relief. "I'm sure there'll be other chances."

"I'm still free to take you fly fishing later, though," he added with a hopeful smile.

I glanced nervously at Cassie, but for once my best friend didn't seem to be bristling at Ewan's friendly overtures. Instead, she looked strangely preoccupied.

"I'd better go and check to see if they want me to continue the painting workshop, since it's raining again and all the guests seem to have wandered off..." she said distractedly as she began drifting towards the side door leading into the castle.

"Hey, you forgot your phone," said Ewan, picking up her mobile from the wrought iron table next to him. He paused, glancing down at the phone screen, then looked back up at her, grinning. "You doing some research on fly fishing?"

Cassie reddened, looking uncomfortable. "Yeah, well... I..."

"You're very welcome to join me and Gemma later, if you're interested?" Ewan said tentatively, obviously nervous given Cassie's previous tendency to bite his head off for any invitation.

"Er... thanks. I'll think about it," Cassie mumbled, before turning and disappearing into the castle.

I stared after my best friend. What on earth had got into her?

CHAPTER TWENTY-FIVE

The rain had started coming down in earnest, and Ewan and I hastily retreated into the shelter of the castle interior. Cassie was nowhere in sight but the Great Hall was full of people, with many ensconced in the various sofas and armchairs clustered around the room. Bruce and Connie were hunched over the vintage chessboard again, and the Wetherby sisters were on their favourite sofa by the windows. One of the staff had lit a fire in the ornate fireplace, and the crackling orange flames gave off a wonderful warmth, as well as lending a cosy glow to the whole area. Suddenly, the thought of sloshing through a cold river with Ewan, halfway up the mountain, seemed a lot less appealing to me.

Several of the guests had ordered Aberglinn

Castle's famous afternoon tea and were now enjoying scones, petits fours, and other delectable treats from their three-tiered cake stands, whilst sipping fragrant tea from delicate china cups. Watching them, my stomach gave a growl. I realised suddenly that it was already mid-afternoon, and not only had I skipped breakfast, but I hadn't had any lunch either.

"Sorry, Ewan, but I need to grab a bite to eat before I do anything else, otherwise I'm going to drop on the spot," I said with a wry laugh.

"Have you not had lunch?" said Ewan, looking aghast. "Ahhh, you must go and eat! Don't rush, take your time. As I said, it won't get dark until nearly ten—" He glanced through the window at the ominous sky outside. "Well, all right, today might be darker earlier because of the rain, but we still have plenty of time. And it might brighten up later. You never know with the Scottish weather," he added with a chuckle. "As my Uncle Mac likes to say: if you don't like the weather in Scotland, wait twenty minutes."

"If it really doesn't brighten up, do you mind if we take a literal rain check?" I asked, giving him a sheepish look. "I think I'd rather curl up with a book in front of that fire than struggle with a rod out in the pouring rain."

"Ahh, once you get into the fish, you won't even notice the rain, trust me," said Ewan, grinning. "But of course. If you'd rather not go, that's fine. Look, why don't I come and find you in a couple of hours and see how you feel then? I've got to go and speak to Mr Mackay, anyway, about some deer I saw browsing on the saplings we've planted on the south side of the estate."

"Okay," I said and watched distractedly as he walked away. Ewan's mention of his boss had reminded me that I still had to tell Inspector Monroe about my suspicions about Angus Mackay and all the evidence and circumstances that pointed to his guilt.

I might as well get it over with first, I thought with a sigh. Catching sight of Izzy carrying a tray towards one of the guests, I stopped her and asked if the inspector was still on site.

"No, miss. He was here this morning, but I think he's gone back to Inverness. He did leave a contact number, though, in case there was anything else we wanted to report," she added. "If you hold on a sec, I'll go and ask Hamish for it..."

She returned a few minutes later with a number scribbled on one of the castle's embossed notepads. I thanked her, then found a quiet spot around the corner, away from the main part of the Great Hall, so that I wouldn't be overheard. Taking out my phone, I paused a moment as I gathered my thoughts. I knew that it was important to prepare my words carefully. Inspector Monroe was already disinclined to suspect Angus Mackay, and I would have to work extra hard to make him listen to my suspicions.

I was so psyched up to argue my case that it was a huge disappointment when a sergeant answered the call and explained that the inspector was currently out of the office.

"Do you know when he'll be back?" I asked.

"No idea, sorry, miss. When he's on an investigation, he can be in and out at all hours."

This was sounding depressingly familiar from my calls to Oxford CID to find Devlin. Heaving a sigh, I gave the sergeant my number and asked him to ask the inspector to call me urgently.

"It's about the investigation here at Aberglinn Castle," I added. "I've got some vital evidence about the identity of the murderer."

The sergeant promised to relay my message and I hung up, feeling deflated. Now that I knew who the killer was likely to be, the knowledge weighed on me. I was desperate to share the information with the police and absolve myself of the responsibility.

Still, there's no point standing around here, waiting. I might as well go and eat first, I reminded myself. Turning in the direction of the dining room, I began pondering the meal with pleasant anticipation. *That pork pie for Lilian looked delicious. I wonder if Morag's got any more left...?*

As I was entering the dining room, I bumped into a couple coming out. It was the young Chinese newlyweds. They were walking with their arms linked together, their heads bent over the screen of the phone that the girl was holding.

"Oh!" she cried as they nearly crashed into me. "I am so sorry! We are looking at photos and we don't see you."

"They must be very good pictures to grab you like that," I said with a teasing smile.

She laughed shyly. "Yes, it is very lucky moment! You know that night we have the special dinner, there is big moon. When we are getting ready for sleeping, I look out of the window in our room, and I see the moon and I think—I must take picture!" She thrust her phone screen towards me. "You see? Very beautiful, no?"

I glanced down at the screen, marvelling at the power of modern technology. Somehow, despite the dark of night, the phone's inbuilt camera had managed to capture a moonlit scene through the window, even down to the subtle details of colour and texture in the nocturnal landscape. The newlyweds were obviously staying in the honeymoon suite on the top floor, and their bedroom window afforded a bird's-eye view of the front of the castle, showing the terrace and front lawn, part of the driveway leading up to the carriage arch, a glimpse of the main door, and the corner of the building, with a slight view of the turrets around the side. The moonlight outlined all the trees and shrubs, turning them into silver figurines, and even highlighted the ornate stonework on the wall of the castle.

"It's absolutely gorgeous," I said with genuine admiration. "What a brilliant moment, captured on camera. You should get it blown up and framed for your wall at home."

The girl nodded eagerly. "Yes! I say this to my boyfrien—I mean, my husband," she said, correcting herself with a self-conscious laugh.

I laughed with her and was about to hand her phone back when I stopped, my eyes catching sight of something in the corner of the photo. Bringing the screen back up to eye level, I peered at the blurry shape in the corner. It was hard to see clearly but it looked like a man...

"Sorry, do you mind if I...?" I muttered to the Chinese girl as I bent over the screen and used my fingers to tap and zoom in on the blurry shape in the image. Yes, I was right. It was a man. Sitting on a stone bench, in the lee of the castle wall, just beyond the main entrance. He was partially obscured by a large bush growing at the side of the castle, but there was something familiar about him... I frowned and tried to zoom in further, but the image had already reached maximum magnification.

"Is something wrong?" asked the Chinese girl.

I looked up. "Oh, sorry, I was just... Do you see this figure here?" I pointed to the blurry shape. "It's a man. I really want to see who he is, but the photo is not in focus..." I sighed in frustration.

"Oh, maybe it is better in another one?" said the girl, taking the phone from me and tapping the screen to show me her whole photo gallery. My eyes widened as I suddenly saw rows upon rows of nearly identical pictures, all showing that same moonlit landscape. Some were taken from slightly different angles, some further back, some zoomed in, some in portrait format and some in landscape, but they all showed pretty much the same scene.

"You took the same photo, like, twenty times?" I said incredulously.

Her husband laughed indulgently and said: "Yu Ming is always like that. Especially when it is something special or beautiful. She wants to get the 'best' photo, so she takes many, many, many of the same thing. Sometimes from different directions, sometimes with different light... When we went to Paris, she took one hundred and fifty-seven shots of the Eiffel Tower!"

Yu Ming gave me a slightly abashed smile. "Because after you go home, you cannot take the picture again. So I want to make sure I get every chance. To catch the moment, you know?" She scrolled down through her photo gallery to show me reams and reams of identical-looking shots. There were multiple copies of the Highland landscape, numerous clones of the castle façade, doubles, triples, quadruples of the Great Hall and other interior rooms, and even duplicate photographs of plates of food the couple had obviously enjoyed. There were also several similar shots and selfies of them posing in front of various backgrounds.

"It's extra important when people are in the photo," Yu Ming said earnestly. "Because sometimes they close their eyes or sometimes they are not smiling, so if you take many copies, there is always one which is good!"

"Wow," I said, looking at her with bemused admiration. I thought of her perfectionist approach and then thought ruefully of my own slapdash attitude to holiday snaps: half a dozen haphazard shots taken at random and barely bothering to check if anything was framed or lit properly, never mind repeating a photo just in case the first one didn't come out well!

The Chinese girl scrolled back to the multiple copies of the night scene from her bedroom window and began examining each one, zooming in and flicking through them at dizzying speed.

"Here," she said at last, handing the phone back to me. "This is the best one. You can see that corner most clearly."

I peered at the screen, and this time was rewarded with a slightly fuzzy but clearly recognisable image of a large, rotund man sitting on the bench, a swirl of smoke curling up in the air above his head.

It was Angus Mackay, smoking his pipe.

I stared at the picture, my thoughts churning. Slowly, almost as if I was afraid to look, I tapped on the picture and selected the option to "Show Details". A list of information filled the screen, displaying things like the photo file size, focal length, aperture, shutter speed, and—most importantly—the time and date the picture had been taken.

I drew a sharp breath.

The photo had been taken at 11:35 p.m. on the night of Aileen's murder.

Quickly, I pulled back out to the gallery and randomly selected several of the other similar shots, including the first and the last. The time stamp on each photo varied slightly by a few minutes or seconds, but overall the photos covered the period between 11:24 p.m. and 11:43 p.m. And Angus Mackay was in every one.

Which meant that the owner of Aberglinn had an alibi.

"Is everything okay?"

I started and looked up to find the Chinese couple watching me in bewilderment.

"Er... yes, sorry," I said, handing the phone back to Yu Ming. "Um... listen, can you do me a favour? Can you please not delete any of these photos for the time being?"

She looked at me in puzzlement. "No delete?"

"Yes, I think the pictures might be important to the murder investigation," I explained.

The couple's eyes widened. "Murder investigation?"

"It's nothing dangerous," I said quickly. "Don't worry. It won't cause trouble for you. It's just... it could be very important evidence for the police."

"Okay," Yu Ming agreed hesitantly. "Do you want me to give you copy of the photos?"

"Thanks, that would be great! Actually, just this

one will be fine," I said, indicating the shot where Angus Mackay could be seen the most clearly.

A few minutes later, with a copy of the picture safely transferred to my phone, Yu Ming and her husband gave me a final troubled look, bade me goodbye, and wandered off. I barely noticed them leave. My mind was still whirling, thinking about the significance of what I'd seen in Yu Ming's photos.

If Angus Mackay was sitting on that bench, smoking his pipe, then he couldn't have been in the library during the time Lilian and Jerry Hudson had overheard the voices.

Which means that he can't be Aileen Fergusson's murderer...

CHAPTER TWENTY-SIX

"Can I help you, miss?"

I blinked and came out of my thoughts to realise that I was standing in the middle of the empty dining room, staring into space. Izzy was standing next to me, watching me quizzically.

"Oh! Er... yes, I was just wondering if I might be able to order a sandwich or something..." I trailed off as I glanced around the dining room and realised that it was deserted. "Oh, sorry, you've probably finished serving lunch and have closed the kitchen—"

"Och, don't worry, we've got a small all-day menu," Izzy assured me. She handed me a gold-embossed card printed with the castle's logo and a list of items. "These are usually served out in the

Great Hall, but I'm sure it'll be fine if you prefer to sit at a table in here."

For a "small" menu, there were a multitude of tempting choices. I deliberated for a moment between the Scotch beef burger in a brioche bun with cheddar, smoked bacon, and seasoned fries, and the Ayrshire honey-roast ham with celeriac remoulade and wholegrain mustard, but finally settled on the "Soup of the Day" with homemade sourdough bread.

When this came, it proved to be a wonderfully warming bowl of leek and potato soup—the perfect antidote to the grey, rainy day. I'd never been a huge fan of leek and potato soup, disliking the usual thick, creamy flavour, but this was completely different to previous versions I'd tasted. With no milk or cream, it was made in a rustic, clear-broth style with chunks of tender potatoes and slices of fragrant leeks steeped in a rich chicken broth. A sprinkle of herbs and a dash of black pepper completed the dish, and accompanied by the fresh crusty bread, still warm from the oven, it was absolute food heaven.

I had barely savoured the last drop when Izzy came over to my table carrying what looked like a whisky tumbler on a plate.

"This is from Morag," she said with a smile. "She says you can't come to the Highlands without trying this."

"What is it?" I asked, eyeing the glass tumbler which seemed to be filled with multiple layers of raspberries interspersed with oats and fresh whipped cream.

"It's called cranachan," Izzy explained. "It's a traditional Scottish dessert. It's steel-cut oats soaked in whisky overnight, and then folded into fresh whipped cream. And then you crush some raspberries with whisky and heather honey, and toast some more oats. And then you put them all in the glass—like, a layer of raspberries, then the cream, then the toasted oats, then more of the raspberries again, and then the cream and the toasted oats..." She indicated the alternating bands in the glass. "There, see? It's delicious. Go on! Try it!"

Picking up the spoon that had come with the glass, I dipped it into the concoction and spooned a mixture of the raspberries, cream, and oats into my mouth. *Mmm...* I closed my eyes for a moment. It was scrumptious, the tangy, juicy flavour of the raspberries melding with the mellow sweetness from the heather honey and the lovely nutty crunch of the toasted oats, and all enhanced by the light, almost fluffy texture of the fresh whipped cream.

"Aye, it's good, isn't it?" said Izzy, giggling and watching my expression.

I nodded vigorously, my mouth too full to speak. Izzy smiled with satisfaction and turned to go, then paused and said:

"I nearly forgot: Morag said to tell you that she'll be doing some baking after lunch so if you'd like to pop into the kitchen when you're finished, you're welcome to join her."

"Oh, that would be brilliant!" I beamed at her.

She left me alone once more and I finished the cranachan in a blissful silence. Still, although the chat with Izzy and the delicious food had been a welcome distraction, I couldn't stop thoughts of the murder case flooding back as I licked my last spoonful of the dessert. I couldn't avoid facing the truth any longer.

I was completely wrong about Angus Mackay, I thought with dismay. *If he has a solid alibi, then he can't be the murderer after all.*

The memory of Cassie talking about Lilian echoed in my mind: *"How do you know you can believe anything she says? She might be really neurotic and imagining things or making stuff up just to appease you."*

I pondered this for a moment. No, I was *sure* there had been someone with Aileen in the library that night. It wasn't just Lilian's assertion; Jerry Hudson had confirmed it as well. He had even seen them—or their shadows, at least.

Then a thought struck me. Taking out my phone, I pulled up the picture that Yu Ming had taken and stared again at the fuzzy figure of Angus Mackay, half hidden in the darkness. Why hadn't I noticed it before? I berated myself. Jerry Hudson had described the second person as having a tall, slim silhouette, but Angus Mackay was a large, rotund man—as evidenced by this photo! So here was another piece of proof that it definitely couldn't have been him with

Aileen in the library that night.

But if it wasn't Mackay, why had Lilian said that it was? Was she lying?

I sat bolt upright as a new thought struck me: what if I had been right in my instinct that Lilian was lying about the "second voice" but wrong in what she was lying *about*? What if she hadn't been trying to cover up and protect someone—instead, she had been lying about overhearing another person talking to Aileen. In actual fact, there was no other person at all...

Because the "second voice" was herself!

A mixture of disquiet and elation filled me as the theory began to solidify in my mind. I remembered seeing Lilian stand up from the harp and being surprised that she was a lot taller than I'd thought. Her rangy, slender figure would easily match the silhouette of the second person that Hudson had seen in the library. I had just never considered it a possibility because I had assumed the silhouette to be a man's.

Lilian had been clever: by quickly introducing the idea of the "second voice" and hinting that it was a man, she had ensured that all my thoughts had centred on this other mystery person and not on *her*. It meant that I hadn't paid much attention to the fact that she had been staying in a room practically next door to the library and could have easily slipped in to murder Aileen and then slipped out again. Instead, all I had thought of was the men in the bar and the staff in the dining room and kitchen, completely forgetting that there had been one other person who had easy access to the library and was, in fact, the closest to the crime scene.

And Lilian has no alibi, I realised ruefully. I hadn't really appreciated that. All I'd had was her word that she had been asleep, and yet I'd never thought to question the truth of that statement.

But what about motive? Well, that had been staring me in the face all along as well. I thought back to the way Lilian had overreacted to Aileen punishing Safa for her fear of cats, and then I thought of Ewan telling me about Lilian's childhood phobia and the cruel nanny who had mocked her for her fears. That first night that we were in the castle, when I'd witnessed the scene between Tariq Al-Mansouri and Aileen Fergusson, the castle manager had mentioned that she had once been a professional nanny. She had also told the Dubai businessman that his kids needed some "tough love"—the very same phrase that Ewan said Lilian's nanny had used to justify her cruel methods!

Yes, it all fits! I thought excitedly. Even if it seemed far-fetched, it wasn't impossible to suppose that Aileen Fergusson had once been Lilian's nanny. She hadn't recognised the scared little girl who had since grown up into a tall, willowy young woman, but Lilian had recognised her. And the harpist, who clearly still struggled with her phobia, had been traumatised to see "history repeating itself" when she had witnessed

Aileen castigating a little girl about her fear of cats. Maybe that was when Lilian had decided that she'd had enough, that she couldn't let this heartless woman continue to abuse more children. It was a worthwhile "excuse" for the woman's murder, which had resonated with Lilian and made her feel justified in her actions.

And her meek, shy demeanour had protected her from suspicion. I thought of the way Cassie had flown to her defence: *"...the poor girl is terrified of her own shadow!"* ... *"Lilian seems very young and vulnerable to me..."*

She had us all fooled, I thought grimly. *I must find Cassie and tell her—*

My phone rang, startling me, and I was flustered to find that it was Inspector Monroe on the line.

"My sergeant said you had some urgent news for me, lassie?" said the inspector. "Something about evidence of the murderer's identity?"

"Yes... no, except... I mean, yes, Inspector," I stammered. "I... um... I think I know who killed Aileen Fergusson."

"Aye?" Inspector Monroe said after a moment as I remained silent.

With the sudden revelation of Lilian's guilt and the change in my thinking, I hadn't had a chance to prepare what I was going to say. Now I found myself struggling to gather my thoughts.

Taking a deep breath, I said: "It's Lilian Monaghan, the girl who was playing the harp that night."

"Lilian Monaghan!" The inspector sounded taken aback. "What makes you say that?"

"It's a lot of little things that I overlooked," I said. "But when you add them all together, it all makes sense."

Quickly, I relayed it all to him—Lilian's cat phobia, her childhood traumas, Aileen's previous career as a professional nanny, the inciting incident with Safa and the stray cat on the night of the murder, and then the clever ruse that Lilian had used to throw suspicion away from herself by inventing a mysterious "other person" who was in the library with Aileen that night.

"...and you know what else? I've just thought of it now: Lilian would have had the perfect weapon!" I added excitedly as I finished. "It was originally thought that Aileen had been garrotted by a rope or cord or something similar, right? But the pathologist then revised his opinion about the murder weapon because Aileen's thick high-neck sweater meant that her skin would have been protected from sharp edges—"

"How did you know that?" cried Inspector Monroe.

"Er... you must have mentioned it to me at some point," I lied hurriedly, not wanting to land Devlin in trouble by admitting that he had used his contacts at Inverness CID to get confidential information for me. Quickly, before Inspector Monroe could question me further, I continued:

"The point is, it means that the murderer *could* have used a wire garrotte after all. Remember, you told me that garrottes were often used by the Mafia in their assassinations, and they used things like piano wire? Well, how about a harp string? They're pretty thick and strong too, aren't they? They would make the perfect garrotting tool. I'll bet Lilian carried spare coils of wire in her bag whenever she performed, in case one of the strings on the instrument broke and needed replacing."

"Hmmm..." Inspector Monroe sounded reluctantly impressed. "Well, it's an interesting theory, lassie, and you could well be right. I hadn't considered a more personal motive. We've been concentrating our efforts on the blackmail angle, since there is clear evidence of regular payments into Fergusson's account—"

"Oh, Aileen *was* definitely blackmailing people— Angus Mackay and Jerry Hudson, to be exact," I said. "But that wasn't the reason she was murdered. It was a more personal, more emotional reason. More like... revenge, in a way. I know it sounds crazy, but I think Lilian killed Aileen as a sort of retribution for all the torment and abuse she had suffered as a little girl. You know how sometimes people who have been bullied and abused for a long time suddenly flip and kill their oppressors? I think it was something like that. And... and maybe in Lilian's mind, she was also protecting other little girls from Aileen's future abuse, you know? I mean, I think she's a bit messed up."

"She certainly doesn't sound like a very stable young lady, if what you're saying is true," said Inspector Monroe wryly. Then his tone turned brisk. "Is Lilian still at the castle?"

"No, she left a couple of hours ago. Ewan—the castle ghillie—took her to the train station." I caught my breath as a thought struck me. "Oh God, Inspector, what if she hasn't gone home? Will you be able to find her if she's taken off—"

"Never fear, lassie, we'll find her," said Inspector Monroe grimly. "I'll send my men out now. If she's committed murder, there won't be anywhere she can run to that we won't find her."

CHAPTER TWENTY-SEVEN

I let out a huge sigh as I hung up on the call with Inspector Monroe. It felt wonderful to offload all my theories and pass the responsibility over to the police—as if a huge weight had been lifted off my shoulders. And while I knew that Lilian hadn't been arrested yet, I didn't doubt Inspector Monroe's ability to bring her to justice.

Wait until I tell Devlin that I cracked the case! I thought with a smile.

Standing up from the table, my smile widened as I suddenly recalled Izzy's invitation to join Morag in the kitchen and watch the head cook do some baking. It seemed the perfect way to "celebrate" solving the mystery, and I hummed a happy tune as I wandered down the hallway to the baize door that led into the castle kitchen.

As I stepped inside, I saw that Morag had a visitor. The head cook was sitting at a large worktable on the far side of the room, her capable hands cupped around a steaming mug, and with her was an elderly man. He was dressed in old tweeds and gum boots, despite the summer season, and wore a flat wool cap over his balding head. There was another steaming mug on the table in front of him, although this one was accompanied by a small flask that I suspected contained Scotland's famous "water of life".

I hesitated and was about to back out of the kitchen when Morag caught sight of me and waved me over enthusiastically.

"Come in! Come in!" she said, smiling warmly. "No need tae be shy, lassie."

"Oh, I don't want to disturb you if you've got a friend visiting—" I indicated the elderly man.

"Och, I'm sure Donal won't mind—will ye, Donal?" she said, leaning closer to the old man and raising her voice. "YE DINNAE MIND IF THE YOUNG LADY JOINS US?"

"I heard ye the first time," said the old man tartly. "I'm nae deaf, ye ken."

"Ye might as well be," grumbled Morag. "Izzy told me she had tae call ye five times afore ye heard her, when ye arrived just noo. Ye need tae get that hearin' aid o' yers checked out. Mebbe ye need a new one."

"My hearin's fine," said the old man indignantly. "S'young people these days. They mumble when they talk. Ye do it yersel' as well."

"I've never mumbled in my life, Donal Mackintosh!" said Morag with a scowl.

Despite the tart words, their exchange had the flavour of good-natured bickering between old friends, and I couldn't help smiling as I joined them at the table.

"Would ye like a cuppa?" Morag asked me. "Or a slice o' cake?" She indicated the fruit loaf on the table.

"Oh, no, thank you. I've just finished eating and I'm stuffed," I said. "That cranachan was delicious, Morag! I'd love to have the recipe to try and recreate it myself at home."

"Oh aye, I can write it doon fer ye," she said comfortably. "But ye'll nae be able tae make the same in England. Aye, ye need oor Scottish cream and Scottish raspberries tae gi' those flavours."

"You're probably right," I said, laughing. "But I'm going to buy some heather honey and Scotch whisky to take home and try to recreate it anyway."

"Well, ye can have a cup o' tea," said Morag firmly, getting up from the table to make me one.

A few minutes later, a large mug was placed before me, but before I could sip the steaming brew, Donal reached over and pulled the mug towards him.

"Noo, lassie, here's summat tae make that tea *really* good," he said to me, his eyes twinkling. "Jus' a wee drop..."

I gulped as I watched him pour a generous glug of

whisky from his flask into my mug. "Er... thank you," I said, wincing internally at the thought of how much the liquid was going to burn.

But to my surprise, when I finally sipped from my mug, I found it to be warm and soothing, with the edge of the whisky mellowed by the sweet tea.

"This is wonderful," I said, smiling at Donal. "Maybe I should start offering whisky with tea as an option in my tearoom!"

"Ye own a tearoom?" said Donal, looking at me with interest.

"Yes, down in the Cotswolds, near Oxford. I offer all sorts of teas—you know, English breakfast, Earl Grey, pure Darjeeling, Assam, Ceylon, even herbal teas and fruit teas, but I never thought of combining whisky with tea."

"Ah, ye can add whisky tae anythin'," said Donal. "S'grand tae use in bakin' too. Nothin' like a chocolate whisky cake—"

"Or whisky banana bread," Morag chimed in. "I made banana bread with the Balvenie you recommended and, my goodness, the guests were goan mad fer it. Kept gettin' requests fer the rest o' the week."

"I'm sure Dora, my baking chef, would love to try out some of these recipes," I said wistfully. "But the only thing is, we wouldn't know which kind of whisky to use—"

"Och, it's easy," scoffed Donal. "Any smooth Scotch from a bourbon cask 'ud go grand wi' bananas. Nice, strong toffee aroma, see? Goes well wi' chocolate too, 'specially a malt wi' vanilla and oak. For almond, ye be wantin' summat that's creamy on the nose, wi' some honey—a twelve-year-old Aberfeldy 'ud do the trick." He nodded approvingly. "And if ye got anythin' wi' berries in it, then ye cannae go wrong with summat like a Tomatin Legacy, finished in port wood. Aye, nothin' like jam tarts wi' a glass o' Tomatin," he said, smacking his lips.

"Donal used tae work at one o' the local distilleries," said Morag, looking with affectionate pride at the old man. "He knows everythin' aboot whisky."

Donal looked embarrassed by the praise. He gave a gruff cough and said: "Well, I best be goan." He rose from his chair, tucked the silver whisky flask back into a pocket in his tweed waistcoat, and tipped his cap at me. "Nice tae meet ye, lassie."

"Are ye wantin' a slice o' cake tae take home?" asked Morag, indicating the fruit loaf on the table again. She glanced regretfully around the kitchen. "I haven't started the other bakin' yet so I haven't much else tae offer ye. And we dinnae have any chanterelles left either."

"S'nae bother," said Donal, waving a hand. "Ewan brought a big bag home t'other night."

My ears perked up. "Ewan?"

Donal nodded and smiled proudly. "Aye, he's a good lad. Always thinkin' o' his uncle. There's nothin' I like better than a plate o' chanterelles, fried wi' a knob o' butter, so he's always bringin' me some from the estate."

"You are Ewan's uncle?" I said, slightly confused. "I thought I always heard Ewan refer to his uncle as 'Mac'…"

"Oh, aye, that's me name: Donal Mackintosh. But me wife always called me 'Mac'." A shadow crossed his face. "S'nice tae have Ewan continue the same." He was silent for a moment, then he straightened his shoulders and gave me a nod. "Well, enjoy yer time in the Highlands, lassie, and p'haps I'll see ye agin."

He let himself out of the rear door of the kitchen and, after he'd gone, Morag gave a sigh and said: "Poor Donal…"

She saw me looking at her curiously and explained, "He lost his wife last year. Aye, she was a wonderful woman. I worry aboot him, withoot her tae look after him. 'Course it's good that Ewan lives with Donal and can keep an eye on him, but s'nae the same as havin' a wife." She shook her head and laughed. "Mind ye, Donal disnae like bein' fussed over. Used tae drive Lesley mad, the way he'd nae listen tae her, 'specially if he'd fallen asleep in front o' the telly and—"

"Lesley?" I looked at her in surprise. "You mean Lesley who used to work here—"

"Oh aye, didnae I tell ye?" said Morag, clucking her tongue. "It's hoo I know Donal. Met him when I first started and he popped in tae see Lesley. Used tae come by noo and then fer a cuppa and a haver.

'Course he stopped comin' after they let her go, and who can blame him, the way they treated her?" Morag said darkly. "But after Lesley passed away, he started comin' agin and I'm glad. Ye need friends, ye know, 'specially as ye get older. I think Donal's made peace with what happened, which is more than I can say fer Ewan."

"What do you mean?" I asked, an uneasy feeling starting to gnaw at me.

"Oh, Ewan's never forgiven Mr Mackay fer firin' his aunt and cuttin' her off withoot the retirement pay she was promised. He hated Aileen too—"

"Ewan hated Aileen?" I said faintly.

"Aye, fair hated her guts, 'specially as she replaced his aunt. See, Ewan lost his parents when he was nae more than a bairn, and he was brought up by Lesley and Donal. Loved them like his own mam and da. And he never believed that Lesley had been fiddlin' the accounts—none o' us did, tae tell ye the truth. But what could we do? Even Ewan, who was always sayin' that Aileen had somethin' tae do with it, had tae put up or shut up if he wanted tae keep his job as ghillie at the castle."

I stared at Morag, digesting her words and trying to ignore the uneasy feeling which had spread to my stomach and was starting to make me feel sick.

I was suddenly remembering the morning after the murder, when Ewan was telling me about his alibi. He had mentioned having a chat with Aileen before leaving the castle, to ask if he could take some chanterelle mushrooms home—and he had specifically said that she refused to let him have any. And yet Donal had just claimed that Ewan had brought home a big bag... *why had Ewan lied to me?*

CHAPTER TWENTY-EIGHT

The police checked Ewan's alibi, I reminded myself frantically. Regardless of whether he took some mushrooms home or not, Ewan had left the castle that night and arrived back home well before the time that Aileen was murdered. In fact, I could still clearly remember Ewan's answer when Devlin had asked him about his movements, that night at the pub in Fort William:

"...the police came round to speak to my uncle this evening and he confirmed that I got home before eleven and didn't go out again after that."

But even as I recalled the words, another scene flashed through my mind: the good-natured bickering between Morag and Donal when I first entered the kitchen. Donal was obviously quite deaf and his hearing aid was unreliable, given Morag's complaints. So could he be trusted to confirm that his nephew "got home before eleven and didn't go out again after that"? After all, if he was prone to falling asleep in front of the TV, like Morag had mentioned, and his hearing aid wasn't working properly, he could easily be unaware if Ewan had left the house again that night.

And Ewan himself had said that, with the empty roads at that time of night, it could take just ten minutes to drive from his house to the castle or vice versa. He could have slipped out, come back to murder Aileen, and then returned home, all without his uncle realising...

I shook myself mentally, clamping down on the thoughts spinning through my mind. *No. Stop. This is crazy! Ewan isn't a murderer! Lilian's the murderer—she has to be! I had it all worked out. It all fits—*

"Are ye all right, lassie?"

I blinked and came out of my thoughts to find Morag watching me with a concerned expression.

"Er... um... yes," I mumbled.

"Dinnae ye be worryin' aboot Donal. He'll be fine. He's tougher than he looks. And noo that Aileen's gone... well, I shouldnae be sayin' this, but things will likely get friendlier aroond here." Morag sighed. "Some say it was because she was a Lowlander, but I think it wouldnae have mattered where she came from. Aileen was just a ruthless coo and—"

"What do you mean, Aileen was a 'Lowlander'?" I cut in. "Does that mean she didn't come from the local area?"

"Och no! Aileen was from Dumfries, doon sooth, near the border with England. Not that there's anythin' wrong with that, mind ye. I know a very nice woman from Dumfries. Married a local lad and settled in Invergarry, not far from here…"

Morag kept talking but I was barely listening anymore. Instead, I was thinking of my theory of Lilian's motive for murder. Everything had hinged on the fact that Aileen had been Lilian's abusive nanny from childhood… but what if I had got it completely wrong?

Conscious of my heart beating uncomfortably in my chest, I said: "Um… Morag, do you know if Aileen spent a lot of time around here? Like, maybe when she was younger?"

"Here? In the Highlands, ye mean? No, she only came up this way a couple o' years ago. Lived doon sooth most o' her life, actually. Family moved doon there fer work and then she went tae college there. Qualified as a professional nanny, I think, and worked in London fer years, afore she got tired o' things and decided tae move up tae Scotland."

I stared at her in silent horror, the last remnants of my theory crumbling around me. If Aileen had only moved to the Highlands a few years earlier, then she definitely couldn't have been Lilian's childhood nanny.

But that doesn't mean Lilian didn't commit the murder, I thought desperately. Even if she wasn't the same woman who had tormented the harpist as a child, couldn't Aileen have stirred up enough bad memories to trigger an attack...? And there was still Lilian's account of the voices in the library. She had definitely been hiding something—I was sure of it. So if she really was innocent, why had she lied?

Trying to ignore the feeling that I was clutching at straws, I mumbled an excuse to Morag and stood up to leave the kitchen. She looked at me in surprise.

"But I thought ye wanted tae watch me do some bakin', lassie?"

"Oh, er... I do, but... um... I just thought of something I need to do. Maybe I can come back tomorrow?"

Without waiting for Morag to reply, I hurried out of the kitchen. I was desperate to talk to Cassie. I knew I could count on my best friend to respond with blunt honesty, and right now I needed someone to help me sort out the confusion of thoughts whirling in my head.

But there was no sign of Cassie anywhere. She wasn't in the Great Hall or in any of the public rooms on the ground floor, and she wasn't in our shared bedroom either, although her phone was on her bed. On an impulse, I rang the number for Graeme's cottage. Mabel answered on the second ring.

"Cassie? No, she's not here with us. She did ring about half an hour ago, though."

"Oh? Did she say if she was going somewhere?"

"No, she wanted to know what we thought of Lilian's story about the voices in the library. We agreed with her, of course."

"What do you mean? Agreed about what?"

"About why Lilian hadn't told the truth, dear."

"Oh, so you all felt that Lilian was lying too! It wasn't just me," I said, elated and relieved.

"Well, yes, anyone could see that the girl was lying and why."

I frowned. "What do you mean? I could see that Lilian was lying and I thought I knew why, but it turned out that I was wrong. Angus Mackay has a solid alibi, so he couldn't have been with Aileen in the library. So then I thought that Lilian must have lied to cover up for herself—that the 'second voice' was actually *her*—but now I'm not so sure either—"

"Don't be silly, dear. Of course it wasn't Lilian in the library," said Mabel impatiently. "Lilian recognised the second voice, but she didn't want to admit it. Girls can be so silly when they're in the throes of calf love. Still, it's hardly surprising that a shy girl like her would be smitten by a handsome, charming chap like that young ghillie."

"Lilian is in love with Ewan?" I gasped.

"Well, of course, dear! It's plain as the nose on your face. She's completely besotted with him. Didn't you see the way she went pink when he even just looked in her direction? And I thought she was going to faint when he offered her a lift and called her 'Lil'.

She could probably have gone home earlier, but I wonder if she hadn't been lingering around the castle in the hope of seeing that young ghillie fellow again."

"Did Cassie notice this too?" I asked, feeling ashamed of my own obtuseness.

"Yes, that was why she rang us up. She wanted to check that we agreed with her theory. She thought that Lilian had lied to cover up for Ewan, because the girl crashed on him."

"Wha—? Oh, you mean Lilian 'had a *crush* on him'."

"'Have a crush'? 'Take a break'? Why do you young people use such outlandish terms for romance?" grumbled Mabel.

Like "smitten" and "calf love" are normal words, I thought, rolling my eyes. "So what else did Cassie say?"

"Hmm... not much else, really. She just wanted to know if we agreed that it was probably Ewan in the library with Aileen that night. Of course, that hardly matters since that nice young fellow couldn't have been the murderer."

"Why do you say that?" I asked, surprised. It was unlike the Old Biddies, and especially the normally sceptical Mabel, to discard someone so readily as a suspect.

"Well, for one thing, he has an alibi, dear. And for another... a lovely young fellow like that? Why on earth would he want to murder Aileen? He had no motive."

Oh yes he did, I thought grimly. And I was surprised that the Old Biddies, for all their skill at extracting local gossip, had missed the link between Ewan and the ex-castle manager. Perhaps they had simply been too focused on the guests' backgrounds and not paid much attention to the staff... or perhaps Lilian wasn't the only one who had been "smitten" by Ewan's charm, I reflected cynically. The Old Biddies had been just as susceptible as I had been.

The only one who saw through Ewan is Cassie, I thought, recalling with shame our argument on the night we were going out to Fort William. Her words echoed in my mind:

"... He could have come back... Alibis can be faked... You just don't want to suspect him because you've got a crush on him... He's just your type, Gemma. All dark and handsome, with those incredibly blue eyes..."

I winced. I might not have had a romantic crush on Ewan, but I had certainly been blinded by his charm and good looks. And yes, okay—maybe I *had* been flattered by his interest in me, and that had made me view him with rose-tinted spectacles...

Oh God, Cassie is really going to enjoy saying 'I told you so' when I see her and admit that she was right all along! I groaned to myself.

My dread of my best friend's ribbing, however, began to fade into genuine concern as she remained nowhere to be found. I searched once more around the castle, checking all the public spaces again and even poking my head into some of the staff offices and utility rooms, and knocking on some of the other guest room doors. But no one had seen Cassie.

"Have you tried looking outside? Maybe she's gone for a walk around the castle grounds?" suggested Hamish when I checked with the reception desk for the third time. "Though I doubt it," he added, casting a look at the driving rain which splattered against the vestibule windows. "But you can never know with guests. We've seen all sorts here. I had one Australian woman who *loved* grey days and being out in the rain and fog," he said with a bemused shrug. "Said it was a nice change from the constant sunshine back home."

Rain definitely didn't hold novelty value for an English girl like Cassie! Still, with every other avenue exhausted, I decided to try the outdoors. Stepping out onto the terrace, I was hit by a blast of cold air that would have done winter proud in several other countries. I shivered, hugging my arms around myself. It was raining heavily now, and the sky had darkened so much that it looked almost like night. I tried to find a sheltered spot under the eaves and peered vainly out into the castle grounds.

It was as if a dark veil had been drawn all around the castle, obscuring the view of the surrounding landscape. I could barely make out the front lawn; the rest of the estate was nothing more than a misty haze. All I could see, higher up, beyond the haze, was the distant dark shapes of the mountains, interspersed with swirls of mist that snaked through the sheets of rain slashing diagonally down from the sky.

This is crazy, I thought. *There's no way Cassie would be out in this!* I turned to go back inside and found that someone had followed me out onto the terrace. It was the little girl, Safa.

"What are you doing?" she asked.

"I was looking for my friend, but she's not here." I made a shooing gesture. "Come on, we'd better get back inside. You're going to get wet."

She ignored me. "Your friend—the art teacher? Miss Cassandra?"

"Yes, that's her."

Safa smiled, showing a gap in her front teeth. "She is nice. She show me how to draw a deer. Baba said he will take me to see deer in the forest."

"That's lovely," I said absent-mindedly, still trying to shepherd the little girl back into the castle.

"Maybe Miss Cassandra will show me how to draw fish next time," Safa continued brightly. "After she comes back from fishing, then she will—"

"Wait." I stopped and stared at the child. "Did you say that Cassie—I mean, Miss Cassandra—has gone fishing?"

Safa nodded. "I see her go. With the Fishing Man."

I felt my heart lurch. "You mean Ewan? You saw Cassie go with Ewan? The tall young man who was teaching fishing the other day?"

Safa nodded again, then she turned and pointed out into the rain. "They go out there. To the river."

I turned and stared out into the wall of rain again. My heart was thudding uncomfortably in my chest and I was trying to ignore the creeping sense of unease which was clinging to me like a damp, suffocating blanket. I wanted to deny it, to argue and protest and find alternative explanations, but in my heart, I knew that voice whispering urgently in my head was right:

Cassie was alone, out in the Scottish Highlands, with a man who was a murderer.

CHAPTER TWENTY-NINE

The pendulum of the grandfather clock at the side of the Great Hall swung with a slow, relentless rhythm: TICK... TICK... TICK. I sat in an armchair nearby, my eyes glued to the face of the clock, watching the hands creep past the numbers with agonising slowness.

Five minutes, seven minutes, twelve...

Outside, the rain droned steadily on, coming down hard and heavy. I turned my head and stared out the nearest window, whilst my heart beat in rhythm with the clock: THUD... THUD... THUD...

Unable to stand the tension any longer, I sprang up from the armchair and began pacing back and forth in front of the clock. *It's fine*, I told myself. *No need to overreact or get paranoid. There doesn't have to be a sinister explanation.*

Bridget had confirmed that one of the fishing rods set aside for guest use was missing from the library. Cassie had obviously just decided to take Ewan up on his fly fishing invitation and they had gone out without me. Then it had started raining so they must have taken shelter somewhere. They were probably just waiting for the rain to stop before making their way back to the castle...

It was all so logical, so reasonable and likely... and yet I couldn't stop the sense of unease nagging at me, like a persistent terrier nipping at my heels. I reached the far wall, turned around, and began pacing back the way I'd come.

"Is everything all right?"

I looked up to see Bruce and Connie, the couple from Texas, watching me with concern from their chairs on either side of the chessboard.

I dredged up a wan smile. "Er... yeah, I'm just a bit worried about my friend. She's out somewhere on the estate, you see..." I gestured towards the nearest window and the pouring rain.

"Alone?" asked Bruce, raising his eyebrows.

"Um... no, she's with Ewan, the castle ghillie. They... er... they went fishing—"

"Oh, now, don't you worry, honey," said Connie soothingly. "That young man seems very capable. I'm sure he'll take good care of your friend. There's probably no one else you'd rather she be out there with."

Oh God. I felt a sudden, crazy urge to laugh at the irony of her words. Hurriedly, I pretended to cough but, before I could reply, my phone rang. I glanced down: it was a number I had called earlier—the number for Inverness CID. Giving the couple an apologetic smile, I turned and walked down a side hallway so that I wouldn't be in earshot of the other guests.

"Hello? Inspector Monroe?" I said hopefully as I answered.

"Miss Rose? Detective Sergeant Taggart here."

"Oh... hi," I said, disappointed. "I was really hoping to speak to Inspector Monroe."

"Inspector Monroe is very busy right now, so he asked me to give you a call," said the sergeant briskly. "You left a message asking him to ring you back?"

"Yes, that's right," I said. "I... um... I have some new information concerning the Aberglinn murder case."

"What kind of new information?"

I hesitated. "I know who the murderer is."

"Aye, Inspector Monroe told me that you rang and spoke to him earlier—"

"Oh no, this is different. I mean, what I said earlier—the person I thought was guilty—was wrong," I said in a small voice. "I know the correct person now."

Even to my own ears, it sounded ridiculous, and I wasn't surprised when Sergeant Taggart grunted in annoyance and said:

"Are you taking the mickey, miss?"

"No! No, I'm completely serious. Look, everyone makes mistakes sometimes, don't they? But I'm sure I've got it right this time. It's Ewan Campbell, the castle ghillie—"

"We've checked Campbell's alibi," said the sergeant, sounding bored. "His uncle confirmed that he got home well before the time Aileen Fergusson was murdered."

"Yes, but his uncle is deaf and his hearing aid doesn't always work. He might not have heard Ewan sneaking out again—"

"Is that your only reason for suspecting that Campbell is the murderer?" said Sergeant Taggart in a scornful tone.

"No, there's also his motive. His aunt was the castle manager before Aileen. In fact, it's possible that she was framed by Aileen and unfairly dismissed. So Ewan probably found out and wanted revenge—"

"This is just you speculating. You have no proof of any of this."

"No, okay, but I do have a witness who can confirm that Ewan was in the library with Aileen that night! Lilian Monaghan, the girl who was playing the harp, heard a man talking to Aileen in the library, and she recognised the voice as belonging to Ewan. She didn't want to identify him before because she's got a crush on him but—"

"Is this the same Lilian Monaghan who you were convinced was the murderer just two hours ago?" said Sergeant Taggart sarcastically.

I flushed. "Okay, I got that wrong, but you have to believe me this time," I pleaded. "My friend's life could be in danger. Please! She's out on the Aberglinn estate somewhere, alone, with Ewan. You need to send some men over now to find her and Ewan, and take him in for questioning—"

"Miss, this is a serious murder investigation," said Sergeant Taggart, starting to sound really annoyed. "We haven't got time to waste following wild goose chases based on your fantasies—"

"They're *not* fantasies!" I almost shouted into the phone. "Please, can you just tell Inspector Monroe everything I've told you and... and at least ask him to call me?"

"Fine. I'll pass the message on."

The line went dead. I exhaled in frustration and stood for a moment in the hallway, wondering what to do. I could wait, of course, for the inspector to return my call or try calling him again after half an hour if I didn't hear back. But somehow, the thought of just sitting around, waiting, made me almost nauseous.

I tried to soothe myself by telling myself that I had no real reason to fear for Cassie's safety. After all, why would Ewan want to harm her? He had no idea that she suspected him.

But even as I had that thought, a new memory

invaded my mind: the way Cassie had been behaving so strangely earlier, her preoccupation with her phone, scrolling and searching for something online...

Furrowing my brow, I cast my mind back as I tried to recall the sequence of events earlier that afternoon. Yes, it had all started after Cassie had helped to carry the tray of food to Ewan's Land Rover. I remembered her fumbling for some time as she leaned in to secure the food on the back seat. Had she seen something then? Something which had made her look for some kind of information online?

Then my heart skipped a beat as the rest of that scene played out in my mind's eye: Ewan coming back from dropping Lilian off and casually picking up Cassie's phone, which had been left on one of the terrace tables. He'd looked at the screen before giving it back to her and made some joke about fly fishing.

Had he seen something which made him realise that Cassie had some knowledge that could incriminate him? Was that why he had engineered to take her out onto the estate, so that he could find an appropriate moment to silence her?

"You're just speculating," I said out loud, deliberately echoing the sergeant's words. But it was no use. It didn't matter that, logically, there was no proof that Cassie could be in danger. Something—some instinct or premonition—was telling me that I had to act.

I have to go out and find her, I decided grimly. *I'll*

never forgive myself if something happened to Cassie and I was just sitting here, waiting...

Whirling, I ran back to the armchair next to the grandfather clock, where I'd left my raincoat. Ignoring the startled looks of the other guests, I yanked it on and then strode through the Great Hall, out to the front vestibule.

"Do you have some gumboots I could borrow?" I asked Hamish.

"Well, yes, but... you're not going out in that?" said Hamish, motioning towards the window where we could see the rain coming down harder than ever.

"Yes, I am. I have to find my friend."

"I'm sure Miss Jenkins is fine! Ewan is a very experienced ghillie and he will have found a spot where they can shelter from the rain—"

"Look, I can't explain, but I need to find my friend and make sure she's okay. Do you know the spot where Ewan normally takes guests to do fly fishing? Can you tell me how to get there?"

Hamish looked at me doubtfully. "Well, yes, there's a track just by the main lawn in front of the castle, which leads through the woods down to the river. You just need to follow the stream through the woods, and eventually it joins up with the river by a little wooden bridge. But I really don't think you should be straying too far from the castle right now, miss. It can be very hard to see in the rain and you could easily slip and fall and hurt yourself. And if the mist drops as well..." He cast another uneasy look out of the window. "Visibility will be practically zero. You could easily get lost and end up halfway up the mountain—"

"I'll be fine," I assured him. "As long as I keep to the stream, I won't stray too far, and I can easily find my way back."

Five minutes later, despite his continued protests, I stood in the castle doorway, bracing myself to step into the deluge. My feet were tucked into borrowed gumboots and the rest of me was bundled up in my raincoat, with the hood pulled firmly up over my head.

I turned to Hamish, hovering anxiously behind me, and said: "There's one thing you can do for me: can you call this number and ask for Detective Inspector Devlin O'Connor? Tell him that I need him to come to the castle urgently."

"Okay," said Hamish, hurriedly scribbling on a hotel notepad. "But what do I say if he asks why—"

"He won't. Devlin will understand," I said, hoping that my instinct was right.

Then I pulled the hood further down over my face and stepped out into the rain.

CHAPTER THIRTY

The track from the main lawn wasn't that hard to find, even in the driving rain, but I was relieved when I finally reached the relative shelter of the woods. I say "relative" because the canopy wasn't really dense enough to keep out the rain completely. Still, at least the tree branches provided a sort of buffer, reducing the downpour to a more bearable "shower".

Not that it really mattered since I was already drenched from head to toe by the time I got there. In the time it took me to get from the castle door to the front lawn and then across the green expanse and finally onto the track leading into the woods, rain had somehow managed to seep past all my waterproof defences and was now trickling unpleasantly down my neck and back and squelching in the borrowed gumboots. My face was completely wet, my hair plastered to my cheeks and forehead, and I could feel my clothes clinging damply to my skin.

But I barely noticed the discomfort as I started briskly down the track. All I was conscious of was the urgent beating of my heart as a voice chanted in my head: *"Hurry... hurry... hurry!"*

I soon discovered, though, that while the thick canopy above helped to block out some of the rain, it also screened out most of the fading light. And as I went deeper and deeper into the trees, I found myself slowing and stumbling in the semi-darkness. My head was swimming with a confusion of sounds: the hissing of the falling rain, the gurgling of the stream next to the track, and the sigh and moan of the wind through the trees, all overlaid with the sound of my own harsh breathing. Twice, I tripped over tree roots and almost fell, and once I thought I'd come across the river at last as I lurched into a pool of ice-cold water, only to find that I had actually stepped into a large puddle formed by a dip in the path.

Climbing back out, I took a moment to get my bearings, then started off again along the track. Finally, after what seemed like ages, I felt the darkness around me begin to recede, and my spirits rose as I saw the tree branches thinning overhead. A few minutes later, I stepped out of the shelter of the trees into a wide-open space and my hood was whipped back by a gust of wind.

I stopped and looked about in confusion. There

was no river in sight. Instead, a bleak landscape stretched around me, dominated by mounds of heather which swayed and shivered in the wind, their haze of purple flowers darkened by the rain. Beyond them, I could see slopes of moor grass and heath rush, interspersed with gorse bushes and areas of barren ground, which rose up into the sharp angles of rocky mountainous terrain.

Belatedly, I realised that the track had actually been ascending for several minutes but I had been too preoccupied to notice. I must have made a mistake after stepping in that puddle and had inadvertently started following a different track from the one by the stream, so that instead of leading to the river in the glen below, the path had brought me up here, out onto open moorland at the foot of the mountains.

Oh God, am I lost? I wondered in dismay, shaking the rain out of my eyes. I peered about again, trying to make sense of the landscape around me. It was hard to see any landmarks as so much was obscured by the mist, which wafted across the view, playing tricks with my sense of distance and perspective. I strained my eyes and thought I could make out the river at last, a good distance away in the glen below me.

Then I heard a scream. It was muffled and echoed strangely in the mist but I recognised the voice.

"*Cassie!*" I gasped, looking wildly around. "Cassie, where are you?"

I started running. The scream had come from downhill, I was sure of that, and I raced down the side of the open moorland in the direction of the river. The ground began to descend sharply, and I clutched wildly at gorse bushes for support as I stumbled and tripped over the uneven terrain. The track back through the woods would have been a gentler and safer descent, but it would have taken too long and I couldn't afford to get lost again.

Then I came to a panting stop as the moor grass gave way suddenly to a rocky scree. Stones and pebbles scattered and rolled away as I stared down at the steep expanse of loose rock in front of me. I gulped. A false step here and I'd go tumbling down the rocky slope, possibly breaking my neck.

Then the sound of another scream pushed all thought from my mind.

"Cassie!" I shouted as I hurled myself down the slope.

My legs wobbled as I began slipping and sliding on the loose stones and gravel. The borrowed gumboots I was wearing were too big, and their rubber soles were totally wrong for this kind of terrain. One leg went out from underneath me and I lost my balance with a frightening swing of the body. I fell back against the slope, clutching desperately with both hands, but I kept sliding, faster and faster. A shower of pebbles scattered down the slope with me. Frantically, I dug my heels in *hard* and finally felt myself grind to a stop. I clung to the side of the scree, panting and sweating, as my heartbeat slowed again and I tried to get my breath back.

Another cry sounded and I jerked my head up to see that the mist had parted to reveal two figures in the river below.

It was Cassie and Ewan standing in midstream, locked in a struggle.

Ewan was behind Cassie with her head in a choke grip, his elbow tight around her neck, whilst she fought and struggled, kicking and biting and screaming. Cassie might have looked like a "pocket Venus", but what she lacked in size, she more than made up for in spirit, and it looked like Ewan was not finding her as easy a victim as he'd anticipated.

She wriggled free suddenly in a sideways move that unbalanced him, causing him to fall over into the water. Then Cassie turned and started to run, but she hadn't taken two steps when Ewan heaved himself out of the water and lunged for her. He grabbed her foot and yanked, pulling her down into the water as well. And then he was on top of her, his hands around her neck, holding her head down below the surface of the rushing river.

"*CASSIE!*" I screamed in horror.

I groped reflexively around for a weapon but the only rocks on the scree slope were small and flinty. In any case, even if I could find something, I knew I was still too far away. Unless I was an Olympic discus thrower, I could never throw anything with enough force and accuracy to hit Ewan.

Sobbing with fear and helplessness, my scrabbling hands encountered something hard in my raincoat pocket. I pulled it out and looked blankly at the giant lipstick in my palm. Then I realised what it was: the novelty flare gun that my mother had given me.

Without thinking, I yanked off the lid and pointed it wildly at the struggling figures in the river. I twisted the device. A bright pink lipstick popped out. *GAAAH!* I twisted frantically in the other direction. There was a small explosion that made me flinch and then a *WHOOSH* as a bolt of orange flames shot out of the end of the "lipstick".

It flew outwards in an arc towards the river. There was no way it could have hit Ewan, of course—as a weapon, it might as well have been useless—but for a moment, it lit the sky with a brilliant orange glow before it fizzled out in a trail of sparks.

Ewan jerked around, distracted, and Cassie gasped with relief as his hands fell away from her throat. I felt a surge of hope. Maybe the distraction would give Cassie the chance to wriggle free? But my hopes were quashed the next moment as Ewan turned back to Cassie and lunged for her again.

"*NOOO!*" I screamed in despair. The flare gun had been my one hope and now it was used up, gone.

I started trying to scramble down the scree slope once more, even though I knew I would never get there in time...

Then a figure burst out of the woods next to the

river: a tall, dark-haired man who plunged into the water and hauled Ewan off Cassie's flailing body.

"Devlin!" I gasped, unable to believe my eyes.

The two men were locked now in a deadly wrestling match, as each tried to overpower the other whilst keeping their balance in the rushing river.

Beyond them, I saw a second figure come running out of the woods, then a third... I watched incredulously as the second figure—a muscular young man—hurried over to Cassie and lifted her to her feet, then gently supported her as he helped her out of the river. The third figure raced towards Devlin and Ewan, but by the time he got to them, the fight was almost over. The ghillie was face down over a large boulder at the water's edge with one arm wrenched behind him, while Devlin held him captive with a classic police wristlock.

I let out a whoop of relief and elation. Eager to join them, I started recklessly down the scree slope again.

"Wait!"

I looked up to see the third figure hurrying towards the bottom of the slope. He was a red-haired young man with a tanned face and friendly blue eyes. "You need to lean backwards," he called. "Throw your weight back... aye, and try crossing switchback—"

"Switch what?" I shouted.

"Move in a zigzag way..." He gestured with his hands. "Hang on... I'm coming up to show you..."

With patient guidance, he showed me the technique to descend a scree slope safely, and several minutes later I breathed a sigh of relief as I finally felt level ground beneath my feet again.

"Gemma!"

I turned to see Devlin rushing towards me. He had a cut lip and a bruise developing on one cheek but otherwise looked fairly unscathed in spite of his recent violent bout in the river. "Are you all right?" he asked urgently.

He stopped suddenly as he arrived next to me, his hands going out for a second, and I felt a sudden urge to fling myself into his arms. But I hesitated, unsure... and the moment was gone. Devlin dropped his hands back to his side and shifted his weight awkwardly, while the red-haired man chuckled and said:

"She's not bad for a beginner, mate. Reckon we could make a mountaineer out of her yet."

"Th-thanks," I said, giving the man a weak smile. I turned to Devlin. "I'm fine. A bit scratched and bruised, that's all. What about Cassie? She's the one who was mauled by a murderer!"

Devlin turned to look across at where my best friend was sitting on a rock by the water's edge. She had a blanket wrapped around her shoulders and was clutching what looked like a silver flask as she talked to the man who had helped her out of the river. I walked over on trembling legs to join her, and Cassie looked up as I arrived. Her face was swollen and cut, and her throat purple with bruises, but she managed a weak smile as I threw my arms around her.

"Oh my God, Cassie—" I cried, struggling to hold back tears.

"I... I'm all right," she said hoarsely. "Just a bit wet."

I hiccupped and laughed at the typically British understatement. "Oh, Cass..."

She gave Devlin a wry look. "Hey, O'Connor—I'm glad you arrived to play hero when you did. For a moment there, I thought I was a 'goner', as the Americans say."

Devlin reached out and gave Cassie's shoulder a squeeze. "You looked like you were putting up a pretty good fight to me," he said mildly. "But I'm glad I could join the party."

"It was bloody lucky we saw the flare," said the young man standing next to Cassie.

"Aye, guided us right to you," agreed the red-haired man.

"The flare?" I started to laugh, slightly hysterically. "Oh my God, are you telling me my mother's stupid lipstick thingy actually saved the day?"

I began giggling uncontrollably. It was as if something had snapped inside me. Once I started laughing, I just couldn't stop and I doubled over, clutching my stomach and cackling like a maniacal witch. Devlin and the two other men eyed me nervously.

"Oh God..." I gasped for a breath, wiping tears

from my eyes. "I'm sorry... I don't know why I'm laughing... it's really not funny but... oh... ohhh..." I dissolved into fresh peals of laughter.

Cassie thrust the silver flask into my hands. "Drink this."

Still gasping and chortling, I raised the flask to my lips and took a deep gulp. Instantly, a fiery punch of smoky flavour hit me, erupting in my mouth and burning down my throat. I coughed and choked on the whisky, then paused as an amazing warmth began spreading through my body. The giggles subsided, the hysteria ebbed, and my breathing slowed. I sat up and looked around me, blinking. Everything seemed clearer, brighter, and yet also enveloped by a warm, calm haze.

Cassie grinned. "Good, huh? You should have seen me when I came out of the river. Shaking like a leaf. But a couple of swallows of that stuff and now I feel like I could run up Ben Nevis." She chuckled. "I reckon the Scots have it right. There's nothing to beat 'the water o' life'."

CHAPTER THIRTY-ONE

The grandfather clock in the Great Hall chimed the hour and I looked across at it with a smile. It was hard to believe that only this time yesterday, I was sitting here, in this very same armchair, panicked and confused—and terrified for Cassie's life.

Now my best friend sat lounging on the sofa next to me, happily munching on a Scottish macaroon accompanied by a mug of tea. Her face and neck still bore the marks of Ewan's assault, but she was looking remarkably recovered from her traumatic experience last night. In fact, instead of falling exhausted into bed when we'd finally returned to the castle—as I would have expected—Cassie had thrown herself into painting a wild, vivid scene of the river, churning with wind and rain, and framed by swirling mist. Perhaps it had been her way of exorcising her demons; it had certainly been one of the most powerful paintings she'd ever created. Whatever the reason, I was incredibly relieved to see her looking so sanguine now.

She caught my eye and said: "What? Gemma, you *have* to stop staring at me like that!"

"Sorry." I gave her a contrite smile. "I'm just so happy and relieved to see you looking okay. And... oh God, I know I've said it already but... I'm *so* sorry, Cassie!" I gave her an anguished look. "I feel so awful for not listening to you about Ewan—"

"Oh, stop it," said Cassie, waving a hand. "Look, to tell you the truth, I didn't really suspect him either to start with."

"But you suggested him as a suspect as soon as—"

"Yeah, but that wasn't because I'd noticed anything suspicious," said Cassie with a sheepish look. "You were right, you know. I was just annoyed and picking on him, cos Ewan was ruining my plans for getting you and Devlin together. I just took against him because he was charming and good-looking and a rival for your attention. I know I accused you of being blind and biased about him but, well, I was biased too, in my own way."

"Your bias turned out to be right, though," I said, grimacing. "And if I hadn't been so blind, I might have noticed something 'off' about him earlier—"

"Aww, you're being too hard on yourself," said

Cassie. "There wasn't really anything 'off' to notice! Ewan fooled us all, and like I said, I didn't *really* have any suspicions about him. I just wanted to bad-mouth him because I didn't like him messing up my plans."

"But something must have made you start to seriously suspect him."

"Yeah, it was luck, really... or bad luck, depending on how you look at it," said Cassie with an ironic look. "It was when I helped to carry that tray of food to Ewan's Land Rover yesterday. I was putting it on the back seat and there was all sorts of junk there, so I had to move some things around to make space for the tray and then figure out how to wedge it in, so that it wouldn't slide or flip over if he swerved... Anyway, I noticed this label which had fallen to the floor of the footwell. It looked like it had been torn off something. Then I realised what it was: a label from a coil of fishing line."

"But Ewan's a ghillie. He must carry loads of spare fishing line in his car," I said, frowning. "I don't see how that—"

"It was the number on the label that caught my eye," Cassie explained. "It was a #14 weight line, see? And I remembered overhearing Ewan talking to his group on the lawn that morning. He said that he doesn't carry that weight of line because it's only for really big game fish, like tuna and marlin, which you don't get in the Scottish Highlands. Well, it made me start to wonder: why would he lie? I remembered you telling me that Inspector Monroe had already dismissed the possibility of fishing line as the murder weapon because it wouldn't be strong enough and would just snap... but I started thinking: what if it was a #14 fishing line? Something that was strong enough to haul in a huge fighting fish like tuna or marlin would surely be strong enough to use as a garrotte."

"Ohhh—is that what you were Googling on your phone?" I cried. "And that's what Ewan saw when he picked up your phone to hand it back to you, wasn't it? I remembered he made some comment about you researching fly fishing and you were really evasive."

"Yeah, I think that's when he started to realise that I could be a danger to him," said Cassie. "He must have realised that I'd seen the discarded #14 line label in his car and was putting two and two together and making five."

"But surely that's still circumstantial evidence—"

"Not if you combine it with Lilian's behaviour," said Cassie. "It was obvious she had a huge crush on Ewan and would do anything for him—"

"How did everyone see that except me?" I groaned.

"Maybe because you had a huge crush on him yourself?" said Cassie with a cheeky look.

I threw a cushion at her. "Shut up! I'm telling you, I never had any romantic interest in Ewan! I liked him, yes, but it was never more than as a friend—"

"Okay, okay, I'm teasing," said Cassie, chuckling. "Anyway, so I was fairly certain that Lilian had recognised Ewan's voice and was covering up to protect him. That meant that he was in the library with Aileen just around the time of the murder! I still didn't know how he'd managed to get around his supposedly rock solid alibi but—"

"*I* do," I said ruefully. "I met his uncle, Donal Mackintosh. He's a lovely man—but very deaf, and his hearing aid doesn't always work properly. Which Ewan knew. So he knew that once his uncle was asleep in front of the TV, he could sneak out to the castle and back home again without anyone knowing better. And when the police questioned his uncle the next morning, Donal gave Ewan a perfectly honest alibi."

I shook my head. "Bloody hell, now that I think about it, Ewan even sort of bragged about it! Remember when he was telling us about doing the trip in ten minutes instead of twenty? That must have been how he came back to the castle to murder Aileen and then got back home again so quickly."

"Yeah, and his ghillie knowledge would have given him a real advantage," said Cassie thoughtfully. "He probably knows the estate better than anyone, so it was a doddle for him to creep into the castle grounds unseen and make his way to the library that night. There's a fire exit at the end of the hallway from the library, isn't there?"

"I wonder how he knew that Aileen would be in the library, though?"

"Oh, Aileen had a habit of helping herself to a 'wee

dram' from the hotel bar and taking it to the library to enjoy last thing at night. Ewan told me that Angus Mackay had been complaining to him about it, because Aileen had been helping herself to more and more expensive single malts from the bar. So he knew her habits and routines."

Cassie sighed. "You know, murder is wrong and all that... but I have to say, if ever someone asked for it, it was Aileen Fergusson. That woman sounded like an absolute cow. So mean and cruel to everyone else, but so greedy and grasping when it came to herself."

"Yeah, I don't think anyone is really that sorry that she's dead. In fact, I even get the impression that some of the staff side with Ewan," I said, thinking of the snatches of conversation I'd overheard around the dining room and kitchen that morning.

"What, they think it was okay to murder her?"

"Oh no, they don't condone murder, of course. It's more like they seem to sympathise with him." I paused, then added, "Although mostly, people just can't believe that he did it. Ewan seems so decent and... and so *nice*." I gave Cassie a shamefaced look. "That's what got me too. I just couldn't imagine how someone like him could do something like that! I mean—I know the reason 'why' now, of course. I know his motive—it was in revenge for what Aileen did to his aunt. But still... it seems a bit extreme."

"Maybe not, if you heard the way he was talking," said Cassie, thinking back. "He found me snooping around his Land Rover, you know; I was trying to find more clues and I just sort of panicked when I turned around and he was standing there. So I started blabbing about how I'd changed my mind and was really keen to try fly fishing after all. I made such a big fuss about it that when he offered to take me down to the river, I couldn't really refuse without looking suspicious. It was only when we were walking along that track in the woods that I started realising how dodgy the whole situation was, being out there alone with him."

She shook her head. "Bloody hell, you know, I really have to thank that little girl Safa. She might be a spoilt brat, but she saved my life. If she hadn't seen me going off with Ewan and then told you..." Cassie looked back up at me and shuddered. "When we got to the river, Ewan started talking about the murder. It was terrifying listening to him because I realised that he was only telling me everything because he had obviously decided to get rid of me."

"Oh Cass..." I said, reaching for her hand.

She waved me off, continuing, "No, no, what I wanted to say was—when I was listening to him, I couldn't help feeling a sort of pity. Aileen *really* shafted Ewan's family—especially his aunt, Lesley, who was like a mother to him. You don't know how much Ewan adored her and looked up to her, especially as she took him in after he was orphaned. And Lesley gave her life to Aberglinn Castle: she had worked here since even before she got married, and her brother—Ewan's father—was a ghillie here.

Ewan was always running around the place when he was growing up, working part-time, helping out..."

The words that Lilian had overheard in the library suddenly came back to me: '...*what this castle means to my family...*'. I had thought that it had to be Angus Mackay talking about the home of his ancestors, but I'd forgotten that there was another family who had devoted their lives to Aberglinn Castle and its estate.

"It must have been awful for Lesley to be fired like that." I spoke my thoughts out loud. "I mean, in a small community like this... all the horrible gossip and looks when she went to church or the village... and then to lose her pension as well, after all those decades of work and loyalty, for something that she didn't even do..."

"Yeah, Ewan said she was devastated. She had really bad depression and he's convinced that was partly what killed her. And all because Aileen got her kicked out so that she could take the job."

"Is that what tipped Ewan over the edge? Did he find proof that Aileen had framed his aunt?"

"Well, sort of. I think he'd been suspicious for a long time but didn't have anything to prove it. It was the chanterelles that brought it all out."

"The chanterelles?"

Cassie nodded. "Ewan told me that he went to ask Aileen if he could take a few home for his uncle because he'd collected a big batch and there were more than enough to spare. But she was completely unreasonable about it and refused to let him have even one. And she said some pretty nasty things too, to make him feel really small."

I recalled the way Aileen had spoken to me that first day in the library and felt a reluctant tug of sympathy. I knew exactly how the castle manager's poisonous tongue could humiliate you.

"So Ewan stormed off, really furious, and I think he just decided he'd had enough," Cassie continued. "He told me that he decided to ignore what Aileen had said and took some chanterelles home anyway. It was like something just snapped, like he didn't care anymore. And he was fuming in the car all the way home—I think he was fantasising about killing her. I don't know if he was really serious about it, but after his uncle nodded off, he came back to the castle."

"So he did plan it—"

"I don't know if he consciously planned it; maybe he just wanted to have it out with Aileen. Although he *did* have that #14 fishing line on him, so maybe subconsciously..." Cassie trailed off. "Anyway, he said they got into an argument, and maybe Aileen had had a bit too much whisky or something, but she basically told Ewan what she did to his aunt. She even laughed about it. I think *that's* what tipped him over the edge."

"*Nemo me impune lacessit,*" I said suddenly.

Cassie looked at me, puzzled. "What?"

"It's Latin for 'No one provokes me with impunity'. It's Scotland's adopted motto—that no one can harm a Scotsman or his family without being punished in return." I shook my head slowly. "Remember on the first day we arrived, Ewan was telling us about it in the car? He laughed at it... but maybe he believed in it more than he realised."

We were silent for several minutes, lost in our own thoughts, and were only roused when a familiar booming voice said:

"Ah... here you are, girls!"

I looked up to see Mabel bearing down on us, with the rest of the Old Biddies toddling behind her. Florence was carrying Muesli's cat carrier again, and I could see my little tabby looking sulkily out of the bars of her cage.

"We've just been chatting to Mr Mackay—" Mabel started to say, but I interrupted her indignantly.

"Hasn't he been arrested as well? I told Inspector Monroe all about the whisky scam that he and Tristan St Clair were running! The police should have taken him in for questioning—"

"They did, dear, and it seems that Angus Mackay himself was a victim of the scam too," said Florence.

"What?" I said, taken by surprise.

"Yes, that nice young man was the mastermind behind the whole thing, can you believe it?" said Glenda with a sigh. "And so handsome too!"

"But I'm sure I heard Mackay selling the scheme to Jerry Hudson," I protested. "He sounded like he was actively trying to bring others in as well. And he definitely let Tristan St Clair stay here for free—"

"Yes, that boy has a clever tongue," said Mabel

with grudging admiration. "Tristan St Clair approached Mackay about the whisky scheme and conned him into thinking that it was a legitimate investment opportunity. In fact, he even persuaded Mackay to sell off some of the castle antiques in order to get funds to invest in the whisky scheme! And then he convinced Mackay that things could be even more profitable if there were more participants in the scheme and that the castle was the perfect base for him to meet other 'potential investors'. So Mackay believed that for every extra person he helped to bring into the scheme, he could earn a percentage of their investment as a sort of 'referral fee'." Mabel snorted with contempt. "Really, Angus Mackay is a dolt! He may not have been guilty of criminal intentions, but he was certainly guilty of being greedy and stupid!"

"I think it's because he was desperate about the castle," said Ethel in her gentle voice. "He desperately needs money to keep Aberglinn going, otherwise he will be forced to sell it. It's been in his family since the thirteenth century and he just can't bear to lose it."

"Yes, especially to a big international company which just wants to dig up the castle grounds to put in swimming pools and tennis courts, and convert the castle itself into a modern resort," said Florence sadly. "Mackay has had offers from hotel chains in Dubai and Asia, and he's been holding out against them so far, but he has been getting really desperate."

"Ooh, yes, desperate people often do silly things and believe all sorts of things that are too good to be true, don't they?" said Glenda.

"Hmph," said Mabel, pursing her lips. "Well, I hope Mackay has learnt a good lesson. He's lucky that the police managed to get his money back out of the 'scheme', even if they didn't manage to stop St Clair absconding—"

"Wait, what?" cried Cassie, aghast. "Are you saying that the slimy sod got away?"

The Old Biddies nodded soberly.

"Yes, when the police went to Tristan St Clair's room this morning, they found it completely empty," Florence said. "All his things were gone—and that girl who was with him too. They must have sneaked off in the night."

"Bugger," I muttered. "I'll never know what St Clair was doing in Jerry Hudson's room now."

"Probably just snooping around, looking for anything he might be able to use as leverage," said Cassie cynically. "You know how these conmen operate. They're good at using any background information they can find to manipulate people."

"So what's Angus Mackay going to do now?" I asked. "Is he going to have to sell the castle?"

Looking around at the majestic beauty of the Great Hall, I felt a pang of pity for the Scotsman. I could just imagine how heartbreaking it would be to have to sell Aberglinn if it had been in my family for generations. And how dreadful if it was bought by some modern conglomeration who tore it down or converted it into some soulless "swanky resort"!

"Oh no, we just heard some wonderful news!" cried Glenda, her eyes sparkling.

"Yes, we were just chatting to Mr Mackay—as I was originally saying," said Mabel, glowering at me, "—and he told us that the Wetherby sisters have approached him and told him that they'd like to invest in the castle."

"Wow, really? You mean they're thinking of buying it?" asked Cassie.

"No, no, they've had such a wonderful time here that they'd like to see it kept exactly as it is now for others to enjoy. So they're going to become a sort of 'silent partner' with Angus Mackay, and they'll provide him with funds to develop and promote the castle hotel."

I wonder if they've run that *past their financial advisor*, I thought with a wry internal smile. Still, it was a wonderful solution, and I felt my spirits lift. It was lovely to think that Aberglinn Castle and its spectacular estate would be preserved in all their natural beauty.

CHAPTER THIRTY-TWO

Cassie gave a wistful sigh as she looked around the Great Hall and—as if she'd been reading my thoughts—said: "It's so beautiful here, and I feel like we've hardly seen the estate properly. It's a shame that we're going home tomorrow."

"Maybe you'll be asked back to run another workshop and we could come again," I said hopefully. "I mean, there's so much of the Scottish Highlands to see yet! I still haven't visited a whisky distillery or tried fly fishing or even seen a deer..."

I trailed off as I saw the Chinese newlyweds come into the Great Hall, wheeling two large cases. They stopped beside us.

"We are leaving today," Yu Ming said regretfully. "I wish we can stay longer but we already book another hotel in Edinburgh." She gave me a shy smile. "It is so nice to meet you."

"Yes, you too!" I said, warmly returning her smile. "If you guys are ever down near Oxford, you must look me up." I gave her the address of my tearoom, then added, "I'm sorry; your stay must have been spoiled by the murder investigation—"

"Oh no! It is very exciting," declared Yu Ming, her eyes sparkling. "It is like being in detective movie! We will always remember this special time in the castle."

"Yes, well, at least you'll have a lot of photos to enjoy when you get back," I said, laughing and pointing at the mobile phone clutched in her hand. "How many have you taken now?"

Yu Ming's husband guffawed and said: "I think she has taken over six thousand photos since we arrived in Scotland."

"Six thousand...!" I spluttered. "I don't think I'd take that many photos in a lifetime!"

Yu Ming laughed, looking both defiant and embarrassed. "It's okay. I can delete many of them." Then she turned to me eagerly. "I don't have photo with you. Can we take together?"

"Oh, er... sure," I said and posed self-consciously with her as she stretched her arm in front of us and expertly snapped a selfie.

"I take one of you and your friend?" she said, gesturing to Cassie. Without waiting for me to reply, she took my phone from my hand and held it up to frame the shot.

"Oh God, I probably look awful," grumbled Cassie, but she reached out and put an affectionate arm around me, and we snuggled together as we posed for the picture.

"Thank you," I said gratefully to Yu Ming. "I hadn't even thought to take a photo with Cassie yet. It'll be a lovely memento of our time in Scotland."

"Also your other friends?" suggested Yu Ming, gesturing to the Old Biddies. "Do you have photo all together?" She looked horrified when I shook my head. "You don't? You must take group photo! Happy memory together!" she cried.

She began hustling us off the sofas and towards the windows which looked out over the front of the castle. "Here... here... this is very nice place for photo. Yes, you stand here... and you in front, you are shorter... and you stand on this side..."

With a camera in her hand, Yu Ming transformed from a shy girl into a veritable army general as she shuffled and arranged us into the perfect configuration for a group shot. I was amused to see that, for once, Mabel seemed to have met her bossy match, and she looked slightly stupefied as she was assembled with the other Old Biddies into a good pose.

Just as Yu Ming lined up the shot, though, there came a petulant "*Meowwrrn!*" from the cat carrier. It was Muesli, and she was indignantly letting us know that she didn't like to be left out!

"Ahh... your cat also!" cried Yu Ming, hurrying

over and unlatching the cage.

The next moment, Muesli was thrust into my arms, and this time I kept a firm grip on her as I held her close. But even my cat seemed to be mesmerised by Yu Ming's photographic zeal, and she nestled obediently against my chest and looked towards the camera.

"Good! Good!" the Chinese girl cried in delight as she took up a position in front of us. She held up my phone camera. "Smile! Say cheese!"

We complied, shifting our weight self-consciously.

"One more!" cried Yu Ming, leaning to the right.

We smiled again.

"Another one!" cried Yu Ming, leaning to the left.

We smirked determinedly.

"Great! Another one! More smiling!" cried Yu Ming, dancing in front of us and snapping maniacally.

Oh my God, how many photos does she need to take? My smile was beginning to feel like a rictus grin, and I could feel my eyes watering from staring so hard at the camera lens. Finally, Yu Ming lowered the phone and we all sighed with relief.

"Maybe we take another one next to the staircase?" she suggested, pointing to the other side of the Great Hall. "Or with the harp?"

"Er... no, no... this is great... thank you," I said, hastily grabbing my phone back from her. "Thank you so much."

She beamed. "You are welcome. I hope we can

come visit your tearoom one day. Bye-bye!"

"Bloody hell, I feel like I need another whisky after that," mumbled Cassie.

Before I could reply, we were interrupted by a high-pitched voice.

"Miss Cassandra! Miss Cassandra!"

We all turned in surprise to see Safa running into the Great Hall, followed by her father. The little girl ran up to us and grabbed Cassie's hand.

"Miss Cassandra—I show Baba your new painting," she said excitedly. "The one you were doing last night. Of the river."

"Oh... er, right," said Cassie, looking uncertainly at the girl and her father. "Sorry, I probably shouldn't have left the easel up in the back parlour, but the paint needed to dry and I thought it wouldn't get in anyone's way—"

"*Wallah*, it is a beautiful painting," said Tariq Al-Mansouri, dipping his head with respect. "It is like a window looking into Scotland."

"Oh... um... thank you," said Cassie, flushing with pleasure.

"I want to buy," said Al-Mansouri. "How much?"

Cassie stared at him. "Well... er... I wasn't really planning to sell it—"

"How much are you offering, Mr Al-Mansouri?" Mabel cut in, giving the Arab businessman an assessing look.

Al-Mansouri narrowed his eyes. "I want Miss Cassandra to name her price."

"Well, this is a unique piece. Miss Jenkins suffered through a traumatic experience to create it, so it is really priceless," retorted Mabel.

Al-Mansouri waved a dismissive hand. "Nothing is priceless. There is always a price."

Mabel sniffed. "I'm not sure you'd be able to afford the price, Mr Al-Mansouri."

It was like waving a red flag at a bull. The businessman's nostril's flared and he said: "I am one of richest men in Dubai. You tell me. I pay."

"Hmm..." said Mabel in a sceptical tone.

"You tell me!" snapped Al-Mansouri. "How much?"

"Twenty-five thousand pounds!" Mabel shot back.

"That is nothing," Al-Mansouri scoffed. "Okay, you give me bank account details. I transfer money now."

Cassie's mouth dropped open and her eyes bugged out of her head. She stood, speechless, gaping at the businessman, until Mabel elbowed her and said: "Your bank details, dear?"

Cassie swallowed, then began fumbling for her phone. A few minutes later, she sank back down on the sofa next to me, looking completely dazed, whilst Al-Mansouri strolled away—his daughter skipping by his side—to claim the new artwork for his mansion.

"Well, bugger me," Cassie muttered. "Twenty-five thousand pounds... that was almost worth getting strangled for!" She laughed giddily and looked at me. "The next time we come to Aberglinn, we could stay in a suite!" Turning to the Old Biddies, she added, "And I'm beginning to think I should hire you as my agent, Mabel!"

Mabel smiled complacently, rubbing her hands with satisfaction. "That was not a bad negotiation, although if I had known that he would have paid so readily, I would have asked for a higher price. Now," she said briskly as the Old Biddies turned to go, "we're off to see Morag in the kitchen. She's promised to show us how to make a proper clootie dumpling."

"Oh!" I cried, sitting upright. "I totally forgot! I was supposed to watch Morag do some baking yesterday and then things went pear-shaped... I'm going to come with you now. It'll be my last chance to take some notes for Dora before we leave tomorrow."

"What about Muesli?" asked Cassie.

I looked down in surprise at the furry bundle on my lap. Muesli had been so quiet, nestling against me, that I'd completely forgotten about her. I was surprised that she hadn't been trying to creep away. Perhaps my little tabby had finally worked out that embarking on an escape act usually ended with her being locked back in her carrier, so she was trying the "calm and obedient" route now to preserve her freedom.

I felt terribly guilty as I picked her up.

"*Meowwrr?*" she said, looking up at me with a pleading expression.

"Aww, Muesli... I'm sorry, but I have to put you back—"

"Why don't you bring her into the kitchen with us?" suggested Glenda.

Florence nodded eagerly. "Morag loves cats. I'm sure she wouldn't mind having Muesli running around."

"Yes, and she'll be safely out of the public areas and away from the other guests," chimed in Ethel.

"I don't know," I said doubtfully. "I'm sure cats aren't supposed to be in the kitchen—"

"Hah! I'm sure Muesli isn't the first and won't be the last," said Cassie with a cynical laugh. "If it's not her, it'll be one of the dozens of strays that Morag is always feeding. Go on, take her with you."

I bit my lip. "All right." As I cuddled my little tabby close and followed the Old Biddies into the castle kitchen, I thought to myself, *I'll only be in there for an hour or so. Surely Muesli can't get into much trouble in that time?*

Little did I know just how little time was needed for a cat to get into trouble, especially when she spotted her nemesis. As we stepped into the kitchen, Morag looked up from the wooden table where she was kneading some dough and smiled in welcome. Arranged at the other end of the table were several cake stands, already brimming with finger sandwiches and delectable sweet treats, ready to be taken out for the day's "Afternoon Tea" service.

"Ahh... ye've come at last—oh, and ye've brought yer kitty!" Morag said in delight as she saw Muesli in my arms. "That's grand! Duff will love a wee friend visitin'; I've just been givin' him some fresh cream..."

She glanced down at the black cat at her feet who

was raising his head from a bowl, licking cream from his whiskers. He did not, however, look remotely pleased at the prospect of a "wee friend" visiting—in fact, he looked furious at seeing a feline interloper in *his* kitchen. His yellow eyes narrowed to slits, his ears went back, and an ominous growl began to emanate from his chest. In two seconds, he had puffed himself up to twice his normal size and was glaring across the kitchen at Muesli, telling her in a blood-curdling yowl to "puss off!"

Muesli bristled, her own fur rising. There was no way she was taking that insult lying down! Wriggling violently, she heaved herself out of my arms and was across the room, snarling a reply.

"Muesli—!" I gasped, lunging after her and clutching empty air.

Morag fell back with a cry of surprise as the two cats circled and sprang after each other. She tripped on the bowl of cream, knocking it over and splattering cream everywhere, then staggered backwards as the two cats leapt up on the wooden table. Billowing clouds of flour filled the air as Muesli chased Duff across the dough, leaving a mess of pawprints on the smooth surface.

"Muesli!" I shouted in dismay.

"Duff!" echoed Morag in outrage.

"The cake stands!" cried the Old Biddies in horror as the two cats charged heedlessly towards the other end of the table.

The next moment, they crashed through the row

of dainty displays, scattering the cake stands like bowling pins. Petits fours and cucumber sandwiches went flying everywhere.

"Aaaagghh!" gurgled Morag.

"Nooooo!" I groaned.

"Ohhhh dear!" lamented the Old Biddies, staring at the culinary carnage.

Then, in the midst of the mess, Muesli paused and sniffed a smoked salmon roll. Her little pink tongue darted out and she tasted it, then she gave a chirrup of delight. Beside her, Duff paused too, then approached cautiously and sniffed the other end of the roll. Then he, too, took an experimental nibble.

The next minute, we all stood and watched incredulously as the two cats huddled happily next to each other, munching their way through the finest hand-smoked Hebridean smoked salmon that Aberglinn Castle had to offer.

"Ahh... will ye look at that," said Morag, smiling down at the cats, everything forgiven. "Aye, there's nothin' like well tidy scran tae bring folk together."

EPILOGUE

The sky above Inverness Airport looked as fresh and blue as when we had arrived in Scotland a few days ago, and I breathed deeply as Cassie and I stepped out of the car. Suddenly, I wished I could pack up the essence of this wild, beautiful country and take it back to Oxford with me.

Well, you might not be able to pack up the essence of Scotland, but you've packed up just about everything else, I thought. After a last-minute shopping spree yesterday afternoon, Cassie and I had struggled to shut our bulging cases after trying to cram in so many gifts and souvenirs. There were bottles of Highland single malt for our fathers, beautiful Celtic silver brooches for our mothers, boxes of buttery shortbread and whisky fudge for friends and family, and even a smart new tartan cat collar for Muesli.

"Bloody hell, I thought you girls only got to Fort William an hour before the shops closed. How on earth did you manage to buy so much?" puffed Devlin, his biceps flexing as he lifted our cases out of the car and set them on the pavement.

Cassie grinned and winked at him. "It's a female superpower. You blokes wouldn't have the stamina to develop it."

"At least we don't have to worry about Muesli's cage as well," I said with a sigh. "The Old Biddies will be taking her back with them when they return later in the week."

Cassie grabbed the handles of both our cases and began wheeling them briskly away. "I'll get our cases checked in," she called over her shoulder, practically running into the airport terminal. "No need to rush if you want to chat!"

Grrrrr. I glared after my friend as she left me and Devlin standing awkwardly facing each other on the pavement. Turning back to him, I said politely:

"Um... thanks for giving us a lift."

"You're welcome." Devlin cleared his throat. "I hope you managed to enjoy your time in Scotland, in spite of the murder—" He broke off with a sudden laugh and said, with a rueful shake of his head: "What am I saying? The murder investigation was probably your favourite part."

"That's not true!" I protested, laughing. "I did

manage to have a lot of 'genuine Scottish experiences' too. Not sure I want to repeat some of them, though," I added dryly, thinking of my time soaked in the rain and stumbling around the open moorlands, lost in the blinding mist.

"At least you've got a good reason to return: to do all the things you've missed," said Devlin with a smile.

"Yeah, I'd really like to learn to enjoy the whisky too," I added. "I thought it was *horrible* when I first tasted it, but then that day by the river..." I thought back, recalling the moment when the fiery nectar in the silver flask had filled me with warmth and calm.

"Well, there's only one way to fix that, you know," said Devlin, his blue eyes twinkling. "Drink a lot more Scotch!"

He hesitated, then said in a rush, "There's a bar back in Oxford with a great selection of single malts. It's not quite the same as a pub in the Scottish Highlands, of course, but... you could get to know some different styles, see what you like..." He paused, looking uncharacteristically unsure of himself. "Maybe... when we're both back... you might like to meet up for a drink there?"

I looked up into his eyes and felt myself warmed in a different way. "Yes... that sounds lovely," I said, a slow smile spreading across my face. "Call me."

***

A bellow of laughter rang out across the tearoom and I looked up with a smile. It was good to hear customers enjoying themselves so heartily. In fact, several different tables all seemed to be full of people laughing uproariously, their faces flushed, their eyes shining, and the whole tearoom seemed to hum with a jovial, ebullient atmosphere. The euphoria was infectious, and I chuckled along, wondering if they were all sharing a common joke.

The sound of china smashing made me spin around, and I hurried over to a nearby table where a man had knocked his teacup onto the floor.

"Man, I'm so sorry!" he cried, rising unsteadily from his chair. "I don't know what happened."

"It's okay. Accidents happen," I said soothingly as I bent to clear up the mess. "If you hang on a moment, I'll fetch you a new cup from the kitchen."

I gathered up the pieces of broken china and carefully carried them to the kitchen, smiling as I passed a mother and child coming out of the far door marked "Toilet". Much as it had pained me at the time, I had to admit that closing the tearoom for a week had been one of the best decisions I'd ever made. Not only had I enjoyed a Scottish adventure, but I had returned to Meadowford-on-Smythe to find my tearoom fitted with gleaming new toilet facilities which had already earned the Little Stables several new five-star reviews.

I pushed my way through the swing door and stepped into the kitchen. Instantly, the rich, mouth-watering smell of fresh baking wafted over me.

"Mm... that smells incredible, Dora," I said, glancing across at my baking chef who was hovering by the oven. "Are you trying another of the Scottish recipes I brought back?"

"Whatever you're baking, Dora, I hope it's another whisky chocolate cake," said Cassie, pushing through the swing door and stepping into the kitchen after me. She brandished her order pad. "Honestly, everyone's going mad for it! People are even ordering seconds, thirds... and everyone says it's absolutely delicious!"

Dora smiled, looking pleased. "Ahh... that's lovely to hear. You're always a bit nervous, you know, when trying a new recipe, and I've never baked with whisky before." She reached across and picked up a near-empty bottle from the counter, then turned to me with an apologetic face. "You'll need to pop to the off-licence again, though, Gemma. We'll need more whisky if I'm going to make more of that cake."

I looked at her in surprise. "Really? But I got two big bottles this morning. Have you used them all up already?"

"Well, I was just following the recipe..." Dora trailed off as she picked up the handwritten sheets I'd brought back from Scotland. She squinted and held the paper out at arm's length, then gasped. "Oh my God! I've just realised... I read the ingredients wrong and I used four times the amount of whisky!"

"What?" I stared at her. Then I thought of all the

flushed faces and uncontrolled giggling at the tables, the unsteady man who had knocked over his teacup... "Oh God, I was wondering why everyone outside was so jolly!"

Cassie burst out laughing. "Are you telling me that the whole tearoom is totally plastered?" she cried, whooping.

"It's not funny, Cass!" I said, trying not guffaw myself. "It'll be awful if people find out."

"Oh, don't worry about it. They'll sober up pretty quickly," said Cassie, still grinning. "Just serve them some strong tea. By the way, this came for you. A courier just dropped it off," she said, handing me a flat cardboard package.

"For me?" I frowned down at the parcel for a moment, then brightened as I saw the sender's address. "Ah... it's from that online photo company."

Quickly, I unwrapped the package to reveal a large photograph frame. Encased was a group shot of me, Cassie, the Old Biddies and Muesli, taken by the windows of the Great Hall in Aberglinn Castle.

"Wow, that's a great shot!" said Cassie, peering over my shoulder.

"Yeah," I agreed, thinking that, while it had been tedious at the time, Yu Ming's fanatical approach really had produced the perfect picture, with everyone smiling and looking at the camera and not a single squint or blurred face in sight. Even Muesli seemed to be simpering into the lens. And behind us was the gorgeous view of the Scottish Highlands framed by the castle windows.

Walking over to the wall, I hung the picture up on a nail, then stepped back and smiled. My gaze took in our happy faces, with smiles that almost outshone the spectacular view of the Highland landscape behind us.

Well, the Scots might have their bellicose Latin motto but for me, there was a better one to embrace: *Amicitia vera illuminat*—real friendship shines.

FINIS

CHOCOLATE WHISKY CAKE RECIPE

This cake can be made with any type whisky, although it would be best to avoid those with strong peaty, smoky flavours and instead choose something which has "sweeter" notes and flavours of caramel and vanilla in the profile. Examples of single malts include the Dalwhinnie 15, Tamdhu 10 and Glenmorangie 12.

However, there is no need to waste an expensive single malt for baking. A cheaper blended Scotch, such as Johnnie Walker Black Label, would work just as well. In addition, American bourbon whiskey would also be a good choice as it has inherent vanilla notes that complement the chocolate.

INGREDIENTS:

For the cake:
- Two large eggs (make sure they are brought to room temperature before use)
- 1 cup (200g) granulated or caster sugar
- 1 cup (200g) brown sugar
- 3/4 cup (180ml) sour cream (make sure to bring to room temperature before use)
- 1/2 cup (125ml) vegetable oil
- 3/4 cup (180ml) water
- 1/4 cup (60ml) whisky
- 1 Tablespoon (20ml) pure vanilla extract
- 2 cups (300g) all-purpose flour
- 3/4 cup (115g) cocoa powder
- 1 teaspoon baking powder
- 1 teaspoon baking soda
- 1/2 teaspoon salt
- 220g dark chocolate, chopped into small pieces

For the whisky ganache:
- 220g dark chocolate, chopped into small pieces
- 1 cup (250ml) double cream *(known as "heavy cream" in the US and "thickened cream" in Australia)*
- 3 tablespoons whisky
- A pinch of salt

INSTRUCTIONS

1. Preheat the oven to 180 degrees Celsius / 350 degrees Fahrenheit.
2. In a large bowl (No. 1), combine the eggs, white sugar, and brown sugar and mix until it forms a smooth paste. If you are using an electric mixer, this should be done on low speed.
3. In a second bowl (No. 2), combine the sour cream, vegetable oil, water, vanilla extract and whisky, and mix until smooth. Set this aside.
4. In a third large bowl (No. 3), sift the flour and cocoa powder, then add the baking soda, baking powder and salt. Mix well and set aside.
5. Now, alternate adding the contents of Bowl 2 (wet ingredients) and Bowl 3 (dry ingredients) to the sugar mixture in the first bowl, using a folding motion. Be very careful not to overmix the batter as this could result in a dense and tough cake. If using an electric mixer, use it on low speed and mix until the ingredients are *just* combined.
6. Finally, add the chopped chocolate pieces, again using a gentle folding motion.
7. Pour the batter—equally divided—into two round 8" cake tins, which have been greased with butter or lined with baking parchment.
8. Place the tins in the oven and bake until the cake is set and a toothpick inserted into the center comes out clean. This will take from 30 to 40 minutes, depending on your oven.

9. Remove the tins from the oven and let the cakes cool in them for 30 minutes, before attempting to remove them from the tins. Then place the extracted cakes on a cooling rack for a further period of time until they are completely cool.

10. While the cakes are cooling, you can start making the ganache: roughly chop up the dark chocolate and place in a bowl.

11. Heat the cream until it just boils. This can be done on the stove or in the microwave. As soon as you see it start to bubble, remove it from the heat and pour it over the chopped up chocolate.

12. Allow the mixture to sit for a minute, then stir vigorously with a whisk until it forms a smooth and glossy ganache. Now, add the whisky and a pinch of salt. Keep mixing until it is combined and smooth again.

13. Wait until the cakes are fully cooled to room temperature, then spread a thin layer of the ganache on top of one cake and lay the other one on top. Use the remainder of the whisky ganache to frost the top and sides of the double layered cake. You can also decorate with additional things such as strawberries or chocolate shavings.

NOTES:

• Depending on how much of a sweet tooth you have, you can choose to use a dark chocolate with a lower percentage of cocoa (eg. 45%) for a sweeter taste or a higher percentage (eg. 70%) for a more bittersweet flavour.

This recipe specifically uses oil in place of butter. This makes the cake more moist and tender. Do not replace with butter as the recipe ratios are adapted for oil and doing so may result in a dry cake.

Ideally use full fat sour cream, as it helps to add moisture without thinning the batter and make the cake more tender. However, if you cannot find full fat, then "light" will work as well.

When measuring the flour and cocoa powder, it is best to use a kitchen scale for most accurate measurements. If you are using measuring cups and utensils, make sure to gently fill and then level the ingredients; do not forcefully pack them into the measuring cup.

Be very mindful about not overmixing the batter, otherwise you will not get a light, fluffy cake.

Make sure not to open the oven door while the cake is baking as this will drop the oven temperature and can affect the rise of the cake.

Always allow cakes to cool completely before frosting with ganache, otherwise it will melt and run, pooling around the cake instead of covering it in an even layer.

Enjoy!

ABOUT THE AUTHOR

USA Today bestselling author H.Y. Hanna writes fun mysteries filled with suspense, humour, and unexpected twists, as well as quirky characters and cats with big personalities! She is known for bringing wonderful settings to life, whether it's the historic city of Oxford, the beautiful English Cotswolds or other exciting places around the world.

After graduating from Oxford University, Hsin-Yi tried her hand at a variety of jobs, including advertising, modelling, teaching English and dog training... before returning to her first love: writing. She worked as a freelance writer for several years and has won awards for her poetry, short stories and journalism.

Hsin-Yi was born in Taiwan and has been a globe-trotter all her life, living in a variety of cultures from the UK to the Middle East, the USA to New Zealand... but is now happily settled in Perth, Western Australia, with her husband and a rescue kitty named Muesli. You can learn more about her and her books at: **www.hyhanna.com**

Sign up to her newsletter to get updates on new releases, exclusive giveaways and other book news!

https://www.hyhanna.com/newsletter